D1505510

TANGLED TIMES

TANGLED TIMES

IRENE BENNETT BROWN

FIVE STAR
A part of Gale, a Cengage Company

LIBRARY OF CONGRESS CATALOGING-IN-PUBLICATION DATA

Names: Brown, Irene Bennett, author.
Title: Tangled times / Irene Bennett Brown.
Description: First edition. | Waterville, Maine : Five Star, a part of Gale, Cengage Learning, [2020] | Series: Nickel Hill series ; 2
Identifiers: LCCN 2019030190 (print) | ISBN 9781432867294 (hardback)
Subjects: GSAFD: Western stories.
Classification: LCC PS3552.R68559 T36 2020 (print) | LCC PS3552.R68559 (ebook) | DDC 813/.54—dc23
LC record available at https://lccn.loc.gov/2019030190
LC ebook record available at https://lccn.loc.gov/2019030191

First Edition. First Printing: March 2020
Find us on Facebook—https://www.facebook.com/FiveStarCengage
Visit our website—http://www.gale.cengage.com/fivestar
Contact Five Star Publishing at FiveStar@cengage.com

Printed in Mexico
Print Number: 01   Print Year: 2020

With love to Shana, Melia, Corey,
and in loving memory to Rourke.
Nothing is more precious than a child.

ACKNOWLEDGEMENTS

It is my pleasure to thank Professor Jim Hoy, of Kansas. His books, *Cowboys and Kansas* and *Flint Hills Cowboys,* have been both a most entertaining and a helpful source of information in writing my Nickel Hill Series. My heartfelt appreciation goes also to the Friends of the Flint Hills. Your beautiful photos of the Flint Hills on Facebook inspire me daily. And thanks, always, to the sweetest helper and computer mechanic ever, my husband, Bob.

CHAPTER ONE

"Pay no mind about the books, this is not your fault, Mr. Belshaw." Jocelyn waited while Skiddy's friendly-faced postmaster checked the smaller mail slots on the wall. She took a deep breath, relished the ink and paper coolness of the post office, compared to the summer sun outside.

He handed her two letters from the service window and smiled. "There you are, all the mail for today, Mrs. Pladson. Sorry about the school books."

"I was in town for lamp oil and errands for Pete when it came to mind that my order of the school books might've come." She loved the *idea* of re-opening the ancient, much-needed schoolhouse on Nickel Hill land, but it was turning into a trial. One thing and another refused to budge as it ought.

Mr. Belshaw stroked his bearded chin, his dark brows tented in a slight frown. "I reckon, this being late summer, school-district offices are bounden with business and running behind." He smiled encouragement. "Betcha your school's books will be here on time, Mrs. Pladson. Remember: 'Neither snow nor rain nor gloom of night . . .'?"

She gave him a wry grin. "I surely hope so." She tucked the letters into her reticule, noting that one was from her and Pete's dear friend, Mrs. Francina Gorham. Several months ago, elderly Mrs. Gorham hired them to manage Nickel Hill Ranch, at the same time, writing them into her will. She hadn't needed to do the latter as far as they were concerned, but Francina would have it no other way. The property, two thousand acres, mostly in waist-high bluestem prairie grass, had belonged to her only child, her son, Whitman—also boss and good friend to Jocelyn at one time. In the sorriest incident Jocelyn ever experienced, Whit had been unjustly killed by an outlaw. Leaving Mrs. Gorham without family.

Curious, Jocelyn shook off the pain of memory and looked again at the second envelope, addressed from a name she didn't recognize, Mrs. Flaudie Malone. It'd come from Long Lane, Missouri, to Mrs. Letty Stern, Dunlap, Kansas. She supposed it had gone to their old farm, hers and Gram's, and was forwarded from there. Grandma Letty had died years ago.

Forgetting the letters for now, Jocelyn told Mr. Belshaw, "Repairs to the school building are almost finished. It'd be a disappointment not to have the books first day, too."

He nodded. "You keep heart, Mrs. Pladson. You're doing a good thing out there at Nickel Hill, bringing life back to that old schoolhouse. Huge ranches being cut up into small holdings these last years is what brought many new families showing up from nowhere to buy or to rent. I know that by the mail." He gave the counter two sharp pats of his hand. "Their young'uns need schooling and no other school close as 'tis. You and Pete taking over the Nickel Hill ranch, *and* the old school, is a blessing, an' that's that."

"Thanks, Mr. Belshaw. Pete and I love it at Nickel Hill, and we're excited about our school." *We want so much to live up to Mrs. Gorham's belief in us. In every way: make the cattle business, the ranch, a profitable operation. And a good living for the family we want more than anything.*

A raspy female voice behind Jocelyn spoke, in more of a statement than question, "You're startin' up again that old school out there on the Nickel Hill place?"

Jocelyn turned and almost collided with a stump of a sour-faced woman in a slat bonnet and a faded, less than clean dress—men's shoes on her feet. She glared at Jocelyn from brittle, dark eyes. She was fragrant with the smell of a horse barn.

"Yes, we are." Jocelyn took a discreet step back. "How are you, Mrs. Taggert?" She'd only met Icel Taggert once, maybe twice, didn't know much about her other than that she was known to be an unfriendly, cranky soul and owner of the Taggert ranch, located a few miles to the southeast of Nickel Hill. And that she had a son, was a widow who'd lost more than one husband. According to gossip, the ranch grew suspiciously with the death of each mate.

Likely an exaggeration, and who wouldn't be cranky in the woman's lonely situation? Jocelyn decided. Left to run a ranch of a thousand acres or so, with only the help of her half-grown son, a boy Jocelyn had yet to meet. Sympathy rose in Jocelyn, her hand lifted toward the poor woman, then lowered. Would Mrs. Taggert be interested in sending the boy to the newly revived school when it opened? Jocelyn leaned in, her voice gentle. "Mrs. Taggert, would your son, I believe I've heard his name is Herman, like to come to our school? It would be some distance to travel, but there will be other students in that area riding their horses to school. Some families will bring their children by wagon; he could ride along with them."

"I suppose it's gonna be a subscription school, folks havin' to pay through the teeth to keep it goin' whether they can afford it or not?" Mrs. Taggert glowered at Jocelyn, rough brown fists planted on her hips.

"No, it isn't a subscription school; no need for it to be. Land and the school building being already available, there's no cost. We've had some donations, and the school district is helping. It would be free. Would you like for him to come? He'd be most welcome, and I'm sure he'd like it. We're going to have some

fine books to study and read stories from, chalk boards for doing numbers and drawing. Simple music lessons . . ."

"You don't know him, or you'd not be askin'. My boy is
overgrowed, too old for school. Book learnin' would be useless
for him, anyhow. He had four years of schoolin' a'ready, and
you'd never know it. Sow's ear, he is."

Jocelyn's brows went up, and she waited for an explanation
of what the woman really meant, biting her lip. "Sow's ear?"

"Ever'body knows you can't make silk from a sow's ear. He's
no account, and always will be. Weak between the ears is what I
mean; most of the time needs somebody else to think for him
and tell him what to do." Mrs. Taggert turned back to peruse
the corkboard of notices on the wall, a deep frown creasing her
sun-browned forehead.

Jocelyn was shocked at how unkindly the woman talked about
her own flesh and blood. "School might be what he needs . . .
would be good for your son," she said to the woman's back.
"How old is he?" Her school board had voted to allow ages
from six to sixteen. A difficult mix, maybe, but such had worked
out in country schools plenty of times. She waited, then jerked
in surprise as Mrs. Taggert swung around, wagging a finger in
her face.

"How old he is don't matter a whit. I need him on the ranch.
There ain't goin' to be no more school for him."

Jocelyn was silent, half mad and plumb flummoxed for the
tick of several seconds. "Mrs. Taggert—Icel—there's going to be
a meeting about the school at my house two days from now.
Would you like to come and learn more about the whole matter
than I have time to tell you right now? I think you might change
your mind." With effort, she put on a warm, if shaky, smile.

"Enough talk." Mrs. Taggert's nostrils flared, and her lips
flattened. "You're not tellin' me what to do, Mrs. Hoighty
Toighty Pladson. I said, no school. None. I ain't got time for no

meetin' with silly"—her coarse hand fluttered—"*lah-de-dah* ladies. I got a ranch to run, with Herman helpin'. An' it ain't easy." She gave Jocelyn a scorching glare, went to the corkboard on the wall, ripped down a cattle-sale notice, sending tacks flying.

Jocelyn conquered an urge to duck. She turned, jaw dropped, with a questioning look at Mr. Belshaw. He shrugged and spread his palms. Together they watched Icel Taggert clomp to the post office door and outside onto the sidewalk, small crumbs of manure-caked straw left in her wake.

"Well, then, I'd better be getting on home." Jocelyn hesitated a few seconds, her feet glued to the floor, still in a quandary over what had just happened. She shook her head and smiled. "Thank you for the mail, Mr. Belshaw. I'll be watching for the shipment of books, and I hope they'll be here soon."

He came forward with a broom and tackled the mess the Widow Taggert had left behind. "If they don't, I'll be looking into the situation, count on that. By the way, Mrs. Pladson, I heard that you're still in the mule business."

She laughed and turned back. "True, but not so much as you'd notice. I have one little new mule colt, out of the mare Pete gave me as a wedding present. I had my red mare, Pretty Redwing, bred to a handsome donkey jack, about the same chestnut color as her. The new addition is cute as a button and lively. We named him Ricochet because he seems to bounce off everything. We just call him Shay." She nodded. "Pete has his cattle and his horses; I have mules: little Shay, and two mules that came with the ranch, Alice and Zenith. In time, I hope to be back into the mule trade, but for now I have plenty to keep me busy." She drew a deep breath. "And then some." Smiling, she told him, "Bye, Mr. Belshaw."

"You take care, Mrs. Pladson, and tell Pete howdy for me." He waved goodbye, and Jocelyn left the post office. She strode swiftly the few paces to where she'd hitched her mule team, Alice, a sorrel she affectionately thought of as an old maid mule, and faithful Zenith, a tall grey. The two were near inseparable, had been in her charge more than a year now, and they felt like family. She climbed into the wagon. "C'mon, mules." Reins in hand, she clicked and backed onto the street and turned in the direction of home. "Hup, Alice. Zenith. Supper's waiting." Stirring dust in the quiet street, her team swung into a jog-trot toward Nickel Hill Ranch.

Humming as she moved about her kitchen, Jocelyn set her pot of pork and noodles on the back of the stove to stay warm and went about her late day chores, first milking Trudy, her cow, and taking the bucket of foaming fresh milk into her kitchen. They didn't have a separator, yet, but when the cream rose to the top, she'd skim it off for a dozen and a half uses, from making pies and puddings, to using it as a face cream. She placed the milk in her prized icebox on the screened back porch, enjoying the chill on her face for a second or two.

Outside again, she tossed dried corn to her twenty hens, a warm wind blowing her skirts and ruffling the chickens' rusty-red feathers. She smiled as they fluttered hither and yon, clucking noisily before settling in to peck at their feed. She took pride in her farm animals, and Pete, never partial to plain farming—ranching his preference—left her to them. Finished, basket in hand, she picked her way through the busy chickens into the small hen house to gather eggs. She'd already "slopped" their two pigs, pouring some of yesterday's skim milk, potato peelings, and other food scraps into their trough.

Finished caring for her mare and the mules, she heard the sounds of an approaching horse and looked up to see Pete ride in from the pastures on his horse, Raven. She waited, watching until he was close. In the shadow of his hat, his face wore a frown of worry. Things hadn't gone well, then, on his ride to the farthest reaches of Nickel Hill grazing. He barely smiled when he looked at her.

"What's wrong, Pete? Has it happened again?"

He removed his hat and wiped sweat from his forehead on his dusty sleeve. "We'll talk about it later, hon." Resting his hat on his knee, he rode into the corral, swung from the saddle as though every bone ached, and freed the black gelding from saddle and bridle. Raven moved to drink at the trough.

From the sag of Pete's shoulders, she could tell that they'd lost more cattle to rustlers, if not calves to a wolf pack. Dread filled her, but she mustered patience until Pete was ready to talk, a habit she'd found worked best in getting along with a new husband as dear to you as life itself.

At supper, hoping to lighten the mood, she related the morning's incident with the Widow Taggert at the post office. Pete chuckled tiredly at the details, rubbed his whiskery jaw, and said jokingly, "God bless that woman; nobody else will."

Jocelyn nodded ruefully. "I feel sorry for her, although it isn't easy, as mean minded as Mrs. Taggert is. Sorrier for her son, Herman. I'm going to try to meet him, Pete, and I'll tell him about school . . . find out how *he* feels about it."

For the next several minutes they ate in weighted silence. From time to time, Jocelyn stole questioning looks at her husband, loving him, wanting so much to be of help. Pete worked hard from sunup to coming sundown—most often later than that. Each day he rode out in a different direction to check for diseased cattle, calves needing to be branded. He scouted for strays and newborn calves, tried to keep a reasonable count on the critters. With all that, he also worked at their home place, cut hay for winter, harvested grain, treated hurt or sick stock in the home pen. He'd also put in a large field of corn at her urging.

Normal times, Pete would be in a good mood, his natural way. This evening he seemed almost beaten. He needed to talk, to share the problem with her so it wasn't so weighty, but she'd not plague him about it. "A strange letter came in the mail today," she told him, carrying the conversation once again, "from a relative I didn't know I had. A Mrs. Flaudie Malone, from Long Lane, Missouri. Real peculiar."

"How's that?" His eyebrows lifted in question while he buttered a biscuit and reached for the dish of plum butter.

"Odd because the letter was written to be read by my Grandma Letty, her *Aunt* Letty. This Maudie Malone person was asking Gram why she hadn't had a letter from her in so long. I have no idea why this person hasn't written before now—or maybe she did and the letters got lost. Goodness, Gram passed to her grave almost seven years ago, when I was sixteen—no, seventeen." Jocelyn rubbed the heel of her hand against her chest and stared sadly toward the kitchen window. "If Gram was still alive, they could visit each other." She swallowed. "I'll have to write and tell this woman that Gram has passed; it won't be welcome news."

Pete washed his biscuit down with a long swallow of coffee. "You mentioned there was a letter from Mrs. Gorham, too. What was on the dear lady's mind? The usual, I suppose? That we ought to be cuddling a little Pladson by now, an' thinking on another one, or ten?" The wrinkles at the corners of his eyes deepened as he grinned.

Jocelyn laughed softly. "Yes. All of that. But she also wrote that she's having some bothersome ailments, nothing to worry about—her words. Not enough to keep her from seeing Shakespearean plays at the Crawford theatre there in Topeka, and such as that."

"Good for her." He placed his fork and knife across his plate, pushed back in his chair, and stretched his legs out.

"Yes," Jocelyn agreed. "She mentioned how much she looks forward to having a 'grandchild' to fuss over while she's able. She hints strongly for evidence that . . . that I'm in the family way." The room went still for a moment as their eyes met. Jocelyn pressed her lips hard to stop them from trembling. "Francina doesn't come right out and say it, but she believes nine months being married is plenty of time to have started a family." *The way Pete and I feel, too, with each month that passes and no sign that I'm with child. For the love of Hannah, I can't be barren, can I? Never bear a child?*

"I suppose she didn't ask a thing about the ranch, this time, either?" Pete broke into her thoughts with an intended change of subject, his eyes sympathetic.

Jocelyn straightened her shoulders. "Not a word. Even though she's the owner, she just isn't that interested in the workings of Nickel Hill. Asked how we were, she wanted to know how the school is coming along. I wish . . ." She hesitated to return to her problem of not conceiving. *Carrying on about wanting a baby doesn't help, even if I want a baby so much it nearly dizzies me out of my mind.* She and Pete were trying. For some, the miracle of creating a new life took time, no doubt. They were probably one of those couples.

He said gently, grinning, "We'll work on that baby thing later tonight, honey. Just don't let me go to sleep over my Stockman magazine or the *Skiddy Reflex.*"

Jocelyn half rose from her chair, motioning him to come closer across the cluttered table. She caught his face in her hands and kissed him firmly on the mouth. "Yes, we blamed sure will." She grinned, sat back down, and took a deep, satisfied breath. She waited a moment or two and then asked, "What happened today, Pete? We've lost more cattle, haven't we?" *How can we ever get ahead this way?*

Pete nodded, his jaw clenched, and a vein in his throat pulsed.

17

"Yep, hon, we've been stolen from again. I found remains of *another* rustled two-year old bull. One that I planned to sell come October. Saw no sign of it at first, just a rotten smell, swarms of flies when I came close. The entrails, head, and hide had been buried. A coyote, turkey vultures, or something had half-dug them back up." He threw his hands in the air with a look of pure fury. "The hide carried the Nickel Hill, our *N-H* connected brand."

The news turned her stomach. Then heat rose in Jocelyn, and she drew slow, steady breaths to control her own anger. "I'm sorry, Pete, I know how important those young bulls are to building up Nickel Hill Ranch. I can hardly stand the thought. Four—no, five—head now that we've lost in the last month or two? It's outrageous!" She stood up and paced, fists clenched at her sides. "How in creation can we put a stop to this? The first two calves"—she cleared her throat—"we figured could've been stolen by a hungry family. We let it go, much as we hated the loss of the money they'd have brought. We can't continue to lose stock, especially if the thieving's for lawless reasons, not a poor family with starving children to feed." She looked at him and shook her head.

"Nope, we damn sure can't, Jocey, pardon my language. Whether Mrs. Gorham cares or not, the loss is hers, and we're accountable and have to make up for it some way."

"Were you able to track who might've done it?" She dropped back into her chair, elbows on the table, drained from this worrisome discussion.

"I found faint wagon tracks in the grass for a short way, but they disappeared, wiped out by a good wind, likely. I'll talk to the county sheriff, report the theft.I If this is happening around the county, he might already have some idea who the culprits are. Trouble is, we have no evidence. Anybody could have killed the animal, took the meat, and left the hide, even us. Showing the head and hide is meaningless. Before this, during a count, I've thought a few of our stock might be missing. *Saying* they are missing, without any proof they were stolen, carries no weight, brings no action."

Mrs. Gorham had financially backed the start-up herd, and they were able to pay her back some of that, from their share of the first stock sale this spring. They needed the stock they'd lost to help pay on the rest, and for necessities to the ranch. Fortunately, Jocelyn was thinking, they had plenty to eat, thanks to her garden, milk from the cow, and eggs from her hens. And they'd have hogs to sell, eventually. But it was their cattle herd that they counted on to be their real income, their living wage. Cattle they were losing too often and with no return.

"I'll keep trying to catch the sorry bast—whoever's doing the stealing, if they try again," Pete was saying. "The Diamond MC ranch—not only Sam McCleary but others like the new fellow, Rowland—are also losing stock to thieves. Nobody has been able to catch the lowlifes at it yet, and that ain't from not trying. We've done everything but hire a stock detective, or 'protection man,' to do the job for us."

Jocelyn stood up and began gathering their dishes and utensils, then hesitated, her thoughts spinning, and her hands stacked full. "So far, we've hired extra help, two or three, or more, cowhands, for a week or two as needed."

"Yeah," he agreed, "with roundup and branding; hired some with haying. Only way we can get it done, a place this size. What're you getting at, Jocey?"

She turned from her place at the sink and leaned back. "We have to have full-time hands, Pete, one or two at least, here on the ranch all the time, that's what. Heaven knows you can't be everywhere at once, watching for thieves, and doing the work, too."

"You're right, Jocey, but we can't afford nobody full time, yet."

"I know." She hesitated. "I'm going to write to Francina later this evening. I could ask . . ."

"No, sweetheart." He was firm. "We aren't asking for anything more of Mrs. Gorham, although we both know she'd jump at the chance to help us with whatever we need. We want to run this operation ourselves, make it pay from our work, without more financial help from Mrs. Gorham, the bank, or anybody else."

Jocelyn turned back to work the sink's hand pump, smiling to herself, relieved. She felt the same, wanted to be independent of their benefactor and ranch owner.

"I'll help you more, Pete." She went to sit on his knee. "I can scout pastures and do more of the barn chores. We're a team, right?" She brushed his hair back, kissed his temple, thinking of the miles of fence they'd been building together around the ranch's perimeter, and sectioned pastures. One of the first things Pete had done when they took over the ranch was to build a couple of stout horse corrals of strong cedar posts and pine railings hauled by wagon from the town of Skiddy.

"You bet, hon." He gave her a hug. "But you do enough already. I'll manage alone for a while longer, then we'll hire somebody full time. I promise." He lifted her from his lap, stood, and hugged her again. "Now I better get on out and see to bedding the stock. Being ranch manager," he turned to tell her, "sure is a hell of a lot more work and responsibility than the hired cowboy I was and long intended to be." He winked.

Jocelyn's heart stilled. Pete was as much artist as cowboy. *He'd wanted to go West, be a wandering cowboy and painter of wild landscapes, westerners at their trades and way of life, and more . . .*
"You don't regret it, though, do you, Pete?" Her voice was subdued. "Giving up your footloose single life? Our getting

married and taking on the Nickel Hill ranch?"

"Not one bit do I regret our marrying, honey. Not ever." Pete slapped on his hat, kissed her cheek, and headed for the door, looking livelier after eating supper, and their conversation.

Jocelyn smiled after him, breathing easier. She wanted them both to love this life, as well as make a success of it. And, with plenty of effort and the right decisions, they would. She was sure of it—mostly. Luck would help.

That night at the kitchen table, with light from her freshly filled coal-oil lamp, her pen and bottle of ink at hand, Jocelyn wrote two letters.

Dear Mrs. Flaudie Malone,

It saddens me to tell you that my grandmother, Letitia Stern, your Aunt Letty Stern, passed from this earthly world some years ago. She was a hard worker, a woman of good humor, and a dear soul altogether. She taught me about farming on a small farm in the Neosho valley here in Kansas. I didn't know that she had written to you back then, but I was a busy young girl on that farm, and she whiled away her days how she would, being sick abed by that time. I wish you could have visited then; she would have liked that, I know. You would be welcome to visit me and my husband, Pete, here at Nickel Hill Ranch any time it pleases you.

With kind regards,
Mrs. Jocelyn Pladson

Finished with the first letter, she wrote next to Mrs. Gorham:

Dearest Friend,

I hope that the ailments you mentioned in your latest letter, though you describe them as of little account, were put to an immediate end by a kindly doctor. Please be well. I know that your good friend and companion, Olympia, takes excellent care of you. Please give her our regards.

It pleases me to tell you that our little schoolhouse is almost ready for the coming horde of young ones. I look forward to the last more than I can say! We have hired a teacher, Miss Addie Denton. She is young, and a city girl, coming here from Topeka, but she has every qualification we could ask for, according to the county school superintendent who recommended her to us. From our hearts, we thank you again for your more than generous donation to the school budget. The amount has covered the cost of desks, blackboards, and other much-needed items. We now await a shipment of schoolbooks.

I wish I could give you the news of a baby on the way, but not yet, though I pray for the same. I keep busy with my garden and canning, putting away many jars of peas, tomatoes, and plum butter. My little mule, Shay, is becoming quite a dear pet, following me around the farm as I do my chores.

We will soon be taking a bunch of healthy calves to market, and I look forward to bringing you a good-sized payment, as well as a chance to have a nice visit. Until then, my very best wishes.

Your friend,
Jocelyn—Pete sends his regards, too.

Not for anything would she write to Francina about rustled cattle, or other worrisome matters on the ranch. Those were Pladson problems and, with luck, would soon be whipped.

She sealed the letters, blew out the lamp, and hurried to bed, where Pete waited.

Jocelyn stood back to allow her four women friends, in starched calico or gingham day dresses and their best bonnets, leave the screened back porch for the large patch of shade under a cottonwood tree close to the creek. With small murmurs of appreciation, they settled at the table she'd moved outside from the kitchen, fingering and remarking on the crocheted tablecloth.

"Did you make this?" Tarsy Webber asked as she settled more comfortably in her chair. Even with child, she was a pretty woman, blonde curls poking from her bonnet, her eyes clear and blue.

"The tablecloth is from a piece of work my Grandma started, and I finished." Jocelyn added with a wry smile, "Despite my fingers being all thumbs at such." She placed a pitcher of ginger tea on the table and, with hands clasped, said, "I'm so glad you all could come for this meeting to talk about the last needs for our school."

"I thought the folks at the school district office said *no* to our school; what happened?" The red-haired speaker, Maggie Rowland, a newcomer to Rolling Prairie, lost interest in her own question when Jocelyn began to cut into a chocolate layer cake. She smiled as her thin, freckled hands accepted a plate holding a slice of cake, then a cup of tea. "Not that I wasn't plumb pleased with the news, and your invitation to be here." She laughed softly as Jocelyn served the others.

"The school district did turn me down, at first," Jocelyn informed them. " 'Not enough money in the budget to support another school this year,' they said. But 'they'd reconsider for next year.' I didn't want to wait." Holding her list in one hand, she gathered her skirts close and took a chair between Mrs. Goody, her neighbor from not far up the road, and Tarsy, both farm women and good friends from the time Jocelyn had met them.

"Then how can it be that we're going ahead with it?" With annoyance, Maggie swatted a fly away from her face.

"We've had a very generous donor, Mrs. Francina Gorham, who owns this ranch—you all know that we're just the managers." She waved for the women to go ahead with their cake and tea and took up her own fork. "When I happened to mention the situation in a letter to her, she wrote back that it was nonsense to put off a badly needed school. She was happy as can be to learn the old school on her property would be reborn, and my plans for it. She insisted on sending a draft to pay for our desks, a *real* blackboard, maps, and charts. With that support, the district folks reconsidered and will supply the necessary schoolbooks, *McGuffey's Primers* and *Eclectic Readers, Webster's Blue Back Spellers, Ray's Eclectic Arithmetic, McNally's Geography,* and *Clark's Grammar.* And, of course, a dictionary." Her audience chorused their pleasure and surprise, while dishes and tableware clinked. She nodded agreement. "We have good reason to be grateful. Our Kansas ancestors, the first settlers, had to make do with whatever books of their own they could donate. An almanac or two, the Bible, old schoolbooks brought from the East, a few songbooks." She took a deep breath and smiled. "I'm quite tickled with all this, as I can see that you are. We should be ready to open the school on time." Flooded with satisfaction, she turned her attention back to her plate.

For a few moments they ate in silence, forks clicking against china. Tarsy Webber set her cup and plate aside and spoke up, her hand resting gently on her middle. "I remember meeting Mrs. Gorham when I went with you to Topeka, Jocelyn, on one of your visits to the dear lady. We should repay her generosity somehow." She hesitated, giving the others a minute to think it over. "Perhaps we could name the school for her?"

"Lands sakes, yes, that's what we should do," sunny-faced Mrs. Goody exclaimed and looked around at the others. "Don't you all think so?" She forked a last large bite of cake.

"I think Gorham School fits perfectly." Jocelyn kept silent that from the start she'd had the idea herself. After a vote, all agreeing, she continued with her announcements. "The pump and windmill have been overhauled to like new, repairs to the schoolhouse itself are almost complete, and a new privy has been built." At that, the women clapped. She clasped her hands to her chest. "We can thank the gentlemen of the community. Chiefly your husbands and mine," she added with a smile, "also known as 'the school board,' along with Clem Kittredge. Oops, I almost forgot: Clem, old as he is, put up fine new swings in the schoolyard."

"What else does Gorham School need to be ready for the youngsters, Jocelyn? We're here to help," Emma Hunter, Jocelyn's book sharing friend, asked.

Jocelyn read off her list. "A water bucket and dipper, a flag for the flag pole, and especially a heating stove—before winter."

"Gordon and I will donate the heating stove," Tarsy Webber said. "We have a Sears potbellied or 'Round Oak' wood stove not being used. It was Gordon's mother's parlor stove before she died. I'll have him take it to the school and set it up."

Mrs. Goody offered to buy a flag and would supply the bucket and dipper.

"I'd like to donate bookshelves," said Emma Hunter. Her eyes sparkled, and her voice warmed; nobody loved books more than Emma. "—and some storybooks for the pupils to read at their leisure. Some of the books—*Little Women,* by Louisa May Alcott, the Ragged Dick series by Horatio Alger, and *Adventures of Huckleberry Finn* by Mark Twain—are well used but can still provide pleasure for years to come. My opinion, of course."

"But those would be for older students; what about the littlest ones?" Mrs. Goody leaned forward, chin in hand.

"For the younger children I'd give a copy of *Mother Goose,* and *Three Little Kittens Nursery Rhymes.*"

"Thanks, all of you. This is wonderful." Jocelyn flicked her pencil against the tabletop as her excitement grew. "When the books, desks, and the rest of the supplies arrive, we'll arrange a day for everyone to be at the schoolhouse to help see that all is in place and ready. A picnic to follow. You'll meet our new teacher; she'll be there. Miss Denton is a young lady from Topeka. She has been to visit the schoolhouse and is eager to teach, although our school will be her first. Our salary of thirty-five dollars a month, about all we can pay right now, is agreeable to her, and she's willing to board around with the students' families."

"Lyman and I were by the old schoolhouse the other day," Mabel Goody said, brushing crumbs of cake from her mouth. "Made us feel good to see that the horse shed behind the school is still there for youngsters who ride their ponies to school, like we did ages ago."

"Me or my husband will drive ours to school in the wagon, far as the school is from us." Maggie Rowland added with a deep sigh, "Wish we lived close enough that our little tribe could walk to school, leave me and Vern to all the work we got to do of a morning."

Emma reached to give Maggie's shoulder a sympathetic stroke. "I've heard there are supposed to be enough schools in a district so that no child must walk more than three miles. We can hardly claim that yet, but Gorham School will help a lot."

"Unless it changes, the count of students we'll have is fourteen." With a feeling of unease, Jocelyn recalled Mrs. Taggert's attitude about their new school. "I wonder if any of you can tell me about young Herman Taggert? I had a worrisome conversation with his mother, Icel, the other day at the post office. It was very peculiar. I asked if Herman might like to attend our school. She was quite ornery in letting me know he wouldn't, he didn't need it, that four years schooling was enough."

"But that's terrible," Emma said. "Every child should have an education, eight years of grammar school. If possible high school, and for some even college."

Jocelyn nodded. "She said cruel things about her own son

that still won't leave my mind. I don't believe I've ever laid eyes on the boy, and Mrs. Taggert only once or twice at stock auctions." Those times Jocelyn had tried to engage Icel in friendly conversation, but Icel pretended not to hear, or snorted and glared and went on about her business.

"Oh, that poor boy." Mrs. Goody shook her head. "My Lyman knew his father, Dooley Taggert, a good, kindly man. Icel is a different story, mean as a snake and to her own son. She always treated a husband—she's had more than one—awful, too, before they died. Some say she was once a nice person but became a different sort from being thrown from a horse, her head smacking into the stone wall around a well. Others said she landed on her head, on hard ground, when she was thrown. Lyman says there is no truth to those stories at all, that she was awful mean as a child, too, when Lyman's folks and hers was neighbors."

"How old is Herman?" Jocelyn wanted to know.

Emma Hunter shrugged. "About fifteen or sixteen. Jess used to take mail he'd picked up in town to the Taggert ranch when Dooley was alive. Jess says the boy, Herman, is a strapping boy, strong—he once lifted a wagon for his pa to fix a wheel—but awful shy, a nervous child, uneasy and afraid around other people. Nobody has ever seen him much. Jess says he might not be school smart, but he'd be hard to match at ranch work. Before his crippled father died, Herman was already doing the work of a man on the place."

"From what I've heard," Tarsy's voice wavered and her eyes shone with tears, "poor Herman is completely under his mother's thumb, or to be more exact, under her whip, her cane, or a shovel if she decides to take one to him for whatever she allows he's done wrong. He may not be dumb at all but beaten down by her bullying." She swallowed. "The few times someone had an opportunity to talk to him, try to help him, get him to leave, he'd just say, quiet as a mouse, that he was all right and to let him and his ma be."

Jocelyn bit her lip and flapped her list in the air. "I thought Icel Taggert might come to our meeting today; I invited her. But I admit I had little hope after hearing her out. It's a strange, sad situation—we need to keep trying to convince the young fellow that we're friends who only want to help." She cleared her throat, cold fingers of dread traveled her spine. "Trouble is, chances of getting past Icel to her son is as likely as a blizzard in July, unless he wants to come to us and makes it happen. I'll see if there isn't some way to get word to him about our school; I'll talk to him personally if I can."

With details of the meeting over, Jocelyn's friends gathered in the kitchen with their empty plates. Mrs. Goody put a teakettle of water on the stove to wash the dishes and said, turning, "You look tired, Jocelyn." She fingered a bit of icing from the cake plate. "I hope you didn't stay up half the night making these delicious fixings."

"Did that early this morning. I'm fine, Mabel. Missed a little sleep last night is all." She pulled out one of the chairs the women had carried in and motioned the others to sit around the table that they'd toted to its place inside by the window. "We've lost another young bull to thieves." She scooted her chair closer. "Worrying about that, and trying to figure out what to do about it, kept me awake."

Maggie Rowland's green eyes flashed. "Vern, and I, have been hit on our ranch, too. We barely got settled in before the thieving started with our herd. We'll be in the poorhouse if it isn't stopped! I don't think we'd have come to these parts at all if we'd known about the rustling running rampant."

"I'd not say it's *rampant*." Mrs. Goody looked solemn, her chubby fingers tapping the table. "We haven't lost any of our stock. Maybe because we're farmers with a small place and can keep an eye out easier than ranchers with miles of land."

Emma spoke. "We haven't lost any, either, at least at last count. I suppose it could happen to us, though, any time. But I hope not. And I hope a way is found to stop the thieving altogether."

"It'd better be stopped"—Maggie's angry gaze flicked from one woman to another—"or we can't stay on in this country."

"You don't need all these worries," Tarsy broke in, a quiet, comforting smile directed at Jocelyn, "if you're ever to have that child you're wanting. You need to be relaxed, that's what my doctor tells me, and worry about less."

Jocelyn did her best not to react in envy of Tarsy, who already had a small son, Jeremy, at home today with her husband, Gordon, and the baby on the way. Mabel, who delivered many of the babies in that area as a midwife, had assisted with the birthing of Jeremy and would likely do the same with Tarsy's second.

"I don't think worry is my problem." Jocelyn ignored the tightening in her chest. "It's natural to be plagued about things that don't go right, and it's common to work to solve them. Everybody does that and should. What with cooking, canning, cleaning house, doing the wash, taking care of my animals . . . You all know what I mean, because you're as burdened with work as I am. It's near impossible to sit down *airy-fairy* and relax—as you say, Tarsy." Chin lifted, she continued, her face warming. "Pete and I've been married more than nine months now, we are so much in love, and we—well, show it. I was certain I'd be with child a month or two after we married, plumb positive—healthy as I am—but no." She shrugged. "Time goes on, and no baby to hold, to love. We both want children, so much." Close to tears, she couldn't say more.

"Well"—Mrs. Goody reached to pat Jocelyn's hand that rested on the table—"there are ways to help matters along, you know." Her eyebrows puckered in concentration as she divulged her secret. "Drinking stinging-nettle tea is said to be good for making a baby happen." She sat back, nodding agreement to her own words—until she became aware of the other women making faces and noises of distaste. Mrs. Goody threw up her hands. "Or raspberry-leaf tea; that'd taste good, and it is *sworn* to do the trick."

There was a short silence. Emma Hunter eyed the others around the table, seeming to bolster herself for this rare, intimate discussion. She plunged in. "A good friend of mine used honey to boost her chances. Don't you know, that Egyptians supplied honey to the god of fertility? They saw honey as the ultimate food of love. Eat honey, Jocelyn. Stir a little cinnamon into the honey. That's believed to—build up your . . . organs . . . readies your body for conception to happen."

"Did the honey treatment work for your friend?" Jocelyn had to know.

"Like a charm. A nine-pound boy!" Emma's smile was wide.

"I'm not sure I believe this remedy is reliable, that I heard about." Tarsy nodded her head hesitantly before facing the others squarely. "But some women think doing a 'baby dance' when there's a full moon is a sure bet to conceiving. They think fertility blooms when the moon is full. You know, it's because of how the moon looks—big and round like how we look when we're carrying." Four sets of eyes tried not to stare at her midsection.

Everyone turned to hear Mrs. Goody, more the expert, again. "Works even better, I've heard, if there's a 'ring of fire' around the moon." She leaned into the circle of women, her face growing pink, and whispered, "It is also said you have better chances of . . . begetting if the woman stands on her head after . . . you know . . . with the mister. Or putting her feet on the headboard . . ."

"What?" Emma shrieked. "Stand on your head? Head-board . . . ?

"Well, I never . . . !" Tarsy exclaimed, crimson faced and hand on her mouth, her eyes dancing as she stared in disbelief at Mabel Goody.

"I never, either!" Mrs. Goody squealed with laughter and nearly rolled from her chair.

The others laughed at her suggestions until tears streamed down their faces, to be repeatedly mopped away.

Jocelyn caught her breath, her spirits lifted from her usual melancholia about her failure to have a child. "I will do the baby dance when the moon is full. I'll drink raspberry-leaf tea."

And be patient and hope.

In the meantime, she was going to pay a visit to the Taggerts, providing she could gather the nerve to face Icel again.

CHAPTER TWO

Told in the past of the location, Jocelyn couldn't say she'd ever actually seen the Taggert home place. Riding slowly up the lane on Redwing, her mare, she saw that the property was overgrown with brush, five-foot-tall weeds, and tall elm trees. Remembering stories about Icel Taggert made her hands clammy, her heart thump, and her neck hurt. She studied in surprise the house she could make out in small patches through the trees and brush. Rundown and in serious disrepair from neglect, she could see that the stone structure had once been grand.

Most of the white paint on the wood portions of the house—the four gables below the steeply pitched roof and side porch with broken gingerbread trim—had worn off from years of wind and neglect. Tall windows stared darkly back at her. The yard was littered with bottles, cans, and other un-nameable trash. She'd seen slight movement near a large, sagging barn to the right, and she rode in that direction, her nose twitching at bad smells in the air.

Passing what looked like a very old orchard behind the house, sounds of ugly grunting turned out to be hogs rooting under the fruit trees, likely for rotting fruit, one a large boar with tusks that told Jocelyn to stay on her horse and to leave soon. The figure near the barn spotted her, raised from tinkering with a hay rake, started to run away, and then turned back. She halted Redwing and waited, heart in her throat. The young man, in worn clothing, a stained and battered hat in hand, scurried toward her.

"You can't c-come here. You leave n-now!" His pale-blue eyes looked frantically toward the aging house, and back to her. Half-crouched he waved his hat for her to turn around. "Go away," he ordered, visibly shaken. "You got to l-leave."

"I'll go, directly." Despite her nervousness, her thumping heart went out to him. "Please, first I'd like for us to talk. You're Herman, aren't you? I'm Mrs. Pladson, and I'm in charge of the Gorham School. I came to invite you to attend there, with other young people. You'd be most welcome if you'd like to come." Redwing danced in place, tossed her head, wanting to leave. Jocelyn gave her a pat, spoke softly under her breath. "We're fine, Wing, just wait."

Herman seemed to shrink still smaller. "Ma would never, ever let me." Head shaking, biting his lip, he told her, "Please go, ma'am. I can't come to no school. Go before—"

Jocelyn heard a soft sound behind her and turned. Icel Taggert pointed a wickedly long-barreled handgun at the vicinity of Jocelyn's heart. Looking the woman directly in the eye, her voice steady with a confidence she didn't remotely feel, Jocelyn said, "Afternoon, Mrs. Taggert. I was here to invite Herman to school, but—"

"You got no business here a'tall, Mrs. Hoighty Toighty Pladson. Turn around and hit the road for home before my trigger finger accidently blasts your brains plumb to Colorado." She motioned the handgun back the way Jocelyn had come. "You get yonderway, now, or I damn sure will shoot you, tryin' to steal my boy off from me!"

"I wasn't—I was only . . ." Jocelyn shook her head in denial, while her stomach roiled. The long barrel didn't move from its target. "Okay." She was sweating profusely. "I'll go." She looked for Herman, hoping to offer a last word of help, but he had vanished. Turning Redwing, she urged the mare into a trot back down the lane. Her scalp tingled knowing that Icel's monstrous weapon was aimed at her back every foot of the way. She flinched when a lark suddenly trilled and flew up from trailside grasses and nearly collided with her nose as it went by. It was minutes before she could breathe easy again.

She hoped Herman would remember her invitation to school and come on his own. Beyond that, Jocelyn knew for certain she'd never come back here—at least not without Pete plus a sheriff. The woman was a dangerous lunatic.

At home, when she described the incident to Pete, he echoed what she'd already decided. "Don't you ever go back there, Jocey." His expression was grim. "The woman is a halfwit, and a halfwit with the Buntline Colt revolver that I've heard she has is deadly."

It was a day too sunny and beautiful not to join Pete in the pasture with his lunch. Humming and singing under her breath a silly Stephen Foster song about how a "man's handsome moustache won him a wife," Jocelyn packed sliced yeast bread and cheese into an empty lard pail, added tomatoes and radishes from her garden, vanilla sugar cookies, and a jar of tea in another pail. She clamped the lids on tight and, still humming, carried the pails to the corrals where she'd saddled and tied her big mule, Zenith, to be ready. Her sorrel mule, Alice, brayed complaint, *"Eeeonk, onk, onk onk."*

Jocelyn put the pails down, turned and laughed. "It's Zenith's turn to be out and about, Alice, so settle down." She hugged Alice's neck and turned when her young mule colt gave her a bump on the hip, "Shay, you little rascal mule." She gave him a carrot from her pocket and stroked his neck. "Keep Alice company and no mischief." Jocelyn hooked the bails of both pails over the saddle horn and swung onto Zenith. "Git up, mule." She gave him a pat and kneed his sides. "Our man needs his dinner."

A half hour later, jog-trotting along under the scorching sun to the far pasture where Pete repaired a windmill and cleaned the pond, she lost interest in singing about the "man's handsome moustache" and enjoyed the silence broken only by the clack of grasshoppers in the oceans of grass, a bird caroling from a crop of limestone as she passed. The heat sent sweat in rivulets down the sides of her face and wet her hair. She wiped her forearm across her face, doing little good. *The windmill's shade was going to be blessed welcome.*

They were almost there when Zenith smelled water from the shallow, almost empty, pond. He broke into a fast trot, almost bouncing Jocelyn off. "Whoa, Zenith, slow down, just a minute! Pete"—she yelped, pulling back on the reins—"help. Come take these dinner pails."

He looked up from where he knelt next to tools for the windmill and started toward her. She flung the pails back to the muddy bank as Zenith trotted into the pond and in one smooth splashing motion rolled over in the water. Frantic, yanking her feet from the stirrups, Jocelyn dove free and landed face down in the pond. She sat up in water that barely covered her lap, wiped her face, and spat. "Blessed mule, couldn't you have waited until I got off?" She spat again.

On the bank, Pete chortled, tried not to laugh, and failed. He leaned down, grabbed the pails, double checked the lids, and moved them to safety farther back from the pond. With a wide grin, he leaped into the water next to Jocelyn and Zenith. He grabbed Jocelyn into his arms and kissed her muddy, wet lips. "Dinner can wait," he said huskily and kissed her again, and again, while Zenith left the pond and went to grazing by its banks.

She returned his kisses, and when she could get her breath,

she said, "Pete, we're sitting in muddy water, for the sake of Hannah."

"It's not," he argued. "I just cleaned the pond and put in fresh water." He sprinkled a palm full of water over her before he kissed her again, holding her tighter. "A little muddy, maybe, but it feels good this hot day, Jocey, and I love you so blamed much you make me crazy." Gently he eased her back.

She squished back in the water. "I guess I'm crazy, too," she whispered, smiling into his eyes and putting her arms around his neck.

On the way home on Zenith, after a lazy lunch with Pete, she wondered if making love in a cattle pond would in any way help toward her dearest dream, a child? It was about the only thing her women friends hadn't suggested; which meant it might work?

"Listen to this . . ." Jocelyn asked of her women friends at the school gathering a few days later. She held up a sheet of paper. "This came with a carton of books from the school district office." She read aloud to the other women placing school supplies on the proper shelves, " *'Rules of Conduct for Teachers.'* " She waited a second for their full attention. " *'You should not keep company with men. You must wear a minimum of two petticoats, preferably more. You must not dye your hair. Your dresses must be no more than two inches above your ankles. You may not loiter downtown.'* Here is the last one, *'keep the stove's fire going.'* Wouldn't she know to do that without being told?" She lowered the sheet of paper. "I wonder if Miss Denton will mind when I give her this?"

"Why would she mind?" Tarsy Webber's brows pinched together, and she wiped a curl back from her cheek. "Since she's young and this is her first school, I'd think she'd want every iota of advice." She waited, hands on her rounded stomach.

"I suppose you're right, Tarsy." Jocelyn held the sheet a moment, being reminded that a little more than two years ago she'd taken a job with a mule drive, normally man's work. Her companions had been the boss, Mrs. Gorham's son, Whit Hanley, and his partner, Sam. Without a doubt she'd been strong minded and independent then. She smiled quietly to herself. Pete would be the first to claim that she hadn't changed a whit in that regard. "The rules seem—well, bossy and . . . and chained."

She walked over to look out the window. Miss Denton talked with a rancher and his wife, giving them her full attention. The pretty young woman stood sedately in a proper brown dress, a small beige hat trimmed with daisies perched on her auburn, bouffant "Gibson girl" up-do. Jocelyn shrugged and placed the list in the top drawer of the teacher's desk, next to notebooks, pens, and bottles of ink. Miss Denton would likely have no quibble with the rules.

Most of the indoor work completed, Jocelyn wandered outside into the noisy, sunny schoolyard. She noticed that most of the children played tag or anty-over, some swinging, laughing and shouting, except one young boy at the wood pile. He ferociously chopped wood. With every swing and *whack* of the axe, he coughed.

Frowning, Jocelyn went over and caught his shoulder, halting him. "Rommy, give me the axe." She nodded toward the well. "Drink some water to stop your coughing." He passed the axe to her reluctantly, his glance finding Miss Denton, the pretty schoolmarm he'd been trying to impress. Rommy and his father, Chester Trayhern, a tall, gaunt, gentle man, had moved to the area recently from Nebraska. The boy's mother had died the previous year, their farm had failed, the pair lived hand to mouth, and Jocelyn felt especially sorry for them.

She chopped wood a moment or two more in Rommy's place, then planted the axe blade deep into a cottonwood log and turned to watch a group of men setting up tables—schoolhouse doors removed and being placed on sawhorses. Yonder from there, standing in the shade cast by the windmill on the schoolyard's newly cut grass, another group of men stood in deep conversation. From the loud voices, arm-waving, and head-tossing, an argument was gaining heat.

A small, white-haired woman in red calico, a pained expression on her face, approached Jocelyn. "Such a perfect day we been havin'." She fingered an ivory brooch at the throat of her dress. "Now the menfolk go to spoilin' it with talk of rustlin' troubles. We're all hurtin' from the thievin' of our cattle, but it seems to me they could fret about it 'nother time." She nodded toward the men by the windmill, where male voices rolled like thunder. From the sound of it, if one rancher had a week or more with *no* loss, another rancher had been hit heavy during that same time, and so on. Nickel Hill Ranch was the latest.

Jocelyn walked closer to the men, wishing they'd stop. Vern Rowland, Maggie's hard-built husband, his thumbs hooked in his suspenders, was saying, "Mine's just a shirttail outfit, not thousands of acres like some of you other ranchers got, but even I can't be ever'where at once. I lost three steers practically under my nose. Reckon it happened in the middle of night, me asleep in my bed. Found where the fence had been cut but then fixed at the hand of an expert so's you could hardly tell right off." He scratched the back of his neck. "My own wagon and horse tracks are all over the place, anyhow, so couldn't find any that was different. Like the rest of you, I didn't find a clue to who might'a done it or where they went, not a one."

"I lost seven prime steers. Taken one or two at a time—a few weeks in between each theft," Sam McCleary, from the large

Diamond MC ranch, growled. "Leaving a man never knowing when or what part of his holdings will be hit next." His angry, red-faced gaze bounced from neighbor to neighbor. "It's damned hard enough making a living in the cattle business without thieves cutting into your herd and taking what they want, no never mind to them—like they got a God-given right."

Having a weighted feeling from Sam McCleary's words, Jocelyn hugged herself. Some of the ranches covered so much rangeland that a theft could take place in daylight in a distant pasture and not a soul around to see it happen. The loss not discovered for days, too late to do something about it.

"Us has got brushy draws on our place is most easy to hit. A rustler can hide from sight, kill and gut an animal in ten minutes, and be long gone before dawn," another rancher muttered. His jaws churned in anger, and he spat a brown stream several feet, missing the back of Emma Hunter's dress hem by inches. Jocelyn frowned, but he was as blind to her opinion as to his aim. And he wasn't finished. "We need us a bunch of vigilantes like them fellas thirty years ago down in Butler County—hung a half dozen or more horse thieves. Took care of that problem."

"That's the last thing we need," Pete growled. "Vigilante justice without fair trials too often ends up with deadly mistakes being made, by formerly good men turned wrongheaded and bloodthirsty."

Clem Kittredge stepped forward and removed his hat, allowing a light breeze to ruffle his thin, grey hair. "Most of you likely don't know that I used to be a law officer." With a gleam in his eye he peered around for their reaction. "Besides my badge, I had naught but a gun and a rope . . . kept track of the whole county from the back of a horse. In them days, nobody objected when I caught cattle rustlers an' made no argument when the judge decided on 'cottonwood justice.' Hangin' 'em. I hereby offer to take up the job again, like the brand inspectors they have now. I'll put an end to the rustlin' for good and all. A protection man, like the walloping-size ranches in Texas and Montana hire to take care of things." He quivered a bit, attempting to straighten his stooped posture taller, while his weathered face creased in a hopeful grin.

In alarm, Jocelyn looked at Pete, standing nearby. Maybe Clem would be as good at the job now as he was then, though doubtful. Whichever, he could be killed. Cattle thieves had no liking for brand inspectors. She was relieved when Pete said, "There won't be a need for you to do that, Clem, but we appreciate the offer. We can take care of this, helping one another by reporting everything we see, and the minute one of us has good evidence to follow, we'll hustle the news of it to the county sheriff." The Skiddy marshal, busy as he often was at other matters, hadn't done them a lot of good.

Clem threw his hands in the air and shook his head, disappointment in his stony expression. Pete clapped a hand on his shoulder. "Sorry, oldtimer. You stand by; if it turns out we need you, we'll send you word."

"Of us all, you got the least of worries, Pete, you and your wife." The speaker was a neighbor, a chicken farmer who kept a few head of cattle, his name Charlie Sloan. He took steps toward Pete, arms crossed on his chest, jealousy a cold glimmer in his eyes. "No mortgage to pay. The beef ain't really yours to start with, so no loss to you, personal. Wish I could say that about where I stand."

Jocelyn was shocked. It was a long story these folks wouldn't know, nor was it any of their business, but she had protested strongly when Mrs. Gorham turned Nickel Hill over to her and Pete, with funds to buy whatever they needed for the beginning of a working ranch, insisting on no returns for herself as owner. Mrs. Gorham's reasons were her own, and she wouldn't budge.

Following the tragic loss of her grown son, who was owner of the ranch and had been Jocelyn's friend and one-time boss, Mrs. Gorham was more than happy to be shed of ties to the ranch, arguing that she had all she needed and more. Profits were shared with her, but she invariably insisted on those payments going back to them or into the ranch.

Uneasiness assailed Jocelyn when she caught further hard looks in Pete's direction. Tarsy's husband, Gordon, on the other hand, was looking red faced at his boot toes. Maggie's husband, Vern, shifted from one foot to the other, face turned the other way. *Holy Hannah, did their good friends also feel her and Pete's position unfair? No,* she decided, *they were embarrassed for them, surely.*

A thick-set rancher whose name was Stub Harker said, "Yep, Pete could be rustling on the side, building his own herd." He smirked as though joking, but his cold, grey eyes said otherwise. "He could'a butchered that young bull for his own table. Buried the hide and head to make it look like somebody else stole it same as they been thievin' from us. Throw the suspicion off him as he then sorted out cows about to calve, runnin' them to a hideaway place for his own start. Two for one."

Pete's jaw tightened, a flash of anger in his eyes, but he kept his calm and said quietly, "And what about the others, the young steers that came up missing at Nickel Hill Ranch? I suppose you figure that I have those hidden somewhere, too, Stub? Sure wish I knew where that'd be."

"It could happen," Stub blustered, grinning sheepishly now. "Or you could'a took 'em to auction, made out the steers was your own, an' nobody else's, pocketed *all* the money for yourself. Told the ranch owner the beeves was stolen an' weren't never found." He turned toward Sloan, barking a laugh. "That could'a happened, right, Charlie? Happens all the time. Rustler finds himself a few steers wandered off their home pastures. Re-

41

brands them with a runnin' iron, sells 'em at an auction several miles off. If a brand detective there ain't payin' enough mind to what's goin' on, to make sure the seller is the rightful owner of the critters, or bein' crooked his ownself and part of the takin', it's a done deal."

Pete shook his head at the man's ignorance, the fool's accusations covered by a greasy smile. Before he could speak, Clem Kittredge huffed, "You, Harker, and you, Charlie Sloan, sound darned experienced in rustling, hell if you don't. If you ain't stealin' cattle yourselves, then you ought to watch your mouth." He muttered under his breath, "If I had a badge . . . !"

Jocelyn stepped into the circle and said sharply, "Enough of this. You all know Pete and I aren't thieves, or should know, so stop the nonsense. This day is supposed to be a happy time, getting our school ready. Now come get yourselves a plate. It's time to eat and no more senseless blaming, please."

Pete tipped his hat down low in embarrassment at his wife's intervention. He frowned and opened his mouth to say something. A grin replaced his frown when a line of ranchers, led by Sam McCleary, removed their hats to Jocelyn, mumbled apologies, and began to shuffle toward the long table now covered with bowls of beans, platters of chicken, ham, and beef, baskets heaped with fresh bread, and rows of cakes and pies. Pete winked at Jocelyn.

She lifted her head in acceptance of his unspoken praise, while fighting back a winner's smile. Not that the thieving problem was solved. The haunting nightmare most of them suffered remained unchanged.

CHAPTER THREE

"Sure hated to sell off those four-year-old steers and the young bulls last week." Pete, his expression dark, shook the lines on the mule team's backs, and the rumbling wagon picked up speed toward Skiddy, where Jocelyn would catch the train to Topeka for a visit with Francina Gorham. He grunted. "But better to sell for less money than try to keep stock until January or next spring and have them stolen." He continued to scowl into the distance.

Jocelyn couldn't blame him for his fury at being forced by rustling problems to sell early; she felt the same. Even so, "It was the right thing to do," she assured him. "We kept most of our mama cows and their young calves, selling the few older cows along with the others. I'm sure we can build a bigger, stronger herd as it is. We have plenty enough to be thankful for, Pete."

He turned, grinned at her, and shrugged. "Right as rain, as always, honey."

"For starters, we have this beautiful October day." She motioned toward the wide blue sky adorned with a few floating white clouds. The breeze was light, but cooling. Birds chirped, and the air was filled with the pleasant aroma of alfalfa and curing bluestem grass. She especially liked this chance for her and Pete to talk, opportunities on the ranch being scarce as teats on a gander, as Grandma Letty would say. They were both so busy.

She continued her count of blessings. "I'm glad to be taking a payment to Mrs. Gorham, and this time I'll see that she keeps it or else." She was still for a few minutes. "My little school is working out, and I'm pleased as the dickens about that. Miss Denton is proving to be a good teacher, and the youngsters love her."

She admitted, "There was that schoolyard mishap—the very first week—little Jimmy Dary swinging too high and falling off the swing, breaking his arm. Miss Denton was quick to handle the situation, though. Made a sling from her scarf to support Jimmy's arm, put an older child in charge of giving the reading lesson, and in a hurry took Jimmy home on his pony. The family took him on to the doctor. Heard the other day his arm's practically healed." She looked at Pete. "I hope he was an example to the other young'uns to not be so reckless on the swings; that'd be a blessing. Some students have missed school to help with early harvest at home, as is necessary. Rommy Trayhern was out a few days due to a bad cold. Otherwise," she finished, "the school carries on quite well."

"Wish I was going all the way to Topeka with you, visit Mrs. Gorham, myself." Pete patted her knee. "Tell her I'll come with you next time, and we'll make it soon."

Jocelyn leaned into him, which set her hat askew. She pulled away and fixed her hat as they bumped along. "Francina Gorham likes you, Pete, and I know how much you care for her." She looked at him and caught his nod. "She'll understand that you can't be away from the ranch any longer than to take me to Skiddy to catch the train." Pete had need for the team and wagon at Nickel Hill, otherwise she could have driven herself in and left the rig at the Skiddy livery until her return—requiring payment not to be found in their tight budget.

They drove along for some time in companionable silence, Pete's hand holding hers between them.

"What in the name of Hannah is that?" Jocelyn questioned a

while later, her eyes on the balloon of dust moving toward them on the road. "A rider?" *Coming so fast and hard.* She stared ahead, biting the inside of her cheek in concern.

"Yep. Somebody coming hell bent for leather like that, gotta be trouble. Hup, Alice, Zenith, c'mon, mules." Pete slapped the reins hard, and the mules lunged in their harness and swung into a run.

"Big horse. The rider's small . . . must be a child. The poor young'un. Scared of something or out of his young mind to ride like that." Jocelyn sat forward, straining to make out who the rider might be. "What on earth?" she questioned moments later. "It's the Trayhern boy, Rommy." She gripped the seat with one hand and shaded her eyes against dust and sun with the other. "Yes, it's him, on Handsome, that brown, jug-headed horse that he rides to school." Her heart palpitating, Jocelyn muttered under her breath to herself, "Ugly that horse might be, but he knows his job." *Providing the boy and horse didn't spill and break both their necks.*

Horse and rider slid to a halt in a cloud of dust alongside the Pladsons' wagon, Rommy gripping the reins of his sweating mount. "They—they . . ." He bent over the saddle horn, his breath coming in bursts, unable to speak. He coughed hard, tried again to speak. "P-pa . . ."

Jocelyn scrambled from the wagon and hurried around the back to the boy on the other side, still astride. She controlled her own alarm and patted Rommy's leg, could feel his shaking. "Son, calm down. Breathe easy for a minute. There now, no hurry."

"It's my Pa. You g-got to help him, Mrs. Pladson. Mr. Pladson." His face was white as clabber. His next words were nearly buried in a fit of coughing. "Th-they're meanin' "—*cough*—"to-to-to"—*cough*—"hang my"—*cough*—"p-pa."

Chills ran down Jocelyn's spine, the boy's words leaving her in shock. Hang Mr. Trayhern, that gentle, quiet fellow? Pete had climbed from the wagon to stand beside Jocelyn. He said gently, "Boy, you need to calm down. Now, who is . . . threatening to hang your father?"

Rommy took a deep breath, swallowed, wet his lips, and motioned back the way he'd come and blurted, "Drunk as skunks cowboys from Sam McCleary's ranch. They claim—they claim—Pa's doin' all—all the rustlin' been happenin'."

Jocelyn caught Pete's arm, waited for more from Rommy, his cough to ease.

"But that ain't so," he told them, panting. "Them snockered cowboys won't listen to nothin'. They're claimin' they'll burn our shack with Pa inside if he don't come out so they can hang him." A tear trailed down his cheek, and he gulped several long breaths. "I slipped out the back door quick. Don't think they saw me. Pa told them he had a gun, but he don't. He said to find help, 'cause he can't hold them off long with yellin' words back at them. We got to hurry."

Moving quickly, Pete tied the boy's homely animal to the back of the wagon and motioned for Rommy to climb onto the seat next to Jocelyn. She blurted to Pete, "Rommy and his father live on ahead just a couple of miles off the main road to Skiddy." She pictured the tiny shack built by a homesteader who'd given up, deserted the claim, and headed back to Ohio where he came from. Movers, from time to time, had taken possession of the abandoned hovel for shelter.

A half mile from the shack, they could see ahead the curling smoke and brief flames growing larger. Jocelyn gasped and put her arms about Rommy's narrow shoulders, holding tight as Pete drove the team harder, the wagon bouncing in and out of ruts in the road. She looked down at Rommy's white face, frozen with shock; his lips moved, but no words came. Her own heartbeat racing, Jocelyn cleared her throat, attempted to keep her voice steady. "Your pa likely came out of the house in time, Rommy. We'll make them stop. He'll be all right." In the folds of her skirt she tightly crossed her fingers and prayed that to be true.

In the distance, they could see riders milling before the fire, which fortunately didn't look to be spreading. Yet. "Damn fools!" Pete muttered when several shots rang out. There was a momentary silence, then more shots. Pete slapped the lines hard over the mule team.

As they came closer to the scene, Jocelyn's mouth slackened in disbelief. Three or four horseback cowboys, clearly drunk, churned up dust by the fire as they laughed and hurrahed Mr. Trayhern. He sat slumped in the dirt, holding his booted right foot. Blood welled from bullet holes in the scuffed, beaten leather. Behind him, the hut was burning down to a pile of red coals and tongues of flame.

A tall, reedy cowboy, a rusty-colored moustache curled around the corners of his mouth, was so drunk he sloped off his horse, wagged his revolver, and yelled, "Come on, stand up, thief. We wanna see you dance some more. Only shot you in one foot; you still got a foot to dance on. Stand up, cow thief, or we'll shoot you dead and bury you right where you're sittin'."

Slowly, Trayhern staggered up to stand on one foot. He hopped in place, blood from the other booted foot trickling into the dust.

"Stop this, every one of you! Put those blamed guns away." Pete grabbed his rifle from below the seat. "Sit back down, Mr. Trayhern," he added in a tight but kindly tone, "and wait." He tossed the reins to Jocelyn and rifle in hand leaped from the wagon while it still moved. "You damn fools. This man could bleed to death from what you're doing, and every one of you could land in jail for murder. If you weren't so corned out of your minds, you'd know that's a fact."

Jocelyn braked the wagon and scrambled to the ground.

Rommy ran ahead of her to his father and threw himself down beside him. "Pa, are you goin' to be all right?" His voice squeaked. "They shot you?"

Jocelyn knelt near Trayhern's feet and as carefully as possible pulled off his bloody, bullet-ruined boot. She whipped off her scarf. "I'll tie this on to stop the bleeding, but we need to get you to a doctor, Mr. Trayhern."

A second rider looked at them with one eye closed, his voice whiskey-thick and mournful. "He's the rustler stole all our cattle, Pete. He deserves to *hang*. We was fixin' to shake out a rope, an' you can't st-stop us, Pladson. No need to try."

"He stole cattle?" Pete said, looking around with disgust. "Yeah and where are they, you fools? I don't see them." The small corral beyond the smoldering remains of the small shack contained a grey horse; the pastures in every direction were empty. Rommy had told the truth?

"Well, sure as hell he wouldn't keep them here." The third cowboy weaved in the saddle, his head turned slowly, bleary gaze taking in the far distances. "They's hidden off some place. We mean to make him tell us where, a'fore we hang 'im. We got proof he's the one doin' the thievin'. Take a look: there's a fresh hide carryin' the Diamond MC brand in that old wagon yonder, under a bloody tarp. You can help us, Pete."

"That I'll do; it's what I'm here for," Pete told them after a moment's consideration. "You say he's a thief. I say there could be some doubt about that, and it's up to the law to determine the facts. My wife and I are on our way to Skiddy. If it's true what you say about proof, we'll take Mr. Trayhern along with us and turn him over to the marshal. The law can decide what's going to happen. In the process I'll be saving all your behinds from a charge of assault and intent to murder. Now get on out of here." He gripped the rifle and raised it slightly, his finger on the trigger. "Back to the MC where you belong. Be glad you're not behind bars come morning. Go on, before I really lose my temper!" They began to slowly wheel their horses but showed no urge to hurry.

"Bring me your daddy's horse," Pete moved to tell the boy, a tightness in his face as he stared after the grumbling MC cowboys, then looked back on Rommy. "We'll tie his mount to the back of the wagon with yours. We'll be on our way soon as I can shovel enough dirt to make sure the fire goes out." He leaned to pull Rommy to his feet, patted his shoulder, and returned to the wagon, where he grabbed a shovel from the wagon bed and went to work.

Jocelyn grabbed the bloody tarp from the Trayhern wagon, helping Pete by smothering any new flame that sprang up in the remains of the cabin.

Rommy gave Pete a grateful look, ran to the corral, and shortly returned leading the dapple-grey horse, now saddled. Wiping tears trailing down his dusty face, Rommy stopped, stunned, and asked Pete, "Do you hafta?" Pete had taken a bit of rawhide kept in the wagon for assorted needs on the ranch and was tying Trayhern's hands behind him.

"Yes, I do," Pete told Rommy over his shoulder as he helped Trayhern into the wagon bed.

Jocelyn explained quietly to the boy, "First, we need to make sure this looks right to those sotted cowboys." She nodded to where two of the four riders slowed their horses to a near stop, peered over their shoulder, clearly disgruntled by Pete's demand that they let him take over. Hiding her worry, she continued, telling Rommy, "They've gone too far injuring your pa, being drunk, but they mean well, trying to stop the thieving that's been going on. Also, we have to keep your pa tied until we hear his side of all this."

Pete went back to the smoking pile and spent another several minutes making sure the fire was out; luckily the small shack sat in a dirt yard devoid of grass, and a light breeze hadn't carried earlier flames to the pastures. Then they were on their way, Pete shaking the lines to hurry the mules.

As their wagon rolled on toward Skiddy, Chester Trayhern sat tied up in the back of the wagon and explained to Jocelyn and Pete, "It's a fact they found a Diamond MC hide under that tarp in my wagon. I confessed to them rascals that I stole the steer, to feed my boy, here." He shouldered toward Rommy, close beside him. "After bein' low on vittles for weeks, we was about to look starvation plain in the face. I never took no other cattle. Just the one, on that big ranch that's got so many, hopin' it'd not be missed."

Pete asked over his shoulder, his expression stern, "Would you have stolen more—if you hadn't been caught?"

Silence ticked by. "Probably I would. One or two beeves more, maybe. Starvin' ain't easy to take on for nobody." Regret shadowed his face. "I'm sorry about what I done, but nothin' seems right since I lost my wife to consumption, a year back. Me and the boy was lookin' for a new start when we come to Kansas, but I ain't found much in the way of payin' work."

Pete sighed. "I might've found work for you at Nickel Hill, but now you've admitted you rustled a steer, and the way things are around this country these days, I don't think you'd be welcome hereabouts. I don't want you dancing to bullets again. Or worse, victim of a necktie party."

"No, sir, I don't want that, neither. But if I go to jail over this one steer, what's gonna happen to my boy? Who'll take care of him? The place we were livin' ain't even there no more. Nothin' but smokin' ashes on the ground."

"You'd do anything to stay together?" Jocelyn turned to ask hesitantly over her shoulder. Eyeing Trayhern, she wiped her perspiring forehead with her handkerchief.

" 'Course I would. An' that ain't goin' to happen with me in jail. I'd like to take the boy back to Weepin' Water; that's a town in Cass County, Nebraska, we come from. Probably should've stayed there, but I was grievin' bad from losin' my wife. The boy grievin', too, over not having his ma no more."

"I have to think on this," Pete said, his hand in the air as if to ward off something.

Jocelyn leaned close to him and whispered, "Let's take Mr. Trayhern to the doctor, but not to the marshal. I want to let them go, back to Weeping Water, if that's what they want." He frowned for a second and patted her knee. "I've reckoned on something like that myself."

Doctor Fraser Ashwood, a kindly, crinkle-eyed fellow, shook his head over Mr. Trayhern's wounded foot as he washed it over a basin. "Blessed lucky, Mr. Trayhern, I can tell you that." He patted the foot dry with a white cloth and quickly followed with careful stitches, and an application of ointment. "It's a miracle no bones are shattered, seeing as how the end of your third toe is shot off, and another bullet plowed here through the fleshy part of your right heel."

Jocelyn, her arm around Rommy's shoulder, nodded agreement. *The fools could have killed Mr. Trayhern, drunk as they were and if a bullet went astray.*

The doctor reached for bandaging cloth. "You understand that you have to stay off this foot a week or so, Mr. Trayhern? Allow it to heal?"

He looked at Rommy's father for a long moment, but Trayhern, his expression blank, said no more than a solemn, "Thank'ya, Doc."

Back outside with the wagon and horses, Pete advised, "I wouldn't stay around here in Skiddy for too long, Mr. Trayhern.

Tempers are running high over the rustling going on, but the doctor's right about the need to heal. Maybe a day or two, if you keep out of sight, let the boy run errands for you. Rommy should do his best to keep from being noticed, too."

"Don't intend to stay here atall. Me and the boy are ridin' on for Nebraska, right now, if you'll give me a boost onto my horse."

Pete stood silent, shoulders dropped.

"Weepin' Water is straight north of here." Trayhern waved his arm and pointed. "We can be at my brother's, Dirk Trayhern's, little farm in a week, maybe a mite longer."

Jocelyn's crossed arms gripped her shoulders in worry. Her skirts tossed lightly in a breeze as she stood wishing none of this was happening.

Trayhern struggled to mount the grey. Pete sighed and helped him up. In the saddle, reins in hand, Trayhern looked down at Pete and Jocelyn. "God bless you, Mr. Pladson, Mrs. Pladson. I'll never be able to thank you enough."

He waved away the handful of bills that Jocelyn took from her reticule and held up to him. Payment to Mrs. Gorham today would be less than she and Pete intended, but they'd make it up in the future. "Take it, please," she argued, "For you, and the boy. You're going to need it." When both she and Pete continued to insist, Trayhern accepted the money, his chin trembling.

"You all saved me from jail, and likely saved my life from those whiskey-soaked cowboys, by comin' along when you did. Now this," he waved the money. "C'mon, boy, we're goin' back to Weepin' Water. Ain't nothin' here for us." He took off at a trot, his son heeling Handsome's sides to catch up. Rommy looked back at Jocelyn and Pete, gratitude on his face, but reluctance to be leaving showed at the same time. He waved hesitantly.

"You'll be all right, Rommy," Jocelyn called, waving back and hanging onto her hat with the other hand to keep it from catching in a rising wind. "Take care of your father . . . take care of yourself." She swallowed against a tightness in her throat and fought the urge to run after them, bring them back so she could take care of them until their fortunes improved. Rommy had loved school; he'd admired Miss Denton with his whole young soul, was fitting in well. But returning to their old home, under the circumstance, was for the best considering the whole rustling affair.

Wasn't it? She fought the wind and her hat another moment. *Oh, right now I can't be sure of anything, except that if I don't hurry, the train will leave without me. Hatless.*

Chapter Four

It was late afternoon before Jocelyn arrived in Topeka, still shaken from the afternoon's events with Mr. Trayhern and Rommy. Being with her sweet, fragile host, Mrs. Francina Gorham, and Francina's good friend and housemate, Olympia, was a welcome change. They sat happily conversing in the shade of the cottage's porch that faced the nice park across the street. Despite the heat of late day, birds and locusts found cause to sing. Fragrance filled the air from the white clematis that climbed the porch posts and purple phlox bursting from pots by the steps.

"I miss life in Gorham House a trifle now and then," Francina was saying, about the mansion where she and Olympia lived when they and Jocelyn first met. "But Olympia and I've grown accustomed to this dear little cottage, and it's so much easier to keep up than Gorham House and the grounds there."

Mrs. Gorham's left arm was stiff and somewhat crooked, from an injury given her by her abusive first husband, Whit Hanley's father, and the limb was of little use in major physical tasks. Olympia took on most of that, herself.

"We're fine living here," Olympia agreed, in her usual direct, friendly manner. Her rosy face glowed from perspiration. "We've made good friends among the neighbors, and some early mornings we go to the park to sit and listen to birds and watch the sun come up. It's become a pleasant practice."

"Though there'll be less of that when winter comes." Francina's small face screwed in a frown as she fanned herself against today's heat.

"I'm glad for both of you." After a moment of silence, Jocelyn changed the subject. "Francina, you've mentioned in your letters of late that you've not been feeling all the best. It's nothing serious, I hope, and you're seeing a doctor regularly, of course?" She'd noted right away Francina's increased paleness, her shaking hands—but the dear soul was as lovely as ever, her mind lively.

"Pooh! Aging is all it is. I'm not a young belle, don't you know? People wear out with time, just like trees and other forms of nature do. It's natural, nothing to be concerned about." She waved a hand in the air. "Olympia, tell Jocelyn how busy we keep ourselves, never allowing a few aches and pains to bother us."

Olympia laughed softly, but Jocelyn noted her guarded expression at mention of Francina's health. "We do manage to enjoy society's offerings. We both love the performances at the Crawford Theatre downtown and only miss them now and then. We've heard speeches from the eminent Doctor Samuel Crumbine, from Dodge City, who is now a member of the Kansas Board of Health. He's quite concerned about public health, particularly consumption, but also other contagious diseases and the causes of them. Did you know, Jocelyn, that the good doctor has introduced a clever tool called a 'Fly Swatter,' hoping to put an end to those nasty, disease-spreading things?"

"I hadn't heard."

"Yes, it's quite a story. A man named Frank Rose, also a Kansan, first decided to attach a screen to a yardstick, and he called it a 'flybat.' The good doctor, after hearing a chant at a ballgame, 'swat the fly,' 'swat the fly,' improved on the invention and named it the Fly Swatter."

Francina giggled. "Swat the fly!" She waved a hand. "But

enough of that. Another way we keep busy is attending KESA meetings when offered. We're very proud that the Kansas Equal Suffrage Association will not give up until women are given the national vote and other equalities."

"Absolutely," Olympia said, rising from her chair. "Now, excuse me, please, while I go inside and prepare us a small supper."

When she'd gone, Francina asked, "Jocelyn, how is your handsome husband, Pete?" She reached across the arm of her chair to catch Jocelyn's hand in hers. "What's happening on the ranch, and at the school? I love your letters, but I know there is more. I'm interested in knowing it all."

"Pete is—He's wonderful, Francina. Kind and generous to me, good natured and patient with my faults—I couldn't ask for a better husband." She thought of the incident in the pond and couldn't halt the color climbing to her cheeks. She said quickly, "He's constantly at work with the cattle, fixing up what he can at Nickle Hill Ranch, fences and buildings. He's on the school board. Gorham school is coming along just fine as I wrote about in my letters."

"I'm quite pleased with the school's name." Francina gave Jocelyn's hand a little squeeze. She added with a teasing smile, "Makes me feel toffee nosed, very queenly."

"We were honored to name the school for you, Mrs. Gorham!" Jocelyn emphasized with a soft laugh. "It's on the land you own; you've done so much to help us open the school again."

"And that, dear, was *my* honor."

"Now about the ranch." Jocelyn gave a curt nod and brought her reticule up to her lap. "The cattle sale this month earned enough that I can make a payment to you from the ranch's earnings, though unfortunately it's a little short of what Pete and I wanted to give you."

She told her about the Trayherns, finding it necessary to reveal the recent rustling problems at the same time. "We'll have more to give you, after the next sale." She handed the money to Francina only to have it shoved back at her.

"I refuse to take it," Mrs. Gorham said, "absolutely refuse! That poor man and the little boy; you should have given all the money to them, Jocelyn. All of it. Child, what were you thinking? I don't need it, and they do, badly. Send it to this Mr. Trayhern, and his boy Rommy. I'll be most unhappy if you don't."

"But we owe you, Mrs. Gorham. You've already done far too much for me, and Pete, and we insist on paying you back."

"Send it to them!"

"I don't have an address. I only know that they intend to go back to Weeping Water, in Nebraska. A farm town in Cass County."

"That's enough." Francina waved her thin arm, silver bracelets tinkling. "You'll find them."

Jocelyn sighed and returned the money to her reticule. They'd just have to pay her *double*, next time.

"You and Pete are like family, to me, Jocelyn. I wish you would not argue with me about money. It's only paper. The ranch is another thing. I want you to have Nickel Hill for your own. I want your children to have a good life. The ranch is my legacy to them as well as to you and Pete. It's in my will, and when the time comes, and I've gone to my heavenly landing spot, you won't refuse my gift, given with love."

Her delicate face questioned as her glance shifted to Jocelyn's midsection, then politely moved away as she deliberately waited for baby news. A year had now passed since Jocelyn and Pete married.

"I'd love to tell you that I'm with child, Francina, but . . . not yet. We won't give up trying for a family. Pete wants young'uns every bit as much as I do." She hesitated, pondering how much to share. "My friends give advice that's supposed to help the matter. Some suggestions are plumb silly, others not possible." She admitted, "I sat on a pillow after a woman 'with child' had sat on it—that's supposed to work but hasn't yet. Drinking raspberry-leaf tea has been said to be just the thing, but I must wait until those bushes we've planted leaf out and bear fruit, to drink much of that. I've only had a bit from a few berries friends gave me." She sighed. "The doctor says I'm healthy, and there's no physical reason why I can't bear children. That in time it could happen. He tells me to relax and stop worrying about it, but after so many months and no sign at all of a baby, it's hard *not* to worry."

"Your friends gave you advice? Did they tell you about yams?" Francina sat quietly, her hands clasped in her lap, her eyes bright and helpful.

The question brought Jocelyn up short, her smile frozen in place. Sweet Hannah! *Not advice about baby making from Francina, too!* "Yams? No, none of my friends mentioned yams."

"I'm surprised. The advice about yams has been around since I was young and wanting siblings for my son, Whitman. Yams didn't work for me, due to abuse no doubt, the beatings from my first husband. He had the worst temper of anyone I've ever known, and I was a fool to stay with him long as I did. Your Pete is a good man, a wonderful man. You will have a family, I'm sure. You must try eating more yams, though."

"I-I suppose, yes, I can try that," Jocelyn agreed. She and Pete both loved yams, so why not? And what if eating them did help pregnancy happen? She hated being so worried, but how could she not be?

Mrs. Gorham explained, "There is a village in Africa, called Igbo-Boro, or something like that. More sets of twins are born there than any other place in the world, don't you know? The people in Igbo-Boro love to eat yams, a lot of yams. Bushels!

The only apparent reason for such fertility is that strong love of yams. You could have twins, Jocelyn, a good start to your family!"

They sat quietly for a minute or two, and then Francina exclaimed, "Piffle! I should have suggested that Olympia serve yams for our supper."

"That's all right; you've completely convinced me to try yams, and I surely will. I'll eat lots of them when I'm home again."

Mrs. Gorham's face shone with satisfaction, and in her mind's eye she was no doubt already hemstitching a baby blanket.

Having come late to the city, Jocelyn stayed the night with Francina and Olympia and would take the morning train back to Skiddy. She found it difficult to go to sleep, the night was so warm. Her mind wandered to Olympia's *baby advice* that she'd given Jocelyn, following supper. She'd urged Jocelyn to at least try *Lydia Pinkham's Vegetable Compound*, a root and herb remedy, which was a bit odd, since the pink tonic was meant to relieve the pain of a woman's "monthlies" and upsets connected with "the change of life," the first of which wasn't a particular bother and the latter still in the far distant future. Jocelyn had heard the tonic also contained a goodly amount of alcohol, which probably would make a woman feel better. More relaxed, romantic?

It might not be any harm to try the tonic. Olympia had been very earnest in her telling of her daughter's experience with it. "My daughter, Julia, wanted a baby girl in the worst way. She was told that taking Lydia Pinkham's elixir would make that happen. It did. I have the sweetest little granddaughter you ever saw, due to *Lydia Pinkham's Vegetable Compound*. Of course, they've moved too far away to see them often; they live in Indiana. I'll stay here in Kansas as long as Francina needs me, but eventually I expect I'll move to Indiana."

Next morning, Jocelyn took a walk in the park with her friends. Unfortunately, there were mothers with frilly dressed, pink-cheeked babies in prams and baby carriages each direction she looked, and it was hard to hide feelings of unfairness and tears of jealousy that threatened. Hard to laugh and talk with a lump in her throat. Soon after, she hugged the two women and told them goodbye; it was time for her to return home.

When Pete met her at the train station back in Skiddy, Jocelyn told him, pulling back from his hug, "I want to stop at the general store before we go home. I need to buy some yams, there, and Lydia Pinkham's at the drug store."

"What in tarnation is 'Lydia Pinkham's'?" Pete, sensing her excitement, frowned and stood away, hands on his hips. "It's a kind of cloth, right?" His blue eyes glowed with hope that he was right, wanting to please. "I think I might've heard of Lydia Pinkham's—" he studied a second or two. "Is it candy— chocolates in a box? Sure honey, we'll get you some."

"It isn't candy or fabric." She bit her lip to keep from laughing. "It's an herbal tonic. For one thing, it contains unicorn root and other such; it's a woman's medicine."

"You're sick? You didn't tell me—you don't look bad, in fact you look prettier than ever." He gave her a kiss on the cheek. "No fever." He shrugged, still puzzled.

"I'm not sick. I feel fine. I'll tell you more about it tonight." She slipped her arm through his and nestled her cheek against him as they walked to Noack's General Store for the yams, and to the drugstore for the pink elixir—thinking of the night to come. How long might it take for *Lydia Pinkham's Vegetable Compound* and the yams to take effect? She hoped it'd be soon and not turn out to be another unhappy failure.

The first thing Jocelyn did on arriving at home was to take a goodly dose of Lydia Pinkham's and make a sweet potato pie of the yams. Several days later, having given Rommy and his father time to reach their destination, she wrote a draft covering the remaining amount of the payment intended for Mrs. Gorham, put it an envelope addressed to Mr. Chester Trayhern in care of Mr. Dirk Trayhern, General Delivery, Weeping Water, Nebraska. God willing it would reach them, for they'd surely need the money.

In the next few weeks Jocelyn continued to wonder if sending Rommy and his father away was the right thing to do. She missed the boy those times she visited the school, and so did Miss Denton. Talk now was how cattle rustling had dropped off with Trayhern gone. She was convinced that the gunplay had driven fear into the thief or thieves, positive that it was not that the Trayherns had returned to Nebraska. In any event, she was glad the thieving had halted. Hopefully, it wasn't just a lull that'd pick up again.

Following the Thanksgiving program at Gorham School, Jocelyn weaved through noisy youngsters in pilgrim and Indian costume as they headed toward the cloak room and their coats and caps. She joined a group of parents and older folks by the door, a few still consuming pumpkin pie and cider and congratulating Miss Denton for the outstanding rendition of the revered holiday. Jocelyn had just thanked the teacher herself when Clem Kittredge caught her elbow and muttered that he'd like to talk to her, outside. She grabbed her shawl and followed him.

"I think it was Icel Taggert that stole all that cattle been missing the last months," he told her as they stood just around the corner of the schoolhouse. "Maybe her boy helping and some others in cahoots with them."

"Why on earth would you think that, Clem? Mrs. Taggert? She's an odd one and prickly as a basket of tangled knitting needles, but I can't see her stealing our cattle. And thank Hannah rustling troubles finally slowed to a stop."

"It may be stopped for now, but she ought to be investigated and brought in for trial for what she done and before spring and it starts happening again, new calves disappearing from this ranch and that. You might think I'm imagining things, but I ain't. I been thinking on this a bunch lately. It's mighty suspicious how Widow Taggert and her son don't let anyone come near their place. Because they're so unfriendly nobody knows what they could be doin'. While we all turn a blind eye out of sympathy for them," he finished in disgust.

"Clem, you know as well as I do that her being an ornery old woman, and unfriendly to people, doesn't necessarily make her a cattle rustler, too. Icel? I just can't believe you'd think that, Clem." Even as she said it, Jocelyn wondered if Icel Taggert might be hiding something. Like rustled cattle.

"Well, Missy," he lowered his voice. "She's had three husbands. All of 'em died. She got the ranch by marryin' the first husband, then he dies from food poisonin', makin' the ranch and his fancy house hers. Married again, to a poor old man, a lonesome widower, adding his ranch holdin's to hers. He died, they said from old age an' maybe so, but Icel coulda helped that to happen sooner. Dooley Taggert, her last husband, was healthy, doing most of the work on the ranch, gave her the son she has, Herman, but when Dooley got hurt from a fall in the barn, cripplin' him, and couldn't do much work on the ranch, he up an' is gored to death by a bull. Supposedly, Icel and the boy was off doin' somethin', too far from the home-place to save the poor crippled fella. Who shouldn't a been near the bull no way." He leveled his gaze into Jocelyn's eyes. "I don't believe a one of them reasons for the husbands' deaths."

His story had given Jocelyn chills. "I can tell you're serious about this, Clem. And maybe she did have something to do with the loss of the men she married, although that's hard for me to believe. There surely was an investigation to prove that she did, or didn't, get rid of them. Regardless, you believe she's a killer, and now a cattle thief?"

"Yep, I do. And the story I hear from folks is that she's about to lose the ranch, and this time ain't nobody goin' to marry her to save it. Stealin' cattle helps keep the ranch workin'. She also pays dear for the bootleg whiskey she's partial to and sends the boy after. She wants nobody knowin' her true business. But word percolates from here and there, and it ain't no trouble at all puttin' the truth together."

"Other than to take all this to the Skiddy marshal, who must've already looked into the deaths if there was anything suspicious when they happened, I don't know what else can be done."

"They could have made me a brand inspector. I'd have had it settled one way or the other afore now. That mean old lady thief'd be behind bars."

"Tell the marshal this, Clem, if it will make you feel better. Or go down to Council Grave and see the county sheriff about it. But don't you try to do anything about your suspicions by yourself. That woman's reaction to being accused could set her off to doing something dangerous. With her nature, anything could happen. All right? Will you promise not to go anywhere near the Taggert place?"

He stood rigid, looking at the ground, everything about him indicating he wanted to refuse her. "I think a lot of you, Clem; you're decent and well meaning. If she took a notion to shoot you for troubling her, I couldn't bear it. None of the community could. Everybody cares a lot for you, Clem."

He grumbled "aw'right" and set out to get his horse from the shed, but she could see he wasn't happy about making her the promise.

Remembering some recent news that Pete had shared with

her, she called after him, "You do know that since the other fellow left, the county plans to hire a new brand inspector, a young fellow who's had training in patrolling, how to look for evidence, exercising the law legally, and so forth? They'll find the right man, any day."

His back stiffened like she'd hit him. He halted for a few seconds, then kept going. He led his horse from the shed, climbed into the saddle, and turned toward home without giving her a second glance.

You can't please everybody every time, she reminded herself, her heart sinking. It stung for Clem to scorn her when she'd only wanted to make sure he stayed safe. Sighing, shivering from the chill autumn air, she hurried to help Miss Denton put the schoolhouse back in order and clean up the mess of pie and cider and costumes, now that the last of the children and their parents were leaving in their wagons or on horseback.

She wished Clem hadn't brought up the subject of Icel Taggert. She had so many things she needed to keep her mind on. Maggoty thoughts about that hard woman wasn't one of them.

CHAPTER FIVE

Jocelyn had just taken a second pumpkin pie from the oven when she heard the mail carrier's horse-drawn buggy rattling up the lane. She wiped her hands on her apron, smoothed her hair, and went to meet the carrier. Rural Free Delivery was new in their part of the country, and RFD was so much better than having to wait for a trip to town to get the mail. Or depend on a neighbor if they went to town.

The carrier had drawn his buggy to a halt, was rooting in a large leather bag until he found what he was looking for, and held the mail out to her. "Letter for you, Mrs. Pladson." Likely from poor eyesight, he held it at arm's length, reading the envelope. "Comes all the way from someplace called Long Lane, in Missoura." For some reason, he reminded her of a small brown squirrel, beady-eyed, with his head swiveling sharply to look from the letter to her, and back to the letter.

"Thank you, Mr. . . ." She could never remember his name. Was it Hobb Rankin or Hobb Raynor or something else entirely? "Thank you—sir. I appreciate your bringing the mail to my house. Would you like to come in for a cup of coffee and a slice of pie?"

"Would surely like to but have to be on my way. I thought maybe, that you'd . . . well, open it and share the news. If it's good news or bad, funny or sad, I'm here to help you with whatever it is. Part of my job," he fabricated with a wide, hopeful grin.

"Oh—sure." Jocelyn opened the letter, quickly scanned it, a first line that read, *My Aunt Letty left this Nickel Hill ranch to YOU, and we weren't told nothing about it?*

"In the name of Sweet Hannah, I can hardly believe this. From a relative"—she waved the sheet of paper—"a body I've never met or know anything about. I had to tell her a while ago that my grandmother, who was also her aunt, had passed. Now, for goodness sake, without a word of condolence, being sorry for Gram's death, she wants to know what she has coming from Gram's will! Property or cash, maybe jewelry of value?" It was a moment before she realized she'd spilled foolish family details she'd normally keep to herself, and Pete.

It was this little brown squirrel of a man waiting greedily for news that had caused her to spill what should be of no mind to him.

He was looking at her intently, saying, "Well, you know how it is with some folks; they get plumb greedy for what's left when somebody takes their last sleep." His face wrinkled in curiosity. "Did your grandmother have wealth or goods, or fine animals that should go to them? If you don't mind my askin'?"

I do mind. But, with a sigh, answered, "No. Not a thing." Unless you counted a tobacco can of seeds she'd already planted and harvested, plus a half-finished piece of crochet work. The farm had been in Jocelyn's name, which she and her father worked until it was lost to the bank. Papa had died soon after that; there was nothing left. The most she had to remember of Gram was her crochet that she'd finished into a small tablecloth. "Nothing," she repeated to . . . whatever his name was. "I'll be getting back to my kitchen and allow you to be on your way."

Jocelyn took the letter to the house and sat down, hard. She reread the letter. Whatever was she going to tell this person, that she'd believe? The truth, she decided. That was all she could do. With her jaw set, teeth clenched, and her feet tapping under the table, she wrote yet another letter to this woman who was really beginning to fry her manners to a crisp.

Dear Mrs. Malone, (or would you like me to use your given name, Flaudie?)

I'm sorry to have to tell you that Letty, (my grandmother, your aunt) left no will. She would have had very little to pass along to relatives in any case, and most definitely no ranch. Not to say that she wasn't a grand person; she was, and very hard working as a washerwoman in Kansas City. You may have known that she, and I, lived there years ago, in the city? When I was twelve, I took my ailing grandmother to live on my father's Neosho Valley farm, here in Kansas. Unfortunately, the bank took over that property in time. No need my going into detail about that, except to say that Papa was not the best of farmers, and times were hard for everybody.

My husband, Pete, and I welcome you to come visit us at our home, should you ever come to Kansas. We are MANAGERS of Nickel Hill Ranch, not owners. The ranch is a few miles west of Skiddy, Kansas. Pleasant country, even if I do say so.

Again, I wish I had better news to give.

Kind regards,
Jocelyn Royal Pladson

She felt a touch guilty for not mentioning the crocheted tablecloth, but in truth it was more hers than Grandma Letty's. Her work and crochet thread had finished it. The tobacco can of seed that had been Gram's was long since planted in Jocelyn's first garden at Nickel Hill. For fair certain neither was what Flaudie Malone was after, anyhow.

"No, Shay, you can't go." Jocelyn tussled her mule colt back into the corral and locked the gate. She straightened her broad-brimmed hat, an old one of Pete's, that had come askew. "You stay here with your mama, Wing." She nodded toward her chestnut mare, Redwing, whose head turned to face Jocelyn but didn't seem that concerned about her baby. "I'm riding Alice, today, and taking Zenith along because it's been a while for him, too." Fact was her mules hated to be separated, but Alice was a touch better about it than Zenith. She spoke to the animals as though they understood. She figured they did understand some of what she said, from her tone. "You two will get your turn, promise."

She swung aboard, tied her canteen of warm coffee to the saddle horn, gave Alice a pat, clicked her tongue, and reins in hand set off in the bright but chilly December afternoon to check the southeast pasture for the possibility of a sick cow, or a new calf born out of season, either or both needing attention. And maybe spot a cedar tree in a gully that later could be cut for a Christmas tree. Only incidentally was it the same direction as the Triangle T, Icel Taggert's ranch land, an area she preferred to keep her distance from.

As she rode, she was filled with a feeling of contentment. She'd loved the little farm in her past, but she loved this ranch even more. In summer, the waving endless pastures of tall bluestem grass, the red dots of grazing Hereford cattle and half-grown calves, the immense blue sky cupped over all to her was the most beautiful thing in the world. Watching the reunion of a younger, bawling calf separated from its mama, taking its dinner, touched her heart. Today, in December, the scattered cows fed on old grass, drank at the ponds that so far weren't iced over. Should there be snow, later, she and Pete would load hay on a wagon hitched up to her mule team and take it to the cattle.

She snugged her chin down into the collar of her old wool coat. As she rode along, her mind turned to Pete's mission today. He'd ridden up to Geary county and the 7Cs Ranch, where he used to be a hired hand, to talk to his old friend, Red, who still rode for the brand. It was in Pete's mind to hire Red to work for him and Jocelyn, providing that Red's boss and his wife, the Currans, could spare Red and he was willing. The problem, as Jocelyn saw it, was that close friends though Pete and Red Miller were, they were different, more so now that Pete was married. She liked happy-go-lucky Red well enough, but he still lived the wild and free way of life that Pete had left behind: riding hell bent for town on Saturday nights, near drowning himself in liquor, getting in fights, chasing women.

Though Red seemed happy enough that Pete and Jocelyn married, afterward he resented that Pete couldn't, or wouldn't, join him on his Saturday night carousing. She liked to believe that Pete preferred staying home with her, but she also knew that he was often dead tired from full responsibility for the ranch, along with her help. No more was he just a fiddle-foot hired hand. She didn't like being contrary to his plan to hire Red; they did need more help. Especially come spring calving time, late spring branding, summer haying, and all the rest. *But blame it, I can't help but hope that his plan would come to naught. That he'd hire someone else. More than one hand if they could, but not Red.*

As she topped a slight rise, Jocelyn was surprised to see a drifting horse, saddle empty, stirrups dangling. A better look and she could see that it was Clem Kittredge's grey gelding, Storm, but no sign of Clem himself. Alarm tightened in her chest. Why would Storm be here on Nickel Hill range without a rider, and where in the name of sweet Hannah was Clem? She heeled Alice into a fast trot to where she could catch Storm's reins, Zenith trotting along behind.

She reached a shallow draw and, looking down, saw Clem's crumpled body at the bottom. She slid from Alice's back and raced down to where Clem lay. Blood had pooled into the grass from the back of his head. She dropped to her knees, and her hands traveled over him lightly, searching for broken bones. "Clem! What happened?" Under her fingers, his heart faintly thumped. His eyes were closed; he was still as stone. After a moment's conjecture, she slowly, carefully, lifted his head for a look. A sticky knot on the back of his head filled her palm. She bit her lip to keep from crying out.

Snatching off her neckerchief, she wiped the blood from Clem's neck. "Please wake up, Clem, please," she whispered.

She lifted one of his hands and then the other, patted them, shook him a little, frantic for something to bring him around. After a few minutes, his body moved slightly, and his eyelids fluttered. She heaved a deep sigh, sat back on her heels, her skirt tight around her ankles, and watched him for a few seconds.

His eyes slowly opened. He blinked, looked around, and focused on her face. He squinted. "Jocelyn? W-what the hell . . . ?" His hand shook as he reached toward his head.

She caught his hand, smiled down at him, and cleared her throat. "You've been hurt, Clem. Just lay still another minute or two. I have coffee, probably cold, for you when you're ready."

He licked his lips and mumbled, "Th-thirsty."

"Don't move; I'll get the canteen."

With her arm under his neck, she lifted her canteen to his lips. He sipped, once, twice, then frowned and reached a shaking hand to push the canteen away.

"Whiskey!" His pale lips quivered.

"For pity's sake, Clem, I don't have whiskey, I have coffee. Please, drink a bit more."

It was several minutes, but it seemed ages to Jocelyn, before he was able to sit up on his own. In that time, she'd removed his neckerchief and wrapped it around his head to help stop the bleeding. He rubbed his face with a shaking hand and looked around, his eyes questioning.

"Can you remember how this happened, Clem? Why are you

here in our pasture—why didn't you come to the house? I've been there all morning."

"I—I come," he stammered, still looking confused, "to help y-you and P-ete."

"Help us?" And then it dawned on her. Clem had recently renewed his old job, as brand inspector, *unofficially*. Pete had told her how Clem had been traveling around, asking questions of ranch neighbors, looking for clues regarding missing cattle. His request to examine brands on their stock, looking for signs of rebranding with a hot iron, hadn't always been welcomed. Pete and others had told him to stop before he got into serious trouble. Unfortunately, he'd taken to sneaking onto their ranch lands still with the same quest, to find and punish cattle thieves. *To prove that he could, despite his promise not to, bless his soul.*

When she asked him, point blank, if that was what he'd been doing, he nodded and grimaced from the pain. "I kinda remember that I was headed down into this here draw to have a better looksee at what might'a been ashes. Just a handful or two of ashes, that somebody'd tried to hide, I thought. A fire lit for a hot iron, to change your *N-H* connected brand to somebody else's own brand. 'Bout then, yeah, I thought I heard somethin' behind me. I never got to turn around and look. Somethin' slammed into my head right smart and I . . . I, well hell, that's all I remember. I musta' been slugged with a gun butt, or rock, givin' me this killin' pain in my head."

"You didn't get sight at all of who it might've been? Did they say anything, a voice you might remember?"

"Nary a thing. Coulda' been a ghost, they was so quiet and quick." He touched his head lightly. "Other than the hard hittin'." He sighed. "Sure wish you had some whiskey."

"I wish I did, too, Clem. A medicinal sip or two would surely make you feel better. As it is, it won't hurt you to drink some more coffee. Just rest here a few more minutes. I'll bring Storm and round up my two mules."

"Bring my saddlebag," he called after her, "and I'll show you the clues I picked up today."

Jocelyn glanced back at him, shoulders lifting. *Clues?*

Showing more life moments later, Clem pulled a faded, brown shirt, reeking of old sweat and dirty, from the saddlebag. "Looka' here." He pointed at darker brown spots on the shirt. "These are likely blood. I'd say from a thief tryin' to get away over the fencin' fast, or a tangle with a mad cow. Or a horned young bull he was tryin' to steal, gored him."

Jocelyn nodded. "You could be right, I suppose. Any of those things could have happened. Or blood might've come from removing the hide from a critter, as well." Who the shirt belonged to was more the question. Along with the when and why.

"I found these, too." His trembling hand dug into his coat pocket and brought out a fistful of cigarette papers. "I found these by your stone fence. And this." He held up the wrapper for roll-your-own cigarettes. "Coulda' been blown there by the wind or dropped by a cow thief." He looked at the ground around him. "Don't see no sign of ashes, now. No tracks, neither, from whoever hit me. Raked somehow and smoothed everthin' out, looks to me."

"I wish otherwise, but I'm afraid that the shirt and that brand of cigarette papers could've belonged to just about any man, and not necessarily a thief," Jocelyn said carefully.

"Mebbe, and mebbe not," he retorted with fire, his hand fidgeting toward his head wound. "I believe they *are* important, and I'm keepin' 'em here"—he patted his coat pocket and the shirt tucked under his arm—"to show the marshal."

"That's fine, Clem, because you could be right about their importance, in some way. Me and my mules are going to escort you home." She picked up his hat and watched him place it gingerly on his head. "Then, as soon as we can, Pete and I will make a count to find out if any more of our stock has been taken. I know you mean well, Clem, and I want you to know that we appreciate your efforts to help find the cattle thieves."

"Probably them Taggerts done it, the widow woman and her son," he said, with a squint-eyed frown in the direction of the Taggert ranch. "I don't need no . . . woman helping me . . . onto old Storm," he panted, struggling, as Jocelyn helped him mount up minutes later.

"Fine," she said, stepping away now that he was in the saddle, boots in the stirrups, reins in hand. She turned toward her mule and with a hand shading her eyes watched riders coming their way.

Clem had also spotted them. "Trouble comin'," he said, "Sam McCleary and his bunch." He cleared his throat, worry in his eyes. "Now, Mrs. Pladson, you tell them I'm innocent. I ain't done nothin' wrong."

She frowned but nodded. As they approached, she noted that the three riders with Sam were the same hands, drunk then, who'd made Mr. Trayhern dance to their gunfire. By now, it was known by most thereabouts that Trayhern and his boy had left the county, some feeling positive that Chester Trayhern had been the rustler stealing from them all, a few angered that Trayhern hadn't served jail time.

"Good afternoon, Sam. What can we do for you?" Jocelyn's smile wavered. Zenith started to mosey over and join their horses, and she pulled him in place.

"Got no business with you, Mrs. Pladson. Just Clem. We trailed him here. For all we knew, starting out, we were trailing a thief after Diamond MC beef. Soon as we figured it was him, we came on to remind him to stay off our range, mind his own business, or risk taking a bullet by accident."

"You and your boys got all that wrong," Clem said stoutly.

His bandaged head lifted, and he limbered up his neck and shoulders as if to fight from the saddle. He grimaced and sent a wad of spit flying off to the side. "Maybe some folks can ignore what's goin' on; I can't. I'm doin' my part seeing that this rustlin' business comes to an end." He blew out a noisy breath and glared around at Sam and his riders. "It's no harm 'cept to the guilty that I watch for signs of a hot iron being used on stolen cattle."

"Look, you blamed old coot!" Sam's face turned crimson. "You ain't needed. Hear that? You keep this up, and you're bound to get hurt more than whatever happened now to your damned head. The Diamond MC can take care of its own affairs."

"Clem was just visiting," Jocelyn broke in with a lie, forcing a friendly tone, but with a hard eye toward Sam's companions. "Nice to see you all today, Sam, but this is Nickel Hill range land you're on, and, like you, we can take care of *our* problems."

His weather-beaten face turned a deeper red, and his eyes flashed fury as he considered for a moment. He lifted the reins and clicked to his horse. "So you say. Good day, Mrs. Pladson." He touched his hat brim, turned his horse, and motioned for his hands to follow. Over his shoulder he said, "I won't be warnin' you again, Kittredge. This snooping where you don't belong had better end. For your own good."

Clem leaned toward Jocelyn and said under his breath, "It could be McCleary's riders doin' the thievin', and Sam don't even know it."

Jocelyn shushed him with a frown. "Time will tell," she said quietly. *A short while ago it was the Taggerts who were guilty of rustling; now it was McCleary's men.* She needed to get Clem home and in the care of his family. In the meantime, he was right about one thing: whoever was behind the rustling needed to be found out and severely dealt with. Before someone else got hurt—or killed.

CHAPTER SIX

They set off for Clem's place, and Jocelyn told him, "If you start feeling dizzy or faint, say something, Clem. We don't want you falling off your horse." They moved slowly, their mounts at a walk, Zenith following close behind Alice.

"Dadgummit, Missus, I've been through more in my life than you'll ever know. I don't never get *dizzy*, or *faint*," he mimicked the last words. Seeing her hurt expression, he added, "But if I do, I'll tell ya'."

"Good grief, Clem, you were knocked out cold, for how long neither of us know. I was careful, examining your head and stopping the bleeding, not wanting to do more damage, but you could have a skull fracture, or worse. Maybe we should be going to town so the Doc can see to your injury?" She looked at him in a deep study.

"No, I want to go home. My head hurts some, is all." He slid a little sideways in the saddle, then righted himself carefully. His shoulders sagged, and his eyes wanted to close.

A little pain wasn't all. Clem was sleepy to the point of falling more than once. Each time, Jocelyn had to speak sharply to wake him, right him in the saddle, and hold him there as they rode along. She wished now that they'd gone straight into Skiddy and the doctor, but now they were closer to his ranch where he at least could go to bed and get some rest.

The Circle Bar K ranch headquarters finally came into

view—a small stone house, large barns, horse corrals and cattle pens, plus the usual smaller outbuildings. Clem's blue shepherd dog, Pal, came barking to meet them. Molly Marie, his grand-daughter, left off removing clothes from the clothesline and hurried toward them, a worried frown on her young face.

Clem waved away Jocelyn's help dismounting and nearly fell to the ground.

"What on earth happened?" Molly Marie asked and grabbed her grandfather's arm, holding him up, her eyes on the bloody neckerchief tied around his head.

Jocelyn explained quickly, about finding Clem in the draw unconscious—having been struck from behind and with no idea who his attacker was. "Is Ned home?" Jocelyn asked. "Could he ride for the doctor?"

Inside, the women got the old man into bed. Ned came from the barn in answer to Molly Marie's call. After hearing their brief explanation, he nodded and patted Clem's shoulder. "Don't worry, Grandpa, you're going to be all right. Doc Ashwood will see to that." He winked at Molly Marie, gave Jocelyn's arm a pat, and hurried from the room.

"D-don't n-need no d-doctor, dadgummit!"

Molly Marie looked down at her white-faced grandfather, his eyes closed. "Hush up, Grandpa, honey. We're in charge now. You probably haven't eaten all day. I'm bringing you tea and a bowl of soup. Now you lay quiet, and no fussing."

He mumbled, "Shirt . . . p-papers . . ."

Jocelyn stroked his arm. "Those'll be taken care of, Clem, I promise." She removed the cigarette papers from his coat pocket and signaled to Molly Marie it was nothing to worry about. Outside, she picked up the grungy, blood-spotted shirt that had fallen to the ground when they assisted Clem from the saddle.

With a deep frown, she held the shirt up and asked herself, "Now, what, and who?"

For the next several days, Jocelyn went to see Clem as often as she could. Molly Marie and Ned followed Doc Ashwood's orders and kept close watch on their grandfather, making sure he didn't get dizzy and fall. Other than that, the doctor expected Clem to recover just fine after four or five days' rest. There'd been a break in the skin, where the doctor placed a few stitches, but he'd found no indication of skull fracture. Headache powders helped ease the pain overall.

In between times, Jocelyn did necessary tasks at home and took care of minor matters at Gorham School—Addie Denton would be returning to Topeka soon for Christmas, her students to their homes for a week of no school. Added to that were her preparations for the holiday at Nickel Hill, beginning with a return trip to find a Christmas tree, which turned out to be a scrawny cedar that looked more like an ugly bush than a tree. Strings of popcorn and cranberries and bows of indigo yarn helped a lot. Pete had invited Red, who from now on would be working for them, and Jocelyn had invited the Goodys, to join them for Christmas day dinner.

Jocelyn hustled about the kitchen, enjoying the aromas of her meal—beef roast in the oven, ham and corn pudding in the warming oven, cranberries stewing on top of the stove—she shouldn't have used so many cranberries for the tree; there might not be enough. Thank goodness the mince pies and apple cake were baked and cooling. At the sound of harness bells tinkling up the lane, she had to smile. A light snow had fallen Christmas Eve and this morning, but not enough to keep Mabel and Lyman from traveling the few miles from their farm in their buggy.

Moments later, the Goodys were at the door, cheeks and

noses red from the cold, their hats and shoulders dusted lightly with snow. "Punkin pie," Mabel said, handing the pie to Jocelyn, "and Lyman has the brown sugar candy I made."

"Thank you so much, Mabel. You didn't need to do this, but we'll enjoy the pie and candy, I know."

Lyman handed Jocelyn the small basket of candy and joined Pete to put the Goodys' team up and check on the Nickel Hill stock.

"Did Pete like his shirt?" Mabel wanted to know as she removed her hat and coat. She had helped Jocelyn make a blue wool shirt for Pete's Christmas present and a white neckerchief to go with it. They'd opened their presents last night.

"He's real tickled, and he's wearing it today. Come see my present from him." She hung Mabel's hat and coat by the door and led the way into the front room. Wearing a proud smile, she pointed to a painting Pete had hung on the wall an hour earlier.

"Glory be, that's a beautiful picture. You don't tell me Pete painted it himself, do you? I remember you once saying he was a cowboy artist before you got married."

"He did. I love the colors of the sunset, the shadows of the windmill on the pond." Pete admired the art of Frederic Remington, had every intention to travel the West, painting what he saw, before they decided to marry and take on the Nickel Hill Ranch. At times she regretted that his life had to change so much. But she was sure the way he loved drawing and painting, he'd always be doing one or the other when he could. Maybe one day he'd be a professional. He'd sold some drawings in the past.

"But that's here, on Nickel Hill pasture, ain't it?" Mabel was saying. Eyes squinting, she moved closer to the painting. "Pretty little pond."

"It is," Jocelyn answered, feeling her face color at a special memory of the place. "I wish Pete had more time to paint. He sketches sometimes when he's resting out in the pastures, or at night when the work's all done. He's very good, you can see."

"He sure enough is."

Jocelyn nodded and gave the painting another loving look. "Better get back to my dinner. You can set the table for me, Mabel, if you like."

Just as they were thinking to go ahead and eat without him, Red Miller arrived, unsteady on his feet, eyes glassy and red. Jocelyn's jaw clenched. *Sotted to the gills, and Pete is hiring him to be our hired man?* She took his black hat and tried not to breathe in the strong smell of alcohol he carried.

When Red was drinking—drunk to be more specific—he was full of talk, loud to the point of bellowing, his Kansas twang strong enough to damage listeners' eardrums.

All through dinner, hesitating to take a forkful of food now and then, he told bronc riding stories—how well he rode and his number of injuries and where on his body they occurred, not to mention places where he'd been gored by long-horned steers when trying to take them down. True tales about prairie wind wagons, which was a wagon with sails pushed by the wind—a grand invention and fine means of transportation, until caught by a whirlwind and hurled thirty feet into the air, losing the passenger. Close to weeping, he lamented the passing of Black Kettle, the wild stallion (not the Comanche Chief, another Black Kettle). For two decades, innumerable men had chased the magnificent black stallion, Black Kettle, across the open Kansas plains.

Jocelyn sent an apologetic glance at her guests and found that Mabel and Lyman were as rapt as if Red Miller were Lincoln talking Gettysburg. *Well then.* She smiled her relief and paid more heed to Red's rambling stories.

"You remember Black Kettle, don't you, Pete?" Red asked, waving his hand and nearly knocking over his coffee that had been sitting untouched and growing cold.

"Sure do. Drew a picture of him once, using the information from stories I heard about ol' Black Kettle. He was a beaut, and for all those years of trying, nobody could catch him." He looked at his listeners, a frown creased his brow. "After he was caught and an effort made to bust him, Black Kettle was sold three or four times, the first time being used on a breaking plow."

"Blamed sad ending for a horse like that," Lyman said, and the others nodded agreement.

"Yep," Pete said, "that beautiful wild beast, glossy coal black with mane and tail so long they nearly touched the ground when he was standing, died at the age of thirty years. That was about five years ago. Owned then by an old farmer name of Harlan Day."

Red was silent for about thirty seconds and then began on stories about buried treasure in Kansas. "There is a Dutch oven full of gold nobody's found yet." He explained, voice booming, "This bunch'a wagon train immigrants was comin' back from California where they struck it rich. They was bein' chased by Indians and was about to be attacked right about where the town of Kinsley is now, in Edwards County. Durn quick they put their gold in that Dutch oven kettle and—"—he bellowed to a finish—"buried it under a little tree along the Arkansas River so them Indians wouldn't get it."

"What happened to the folks who buried their gold?" Mabel babbled with excitement over a mouthful of buttered yeast roll. "Did they come back later for their gold and lived rich?"

"Story has it they was all killed but for a little girl eight years old who was taken by the Indians," he said with a bleak expression. "Some other folks who'd been with them come along and buried the others close by. Calculations are that the little girl in years to come told about the Dutch oven full of gold, but it wasn't never found where she thought it'd be." He scooted his chair back and turned to Pete. "Pete, you got any whiskey? My mouth is runnin' dry."

"Afraid you've already had a'plenty, Red. Drink some of Jocey's coffee, why don't you?"

From Red's expression Pete had suggested cow offal. "No offense, Jocelyn,"—he looked at her with an apologetic smile—"but coffee ain't what I'm after." He staggered to his feet, nearly knocking his chair over. "Pete, you're one lucky son of a gun," he said, switching to yet another subject. "Beautiful wife, this here ranch, and stock to go with it. Everything a man ever wanted, Scot free. Only other way a man gets a start like that is to—to rustle cattle." He chuckled without humor and stood there, weaving. "Pete, an' you, Lyman, let's go on into Skiddy for some tangleleg at the saloon, what d'ya say?"

Neither man moved or spoke. Red snorted in disgust, waved his hands above his head, and stumbled toward the door. He looked back with a bleary glare and mumbled, "Hell with ya'."

"Aren't you going to have some of my punkin pie?" Mabel yelled stressfully after him.

Pete stood up and stretched and started to follow Red. "He won't get no farther than the barn. He'll sleep off all that 'tangleleg' he drank if I have to tie him to the cot out there."

Jocelyn sighed. As much as Red could provoke her with his drinking, she almost—but not quite—felt sorry for him. For his being alone, and drinking heavily to ease the loneliness.

"I'd begun to figger we weren't never going back to the marshal with our rustlin' troubles," Clem said from where he sat in the back of the Pladsons' wagon as they rattled along. "Thought my young'uns weren't never goin' to let me out of bed, neither."

Jocelyn looked at him over her shoulder and smiled. "Molly Marie and Ned were only following the doctor's orders. You're lucky that they took such fine care of you."

"Too good," he mumbled. "Pete," he tapped him on the shoulder, "this time we're goin' to make sure the marshal investigates, or sends us a brand inspector to study out our way, right?" He scooted closer to make sure he'd hear Pete's answer.

"Yup. We won't leave his office until we get his guarantee. We've all suffered too many losses last year. Not going to happen again, for damn sure." Pete gave Jocelyn an easy nod and smiled.

"I sure as Hannah hope so." Jocelyn sighed and rubbed her sweaty palm on her skirt. "I can't help wondering if it's one person or a crooked gang we'll be facing. Not knowing who's behind the rustling makes me nervous. The whole situation can't be resolved too soon for me, the rustling stopped for good and all."

"An' the ones doin' it payin' for their crime," Clem said behind her.

The three of them fell into silence. Pete snapped the lines to urge the mule team to go a little faster.

Arriving in Skiddy, Pete stopped in front of Noack's General Store. Jocelyn climbed from the wagon, basket over her arm, and told them, "I hope you men have good luck talking to the marshal. It'll take me a while to shop for what we need, and I'll want to visit with Mrs. Noack and her husband while I'm at their store, and probably with any friends who might be there. If you're not out here at the wagon or in the store when I'm finished, I'll come find you."

Mrs. Noack, her ample form in a balloon-sleeved, forest-green and charcoal-grey gingham dress, dark hair waved back and fastened in a bun, beamed when Jocelyn entered the store. "Saw through the window, Jocelyn, that you'd come to town. How have you been? You're looking mighty sprightly today, happy."

"You look quite fine yourself, Mrs. Noack. And I am happy.

It's good to leave the ranch, now and then, and come to town. I'm also excited that Pete is having a serious talk with the marshal about the rustling of stock out our way." Red had stayed to patrol the ranch, riding the pastures with an eye for anything out of order.

"That still going on? I hear people's complaints about it when they come to the store. Talking about getting a brand detective if they could afford one. Thought that'd be all taken care of by now. The scallywags found out and dealt with proper by the law."

"There's been less thieving during these winter months, a yearling, or a two-year-old steer stolen off one ranch or another. Sam—Mr. McCleary—was by Nickel Hill the other day, complaining about another theft. All us ranchers worry about calving time come spring when rustling is the worst. Calves by the number are so easy to snatch and take off with, and of course the little critters wouldn't yet be carrying a brand, making ownership next to impossible to prove."

"Unless a calf runs to its mother and the mother claims the calf; I've heard you can't argue with that." Mrs. Noack laughed softly.

Jocelyn nodded with a smile. "That's true." She looked around. "Now, then, let's see what all I need; shelves at home are practically empty." For most of an hour, she gathered supplies: salt, baking soda, baking powder, vanilla extract, and, in larger amounts, beans, sugar, flour, sorghum, coffee, tea—the list was long. Many families were in town, it being Saturday, and once or twice she stopped to visit fondly with a child who attended Gorham School or chatted with their parents.

Leaving her supplies at the store for Pete to carry to the wagon, Jocelyn stepped out onto the plank sidewalk to look for him and Clem. Beyond several storefronts on down the street was the livery, and in front and into the street a crowd of men churned, getting louder by the second. She guessed that's where she would find them and hurried that way.

Several of the ranchers she recognized from past meetings were quite agitated, she saw as she drew close. From the sound and looks of things, matters were about to boil over into fighting physically. Men, some she knew and others she didn't, faced off with each other, shouting epithets, waving their hats, and jabbing fingers in belligerent protest and disagreement. As to be expected, it was all about rustling troubles.

Jocelyn's throat constricted, and the muscles in her shoulders tightened. The marshal should be here, stopping this. She looked for him in the group, but there was no marshal in sight.

Pete spotted her and hurried over. She caught his arm. "What's happening? How did your talk with the marshal go? Why isn't he here?"

"Didn't have a talk with him; the marshal is out of town."

"No! You didn't get to see him? That's terrible. Where in the name of Hannah is he, anyhow?"

"He's in Eskridge to talk to the marshal there, about a man they're holding for robbing the Eskridge bank; the same man is wanted for holding up the Skiddy bank and leaving an unpaid bill at the hotel."

"So he's not here, and we've accomplished nothing by coming."

"Wouldn't say nothing," Pete replied, nodding toward the arguing men. "We're getting down to brass tacks about this rustling problem. You go on back to the wagon, Jocelyn, and stay there, or at the store with Mrs. Noack. This discussion won't last much longer, and I'll come take you home."

She looked at him as though he were daft. "I'm not going to the wagon, Pete; I'm staying right here. This argument involves me as much as anyone else. I want an answer to who is doing the rustling and what to do about it, too. I want to hear what's being said, and I want to have my say, if I feel it's needed."

He took her elbow, clearly not happy about her refusal to go, and muttered, "Stay close to me then. This discussion could turn into a brick-throwing brawl, if not a gunfight."

CHAPTER SEVEN

Jocelyn and Pete entered the roughly circled crowd at the same time a tall, gaunt man with black whiskers and a hard gaze at the ranchers and cowboys shouted in a drum-deep voice, "We've all decided, then, that the thief is most likely *one of us,* somebody we know, right?" A few men shifted nervously, some spat belligerently into the dirt of the street. Others paced, appearing to wish they were somewhere else.

"Sure as hell!" another man standing near Jocelyn echoed. "But who?" He looked around, a scowl buried in his face. He smelled of dust, sweat, and tobacco. She moved a few steps away.

A woman, approaching from the edge of town on the same side of the street, took note of the crowd by the livery, hesitated, and fluttered across to the other side. With a look of alarm, she hurried until the throng was well behind her. She looked back, then hurried back across the street toward Noack's store.

"I suspect somebody working from McCleary's outfit," a runtish butterball with thumbs hooked in his vest and a too large Stetson on his head declared. At that moment, he spotted Sam glaring at him from the far edge of the crowd, and he turned a deep red. "I don't think he's behind it his ownself," he amended, looking scared, "but I'd bet whoever it is works for him and is stealin' from the Diamond MC same as from others. Sam, are you sure about your bunch?" He looked a little sick, waiting for the answer. He pulled out makings for a cigarette, looked at it, and put it back in his vest pocket.

"Damn right, I'm sure. My men are loyal to me, to how I feel about rustling, every one of them." His eyes were flinty, daring any man there to think otherwise. He barked, "They all know, to boot, what I'd do to them if they stole from me. They're not perfect, but they aren't thieves, neither."

A mumble of agreement traveled through the crowd.

Close by, the barber and a bibbed, half-shaved customer came from the barber shop to lean against the hitch rail and listen.

"Icel Taggert and that boy of hers . . ." Clem began and moved into the center of the group, "I've had my suspicions 'bout them for months. They need to be investigated by the marshal, by brand inspectors, or the county sheriff. Widow Taggert won't allow any of us close, but a man with authority and a gun could take care of that problem right quick." He stood there, small and grey, and looked around at the others. "You all know I'm right."

"No, you ain't, Clem," a bulky rancher shouted, waved his battered, dusty hat, then clapped it back on his bald head. "No old lady and her boy can pull off the rustlin' like what's been goin' on. Now that chicken farmer, what's his name . . . ? Yeh, Sloan, Charlie Sloan. Ain't here is he?" He scanned the crowd and nodded, confident. "He has it in for everybody who is better off, has a bigger herd, more range. But I been watchin', and that little old herd of his is growin' too fast to be honest cattle raisin'. Where's he gettin' the stock from, if they ain't stole? Is he swappin' a chicken for beef on the hoof?" The crowd snickered uneasily then grew quiet and gave the man their attention. He grew bolder, angrier. "It's him, and probably some other yahoos workin' with him. Let's sic the marshal onto Sloan."

Several in the crowd of the same mind shouted, shook their

fists, and clamored that, with the marshal out of town today, they had ought to go after Sloan right now.

"Just a minute—" Pete started, but before he could finish, he was interrupted by Sam McCleary.

"I'd put my money on that fat, worthless, Stub Harker." Sam shook his beefy fist. "He's another one who gets mad at other people's success, when he ain't poking jokes about it. He's so lazy, I doubt a steak in his house ever comes from anything but stealing."

The furor continued, neighbor blaming neighbor—Sloan, Harker, other names thrown out at random. The whole matter raised Jocelyn's ire to no end. She poked Pete with her elbow. "Enough of this. I've looked, and none of the men they're blaming are here to at least defend themselves. Naming names without anything sensible to back it up is dead wrong. Make them stop, Pete, or—" She was suddenly jolted by a man running into her. She stumbled, moved away, saw that it was the local newspaper editor, Stanley Murdock. What on earth was he doing here in such a rush?

Murdock held up a hand and shouted for attention. When the angry shouting had settled to a deep unified grumble the editor said, "I'd like to do a write-up for the *Skiddy Reflex* about this assemblage's trouble with cattle thieves. If you'd just gather in closer here, so I can get your names and ask a few questions. Your cause is important to you, of course, but it also means a great deal to everyone raising cattle in the Flint Hills." He beckoned with a hand. "C'mon, now, who is first?"

Jocelyn's heart sank when Clem Kittredge made it to first in line. She told Pete, "I'd bet my life that this is a mistake. A newspaper story will spread the empty suspicions these rabble-rousers are spouting. Why, oh, why couldn't the marshal have been here today? I know he can't be everywhere, but he could've stopped this finger pointing and blaming . . ."

She'd meant her words for Pete only, but the editor, Stanley Murdock, had overheard her. "May I correct you, ma'am, about my wish for a story and take away your worry?" He smiled broadly at her. "A newspaper article can be the safest peace-keeper of all, even before the law. In this case, it will flush the culprits into the hands of justice, or scare them into stopping what they've been doing, mend their ways, probably leave these parts before they're caught and imprisoned." He lifted his pencil to his paper pad. "May I have your name, please, so I can add your opinion to the piece for the *Reflex?*"

"My name is—Never mind my name. And I think *your* opinion's useless hog slop." Pete choked on a laugh and with a scolding look at her, except for the dancing in his eyes, he led her quickly away. A few feet from them, the barber gave Pete's wife a smile and a thumb's-up and escorted his half-shaved customer back into the barber shop.

A week later, Jocelyn held the Skiddy newspaper in her hands and turned to Pete at the kitchen table sipping coffee. "He's done it!"

"Who's done what?"

"The editor of the paper, Pete. What Murdock has written here in the *Skiddy Reflex* is like holding a match to greased kindling. Listen . . ." and she began to read:

STEALING CATTLE IN KANSAS—This past week we came upon a group of fellow citizens in hostile argument on the main street of our fair town. Such was the shouting and fist waving that we expected any moment an eruption of fisticuffs or worse—bloodshed. Drawn guns and bullets flying. With great caution, we went forth to find that the raging comments had to do with cattle rustling that has taken place on numerous ranches around Skiddy.

Victims of these thefts have suffered, no question. They have

*lost stock worth hundreds of dollars, thousands of dollars more
likely, this past year. These ranchers have done everything possible to end the crime against them. They have found, too late,
their fences cut and quickly repaired so as not to be noticed—
cattle gone for good. They have followed windblown tracks that
led nowhere. Brands have been inspected again and again—to
no avail. The work of these criminals is as slippery as that of
cutthroat hoodlums back east.*

*This paper, giving the matter great thought, has come to
suspect that **a group of neighboring ranchers are in
cahoots,** stealing from other neighbors. Working together, they
cover one another's trail and profess to losses they haven't suffered, while adding to their herds. But who are they? The friend
you most trust? The highly respected neighbor? We warn that the
true rustlers might even have been present in the hullabaloo we
witnessed! Dear reader, we warn that such things do happen.*

Verily, this paper, your dependable Skiddy Reflex, *declares
that all things must give way to the plight of these victims of
cattle theft. Now!*

Jocelyn's mouth dried, and she took deep breaths to control
her runaway disbelief and anger, gripping the paper tightly in
lieu of Stanley Murdock's throat. "Pete, this article is going to
make the mistrust and hate already out there worse, a lot
worse." She swallowed and continued. "You know yourself that
many folks believe that if 'it's in the paper' it is gospel truth. *A
group of our friends and neighbors sided to steal from the rest of us?* I
don't believe that for a second. Instead of helping us, this silly
piece"—she crushed the paper into the smallest possible wad
and flung it onto the table—"is only going to cause terrible
trouble, wait and see." She took a deep breath. "And you don't
know how much I wish it'd turn out that I'm dead wrong."

She looked at him, wanting a comforting reply. It didn't come. His worried shrug said he believed as she did.

"Sometimes I purely hate being right," Jocelyn told Pete a few weeks later as they worked in the barn, pitching hay down to the horses and mules, after cleaning water tanks. "Francina wrote to say that the *Reflex*'s story about our rustling problems was reprinted in the Topeka newspapers. She's upset, worried about us."

"Not necessary." He wore a faint smile. "You wrote to her to say that the Murdock fella's write-up is—hog slop?" In another minute he showed his real concern and said quietly, "You told her that there's no gang of cowmen doing this?" He shook a large fork of hay to land in a stall below.

"I did, and I hope she, at least, won't worry. I didn't tell her that from stories coming back to me, the whole matter is growing worse by the day. It is, Pete. At first, folks who read the piece were disgusted by the untruth of it, but now many think editor Murdock might be right. Good people, who you'd think would know better, of a sudden suspicion their neighbors and friends as outlaws." She jabbed her pitchfork hard into the hay, left it there, and waved her arm. "Arguments build over little or nothing. A wandering, unbranded calf is fought over, with no courtesy or clear thinking at all. A fence broken down by a cow wanting to graze the other side is blamed on a neighbor, not the critter—a bloody fistfight happening as a result." Hands on her hips, shaking her head, she groaned in frustration. "Where is all this dangerous stupidity headed, Pete?"

"Wish I knew." A deep frown creased his forehead. "Some of these fools have started to arm themselves against this dang editor's made-up gang of *thieving ranchers*. I've tried talking sense to the addleheads, and so has Sam McCreary, but they argue back that we're probably in cahoots with the cow thieves."

He rubbed the back of his neck and sighed heavily. "One feller even hinted that me and Sam were *leaders* of this imaginary gang."

She laughed bitterly. "How wrong, but frightening, too. Suspicion without fact spreading like blight, turning neighbor against neighbor, good friends against each other. Unbelievable. Poor Mrs. Goody is scared to death, positive that there's going to be a bloody 'uprising' such as those homesteader and cowmen wars in western Kansas a few years back. She warns that when a 'storm of tempers' let go, as they're about to, blood spilling is bound to happen."

"It won't come to that; we'll put a stop to it damn quick now."

"It has to end, Pete, whatever it takes." They sat now, in the hay, forks aside. "At the spelling bee yesterday, Miss Denton told me that children are hearing things at home. They come to school bragging that their pa is going to shoot another child's pa if he doesn't stop raiding their cattle herd! You weren't there, Pete, and can't imagine what it was like, how ugly it is. Parents, who used to be so friendly to one another, were hardly speaking, were barely polite. One woman, a perfect lady most times, threatened to whop another woman over the head with a spelling book for insinuating that her husband was a cow thief. A body could laugh, but it was awful, Pete, good friends leaving the school in a tiff against each other."

"Don't fret yourself, hon. Baby making and building up Nickel Hill are our main doings; we need to be most mindful of that." He leaned toward her, and the clear, steady expression in his eyes turned warm. Feeling a glow inside, she went into his arms. Face upturned for his kiss, she stopped at the squeal and rattle of the barn door opening down below. Jocelyn in the lead, both sighing in displeasure, they headed down the ladder to the barn floor.

Their so-called hired man stood there, glassy-eyed and sickly pale, stumbling from a "brick in his hat" after hours of drinking. Not a rare event.

"Sorry I wasn't here to do chores this mornin'," he said with his typical crooked grin. "Had me a little too much 'tonsil varnish' down to White City last night. Sorta lost my way back here. Ya' might blame the pretty girl I met down there, too." He winked at Jocelyn. "Not prettier than you, though."

"We could've used you," Pete said genially and clapped Red's shoulder. "Have yourself some coffee and biscuits up at the house; then we're going back to work re-roofing this barn."

Jocelyn would have liked to see Pete at least a little nettled by his friend's heedless behavior, but, as always, he took Red as he was, without so much as a frown. In the kitchen, banging the skillet onto the stove, slamming cupboard doors, she fried eggs and bacon for Red and slapped down dishes of butter and jam for his biscuits. She smiled at him with each slam and bang that pained his darn-fool head. Maybe because she'd never been a footloose cowboy, her opinion of Red differed right smart from Pete's.

Most of the time, Red was good natured, and likable. She had a problem, though, with his badgering Pete to join him carousing in town on a Saturday night . . . making fun of Pete being "hog-tied" by her, when it was Pete's choice to stay at the ranch. There were times they didn't see Red for two or three days.

After he finished his breakfast, she stood at the kitchen window and watched Red weave toward the barn.

It made her uneasy to think any such thing, but once or twice she'd considered that Red and possibly a partner or two *might* be the cow thieves plaguing area ranches. In his envy of Pete, he'd said that he'd someday like to build a herd of his own, settle down with a "good" woman at his side. Some of his

Saturday nights away from Nickle Hill, that they believed were drinking sprees in town, might have been rustling binges of their and others' beef. Earlier, too, when he still rode for the 7Cs ranch—which was not far across the line in Geary County—it could've been Red, saddle high in the rustling, driving the cattle from Morris County to hide them up there somewhere, fulfilling his plan to someday have a ranch of his own.

Or maybe the stolen cattle went to a meat packing plant. Butchered beef brought high dollars, the "sellers" toting it in weren't always checked to learn if they were the true owners.

Jocelyn began to feel sick with guilt for her worrisome suspicions. For pity's sake, Red was her husband's best friend, a friend to her, too.

Me? Stooped to finger pointing at a good friend as the probable rustler? She was as bad as the others! If all that she'd been thinking were true, why would Red hire on with them? Red had his faults. He might even have rustled cattle at one time or another, but not from Pete, or from Pete's friends and neighbors. Even if he had, by now other cowboys on the 7Cs, or the boss, Mr. Curran, himself, would have seen something, would have known what was going on. He'd have been caught and jailed. Likely.

In any event, she'd best mind her thoughts more carefully.

CHAPTER EIGHT

They were like young boys, Jocelyn thought on a sunny Sunday afternoon. She sat on the top railing of a cow pen, feeling fresh and pretty in a long, lavender-flowered dress and navy shawl, her hair washed and rolled in the Gibson Girl style, watching Pete and Red at their own home rodeo. For over an hour now, they'd roped calves and rode Red's half-broke bucking horses he'd brought with him when he hired on at Nickel Hill. They raced their mounts out of sight across pastures and back again. It was good to see Pete relaxed and enjoying himself. She smiled at the scene, being able, almost, to forgive Red his wild rowdiness.

She decided to make them a quick cobbler for supper. Humming to herself, she headed for the house, stopping at the root cellar for apples.

A full and busy week of calving followed: seeing that new calves and their mommas were healthy, helping heifers birthing their first calf, if needed, seeing that all were fed well and provided water. Jocelyn was returning to the house with an armload of stove wood, after checking the newest calves, when a young girl astride a shaggy plow horse loped up the lane. Jocelyn recognized Nellie Streeter, a slender youngster in a brown coat and hat, a student from their school. Nellie, a stricken look on her face, slid from her horse and caught Jocelyn's arm.

"Mrs. Pladson, you have to come; Miss Denton needs you,

96

right now." The girl was trembling head to foot, her fluttering hands motioning in the direction of the school.

"What's happened, Nellie, tell me?"

"T-they shot at one another. Boys. Bertie Springer and Eddy Franklin," she panted, "brought guns to school. Eddy's was loaded. Bertie's been hit."

Jocelyn's heart sank. "Ah no!" she cried, throwing the wood to the ground. "Those two are just little boys."

"Yes," Nellie nodded frantically. "First graders. The shoot-out was Bertie's idea. They been arguin' who had the Pa that was stealin' everybody's cattle. You gotta come. Miss Denton says for you to bring flour to stop Bertie's bleedin'; he's bleedin' somethin' awful. Some turmeric if you got it, and clean rags for bandagin'." She gulped for air. "Eddy run off, maybe to home. We don't know for sure where he went, but he's gone."

"I'll be right there," Jocelyn told the girl. "Thank Hannah that my mare is in the corral, ready to ride; I was about to visit my neighbor, Mrs. Goody."

Jocelyn whirled to her clothesline, yanked down clean dish towels, rolled them up, and handed them to Nellie, who was back astride her horse. Then she ran to the house for turmeric and flour. She scooped flour into a clean cloth, knotted it, and snatched the can of spice from her cupboard. Turmeric would help both the pain and healing. If the boy was still alive. Minutes later, she was riding hard to the schoolhouse, young Nellie ahead, the roll of dishtowels under her arm.

Miss Denton sat on the ground, holding the dirty-faced, sobbing boy in her lap. She'd ripped a piece of her petticoat to mop at blood welling from his shoulder. Frightened children made a circle around them; several had tears running down their cheeks. "Is Bertie gonna die?" one small girl asked. "I don't want him to die."

Bertie looked up at the youngster, surprise and panic in his eyes. "I ain't!" he sobbed. "I ain't, no way!"

Jocelyn shook her head. "Bertie isn't going to die." She smiled. "We're taking care of him, and he'll be fine." She knelt beside Miss Denton. Seeing the young woman's white face, she said gently, "I can take him now, Addie." Miss Denton's shaking hands had difficulty letting him go, but she tenderly released the boy into Jocelyn's arms. "Bring water"—Jocelyn looked up at Nellie—"please. The bucket and a dipper." She said to the trembling teacher, "Addie, you should take the other children inside. Or, maybe, send them home for the day?"

When she had the water, she washed the wound clean. From the look of it, the gash was just a bad nick in the flesh but bled profusely nevertheless. She pressed the wet cloth to the wound, checking every few minutes to see the bleeding finally slow. She patted it with turmeric and ripped a small section of clean cloth to pad the wound, then bound it with the rest of the dish towel. She heaved a sigh of relief, and stood up, bringing the boy to his feet. She picked him up and carried him to her mare, Redwing, and put him in the saddle. She told Miss Denton, in the doorway helping children into their coats, "I'll take him home where his mother can see to him. It seems to be just a minor flesh wound, but his parents might want to take him to Doctor Ashwood in town."

Jocelyn climbed up behind the boy, wheeled her mare, and with one arm around the child set off for the Springers' ranch. As they approached fifteen or so minutes later, his mother, who evidently had seen them riding up from her kitchen window, was waiting on the porch. Seeing the blood on the boy's clothing and his white, tear-wet face, she flew down the steps. "What on earth happened?"

"It's not as bad as it looks, Lucy. There was a—an altercation between Bertie and another little boy. There were guns. A bullet struck Bertie's shoulder, but the wound isn't deep, and the bleeding has all but stopped."

"Bullet?" She clapped a hand over her mouth, eyes wide in shock. "A bullet from where? How? Why?"

Feeling a growing fury she could barely control, Jocelyn wondered how to answer. Two little boys, hearing strong talk and mimicking their parents, had each taken a gun to school to shoot it out, over cattle being stolen. *Children!*

Two evenings later, Jocelyn surveyed the crowded schoolhouse with relief and hope. Ranchers and their wives had come from miles around, to this meeting she and Pete had called. Their plan was to end feuding among neighbors, as well as the rustling problem, once and for all. Folks were still coming through the door. Men rose and gave their seats to women and joined other males lined up against the back wall. Strain showed in nearly every face.

At the front of the room, Pete leaned back against Miss Denton's desk, his legs crossed at his booted ankles, a quiet grin on his face. "Thank you all for coming," he said, when the door closed behind the last person and the room stilled. "I reckon we all feel the same. That enough is enough." A murmur of agreement filled the room. "These past months we ranchers have lost more cattle than we can afford and have been hard put to stop it. Clem Kittredge was bludgeoned by a lowdown sneak who could've fractured his skull, killed him. One of our school children brought his pa's loaded gun to school and shot another child, trying to take our problem on themselves. One or both could be dead, today, if the good Lord hadn't been looking on."

A man in the crowd spoke. "Me and my wife want to apologize to Bertie and his family, to you all, really. My boy, Eddy, here, wants to let you all know how sorry he is." He drew the boy up to stand beside him. "Go ahead, son."

Pale and taking deep breaths, Eddy spoke. "I'm plumb sorry,

Bertie. Ya'all is my best friend. If I'd a killed you, I couldn't a' stood it." He choked. "Not for one day. That's why I run off and hid 'til Pa found me. I'm sorry." He sat down. Then quickly he stood up again. "Sorry to everybody I caused so much to worry."

His father continued, "Like the rest of us, these little boys had their own problem. One of our cows had been shot and left to rot. Not stolen. Tom Springer takin' revenge, is what we thought, because he was set on the idee we were raiding *his* cow herd. We've talked it out, and I know now that it wasn't him killed the cow; we don't know who did it. Eddy didn't know me and Springer'd made peace; all he knew was that a cow had been killed for a mean reason." He took a deep breath. "That cow was our boy's pet when it was a calf." Soft gasps echoed from the listeners. His jaw firmed. "Shot, left to rot."

A back and forth discussion, most speakers attempting to stay calm, went on for another hour and a half, ending with three men—Pete, Sam McCleary, and Clem Kittredge—elected to take their story to the Skiddy marshal. To insist on his immediate help. Jocelyn would go, too, to tell how she'd found Clem, and about the school incident.

Jocelyn and a cadre of her friends rose and served lemonade and cake. With a full heart she noted folks—for the first time in weeks—smiling at each other in apology, shaking hands and chatting . . . a mood she hoped would last a very long time. In the meantime, there was the call on the Skiddy marshal to be seen to.

"I'm purely sorry you've missed Leo again." Seated behind the Skiddy marshal's desk, Cora Hillis, his wife, patted a stack of papers. "Like I said, we had another attempted holdup at the Skiddy bank." She raised her voice, shook her head in puzzlement. "Most times this is a quiet town, and things like this don't happen. Thank the Lord that Leo cramped this second one in time. He sacked the lowlife back there in our jail for a few days"—she motioned with her head—"on an attempt charge. Time enough that we found out that he'd pulled a big one on the Cornwell bank in Denver." She waved a blunt hand toward the door. "Leo left an hour ago on the stage, taking the prisoner to the Denver law officers. But I can help you." She jerked a drawer open, pulled out a badge, and pinned it on. "I'm his deputy until he's back in the office."

"Uhh . . ." Clem started, then finished, "We need a feller." The bag gripped tight in his hand held the blood-spotted shirt and the cigarette papers.

"I worked with Leo, and I know what to do." Her look was stern. "I grew up on the range, and I know how to read brands. I'm as good as Leo at out-guessing outlaws." She stood up, and they could see that she wore men's pants and a man's baggy shirt. There was a telltale bulge under the shirt. "I read trails as good as an Indian, too," she boasted, coming around the desk.

Jocelyn had no lack of admiration for strong women. She'd heard that even the Pinkerton Detective Agency had women detectives employed with them, but this beat all.

Plain as morning sunshine, this woman was in the family way. "Ma'am," Jocelyn blurted, "are you . . . ?"

The marshal's wife beamed. "Yes'm. Number four."

Pete looked on in disbelief, his smile tight. "Going after outlaws, rustlers, is dangerous business, Mrs. Hillis."

"*Deputy*," she reminded him, hazel eyes flashing. "Deputy Cora Hillis. When the marshal's not here, 'dangerous business' is my job." She started pulling out desk drawers. "Leo has an extra double-action revolver here somewhere." She found the handgun, turned, and grabbed a Springfield rifle from a rack behind her on the wall. "You all wait here while I go grab Otis, back swamping the cells. He minds the desk when neither me

101

nor Leo can be here."

McCleary growled after her, turning for the door, "Beggin'
your pardon, ma'am, but you're not takin' this job for us. It's a
man's job."

She stopped, gave him a flat look, her eyes narrowed . . .
looked about to protest, then changed her mind.

Jocelyn said quickly, stepping toward her, "I believe you, that
you're experienced, Mrs. Hillis, uh, Deputy . . . Cora. But what
about your—your condition? Pete, my husband is right. Taking
on rustler trouble would *not* be safe for—for number four, or
you." It was hard to remain calm; she was green with envy
about the unborn child.

"We were already thinking this was more a case for the county
sheriff," Pete manufactured suddenly, arm around Jocelyn as he
maneuvered her toward the door. "We'll be heading down to
Council Grove for a talk with him." When *Deputy* Cora Hillis
stepped forward to argue, knuckles white on the weapons she
still held, he raised his hand to stop her. "It's settled, ma'am,"
he said quietly, "but we thank you."

Her lips tightened, a few seconds passed, and she nodded.
She reluctantly replaced the rifle to the wall, revolver to the
desk drawer, and slumped into her chair. With a flick of her
hand she waved them off.

As they took the plank walk to where they'd left their horses,
Clem looked back, eyebrows lifted. "Well, if that don't take the
salt offen soda crackers."

"She meant well." Jocelyn defended the marshal's wife, at the
same time wishing she had the good fortune to have children. "I
think Mrs. Hillis—Deputy Cora—is as good a law officer as she
says." She could list a dozen women she'd heard of who "kicked
over the traces" so to speak. To start with, Carrie Chapman
Catt, a teacher and school superintendent from Iowa who
continued to lead the fight for women's suffrage. There was

Colorado's "Mountain Charley," her real name Elsa Jane, who disguised herself as a man to avenge her husband's murder. Nellie Bly, the well-known journalist, posed as an asylum patient to expose awful conditions in such a place. And more. She said to the men, "But we should head home, give our horses a rest, and let folks know what we plan to do next."

The men agreed. They'd leave first thing in the morning for Council Grove.

"But if the law don't end the rustlin' this time, we'll do it ourselves," Sam growled as he swung onto his horse. "Go back to formin' a bunch of vigilantes same as they did in Dodge City to clean out the lawlessness the spring of 1873. When the law can't or won't, takin' the job on ourselves is the only way left."

Pete and Jocelyn looked at one another without responding, but aware of each other's skepticism. The problem with Sam's thinking was that it didn't go far enough. At that time in Dodge, and after killing their first six desperadoes, power went to the vigilantes' heads. Killing came easy, little proof of wrongdoing needed. Violence grew rather than diminished. Two vigilante members killed a man named William Taylor, whose boss was Colonel Richard Dodge, commanding officer at Fort Dodge. The furious officer immediately telegraphed the Kansas governor and received special permission to arrest the two guilty vigilantes. The colonel's men entered Dodge the next day and made the arrest. Two days later the soldiers arrested five more of the worst vigilantes.

Jocelyn drew a deep breath. The Dodge City violence was a good example of why their own problems must be put into the county sheriff's hands, the matter settled lawfully.

Would the county sheriff—she thought his name was George Proctor—remember her, Jocelyn wondered? Not that it mattered; she'd rather forget that terrible day—one of the worst, saddest experiences of her life. Whit Hanley, Francina's son and

Jocelyn's boss on a mule drive, had just been murdered by a brutal outlaw. Even today, remembering, she felt a chill. What a blessing it was, that Pete had been there, too, and helped her through it.

CHAPTER NINE

Sheriff Proctor, lean, middle-aged, friendly, and competent, spent four days of investigation in their area, riding from ranch to ranch, getting acquainted, asking questions, spending time on the range, reading brands.

At the end of it, following a supper at the Pladsons, he told Jocelyn and Pete, and their friends, "I met a lot of nice folks, is about all I can report to you. I looked for earmarks, because they can mean trouble for a cow thief. It's hard to alter both an earmark and a brand that anybody'd believe. To hide the earmark, rustlers in the past would just cut off the ear. Didn't find any of that. I looked for activity on the range, smoke from a small fire where cow thieves would be heating a running iron, like heavy wire, or a cinch ring to make a brand into a completely different one. Looked for ashes, but they're easy to hide by kicking dirt. I even looked for what they call brand picking."

"I've known that to happen in the past," Sam McCleary said. "Thief uses a knife to carve away the hair, or takes pliers and pulls it out, so the brand don't show."

"Yep." The sheriff nodded. "I can't prove anything about maverick calves, either," he continued. "Stealing weaned but unbranded calves is the cow thief's dream. Just drive them off to your own pastures and slap your brand on the calves." He looked at Clem Kittredge seated across the table from him. "Wish I could find the man who assaulted you, and I'd likely have the thief behind all you folks' trouble. Or at least part of the answer; could be a couple or more thieves who work together." He spoke directly to Clem. "The blood-specked shirt and the cigarette papers you found very well could have belonged to who we're looking for, but there's no way to make a connection. Sorry."

"You investigated the Taggerts, like I told you? The rest of us can't get anywhere near the Taggert place, but you with a gun and a badge could've, right?" Clem asked.

"I did, but it took some convincing. Wasn't easy getting through all those hogs, either, that run loose around the house. I went over their pastures thorough, didn't find anything suspicious. Brands on their stock showed no run-overs with a hot iron. Nothing suspicious in the barns. The young fella is timid, hardly got a half-dozen words out of him. He looked sick, scared, or maybe just tired. His Ma talked innocent of any wrongdoing. She'd been nipping at a little rot-gut, was coquettish, tried to make moon-eyes at me, which I tell you came off damn strange." He laughed with disbelief, as did his listeners, and shook his head.

"Tryin' to fool you is what she had in mind," Clem said.

The others nodded in agreement. "Almost had to be." Vern Rowland agreed. "From what I've heard Icel Taggert ain't no pretty young damsel."

The sheriff continued, "I reckon that's what it was, trying to divert me from what I was there for. She invited me to supper, but I had to refuse. I never smelled food so bad, plus the pig odor in my nose, or I might've. It pays to get to know folks well, especially suspects." He shrugged. "Not this time."

"The widow Taggert was tryin' to poison you, Sheriff," Clem said. "That's the kind she is, tryin' to be rid of you same as how she did her three husbands, one after t'other. You're lucky not to eat at her table."

"Maybe they were prepared for your comin', Sheriff. Hid stolen cattle," McCleary said. "Word gets around. You'd already been here in these parts, looking for signs of cattle theft, a day and a half before you checked the Taggerts."

"From what I saw, they looked innocent as babes," the sheriff maintained.

"They could have sold butchered beef," Pete suggested, "although with all our searching, we never found a buyer guilty of dealing with the Taggerts."

"For all we know," Jocelyn suggested, "hidden cattle could have already been sold, one carload at a time. And lucky for them, they were never caught. Probably because we were looking for trouble elsewhere."

"Could be. In their case, or in somebody else's. This investigation isn't over. I'll be coming again, maybe a surprise visit or two, when I can." He said with a wry grin, "The only clues I saw was that many families were eating beef. And yes, I'm aware of the habit in range country of ranchers never eating their own beef. When a steer wanders onto their property, the critter becomes dinner. Back and forth. If any of you think I'm going to untangle all that around here, you can forget it. In that regard, I figure folks are even up. Fine peach pie, Mrs. Pladson."

"We appreciate your help, Sheriff. The rustling has been an ever-growing problem for us, no matter the lengths we all go to, to solve it." She poured more coffee.

"First of all, I recommend everybody quit the squabbling." The sheriff blew on his coffee and took a sip. "Does nobody good. You need to help each other, to my mind. Keep an eye out, regardless of whose pastures, for suspicious activity, or where something's happening that doesn't ring right. Riders you don't recognize. A neighbor's branded cow being sold at an out of the way sale barn, such as that. You'll like to know that in the past, when the law starts poking into problems, the trouble can come to a flat-out halt. The guilty party feels the law breathin' down his neck and leaves the country or gives up the thieving trade rather than get caught, shot, or sent to prison. I can't promise that'll happen this time, but it might."

In the next several weeks, the sheriff made more trips to have a look, question ranchers, learn if there'd been loss of stock to thieves. Sometimes he sent a deputy in his place. As Clem Kittredge put it, "Having the law sniff around puts a clamp on the thievery, sure enough." Not a single rancher had a report of rustled cattle from the time of Sheriff Proctor's first visit. Jocelyn had to wonder, had the law's coming scared the thief or thieves into changing their ways? Or had the rustler been scared into leaving for other parts? There had without doubt been thieves operating in the past months, besides Chester Trayhern, who was guilty of stealing one critter and left Kansas with her and Pete's assistance and sympathy.

In any event, Jocelyn was glad for the lifting of worry, however long it might last. There were still rumbles from locals vowing to form a vigilante group if the sheriff didn't put a stop to the problem. Jocelyn and Pete maintained their argument against it.

"I'm so glad you've come," Miss Denton blurted anxiously when Jocelyn made her regular visit to Gorham School on a bright spring day. They had stepped outside for a private conversation, leaving students to practice their spelling at the blackboard. She caught Jocelyn's hand. "There's a gangly, nearly full-grown boy who is purely scaring me to death and . . ."

A bully? Jocelyn's heart sank. Wasn't the set-to between the two small youngsters packing their fathers' weapons enough? "Tell me about the student, Addie; we'll see what we can do."

"Oh, he isn't one of my students. He's a young man who watches us from time to time. Sometimes from a distance, and we can hardly make him out. Other times, he's closer. When I go out and call to him, he runs away. Recently, he peeked in the window. Set my heart to beating almost out of my chest." Even now, she put a hand to her throat. "The children hadn't seen him that time; I was the only one. When my nerves settled, I told the children to read a story in their books, and I'd be right back. When I went outside, he'd disappeared."

A smile slowly wreathed Jocelyn's face, and she caught Miss Denton's hands. "It's all right. I think I know who it is. His name is Herman Taggert. He's only gone to school through the fourth grade. I think he wants to come to school! To finish what his mother didn't allow him to do. Learn. Read books. Know other youngsters."

"But why doesn't he?" Miss Denton wrinkled her nose and smiled. "He'd be welcome."

"For one thing, he's his mother's right-hand man on their ranch, a hard worker from what I've heard. She claims more schooling wouldn't do him any good, and that he's had enough 'learnin'." Jocelyn bit the inside of her cheek, overcome with a wash of sympathy for Herman. She spoke with anger. "I suspect he's been browbeaten for years. Afraid of her, of what she'll do to him if he goes against what she expects."

"What shall we do? If he wants to come, he should be allowed. There's not much remaining of the school year, but if he came it'd be a good start for next year. And I could give him lesson work to do over the summer. Oh, I hope he comes again and allows me to talk to him."

At least, if he and his mother were the guilty ones, Herman wasn't stealing cattle these days. Was he sneaking away from his mother, and their ranch, now that he had more freedom? Watching the school until he built his nerve to declare what he was after?

Lawbreaker or not, Jocelyn's heart went out to him. *If* he had helped his mother steal cattle, she'd guess it had been under

Icel's dire threat if he didn't mind her orders. She leaned down and plucked a dandelion leaf and tore it to pieces. She said to Addie, "Shall we wait and see? If he keeps coming closer, his courage may push him into speaking to you, and you can take it from there. If you need anything from me, from the men on the school board, let us know. I wish his mother would allow me to come talk about this. I've only met threats when I've tried."

"Thank you, Mrs. Pladson. You've put my mind at ease by explaining what you know about him. And anything I can do for this young man, I will do. There are two other older boys here in school, good fellows who I expect would be kind to him."

Spring work that followed kept Jocelyn and Pete busier than ever. Leaving Red to look after the cattle, they harrowed and planted the corn field and kitchen garden, ridded old manure piles that would invite a fresh invasion of horse flies, cleaned feeders and ponds, and made repairs large and small to the house and outbuildings. Through it all, Jocelyn couldn't take her mind from Herman Taggert and the truth of his wish to attend school. She wanted so much to help him—to find a way—but what?

Cleaning the smelly henhouse was far from Jocelyn's favorite chore, but she worked industriously toward the result that she wanted, washing drink pans, cleaning nests, and filling laying boxes from a pile of fresh bluestem hay.

Humming under her breath, Jocelyn was about to spread an armload of hay for the last laying box. Too late, she saw the snake, felt it strike her left hand before she could move. Terrified, she looked at the fang marks, at the fallen snake writhing away at her feet. Moving quick, she grabbed the manure shovel she'd used earlier and brought the blade down, chopping the head from the snake. Weak kneed, she stumbled to the open door and yelled, "Pete! Come quick, Pete!" She saw no sign of him, was afraid to run, should it send venom further through her veins. She began to shake. "Pete," she tried again. "Red. I need help, please, now!"

They were out of hearing. What was she going to do? She couldn't remember if there had been a sound from the snake, if it had rattled, so it must not've. It was brown, patterned like many snakes. What kind it was, she didn't know. All she knew was that it wasn't the usual, harmless bull snake they often saw. She made her way to the house carefully, holding her quivering hand in front of her.

In the kitchen she found a knife. It would be sharp enough; Pete liked to keep their knives extra sharp. Sitting down at the table, knife in her right hand, teeth clenched, she made two cuts across the fang marks and watched the blood rise and flow. She considered sucking the blood and spitting it out, but she'd heard that might work for some but didn't for others, and they had died. She wiped the blood away carefully with a cloth and let it flow some more.

Pain from the cuts had now set in, and she clamped her jaw against it. At the washstand by the back door, she dipped water and poured it over her hand, flooding the wound over the wash pan until she believed it was good and flushed. If the snake was poisonous, had she done enough? She flushed it more.

Jocelyn, gripped with apprehension, sat as quietly as she could and stared at her hand. At last, she heard Pete's booted feet clumping onto the porch. She called his name, "P-peeete." It sounded more like a puppy's squeak. He came flying through the door, his eyes wide. He kneeled beside her chair. "Honey, what's wrong?"

She held her hand for him to see. "A-a snake bit me on the hand. I was filling laying boxes w-with fresh hay. He was in the hay I'd picked up; I didn't see him until too late. I don't know what kind of snake. I killed the thing, chopped its h-head off."

"Damn! How do you feel, Sweetheart?"

"B-better now. Right after it bit me, I was weak, wobbly. From shock, maybe, not from snake venom? I don't know." She licked her dry lips and explained that she'd cut and flushed the bite. "Would you go look at what remains of the snake, Pete? Maybe you'll know what kind it is, poisonous or n-not."

He came back in a few minutes to tell her. "We think it's either a rat snake, Hon, or a kingsnake; neither is poisonous. I had Red look at it, too, and he says that it is a king snake—you can tell by its small head and the wide, brown triangle patch on its head. I was so damned scared, that it might be a prairie rattlesnake or a copperhead." He took her hand and kissed her fingers. "If it had been, I think you still did the right thing. That you got rid of the poison had there been any."

"You're sure?" Her lip trembled. The cuts on her hand ached.

"Fair certain. But we could try my ma's treatment for rattlesnake bite."

She looked at him questioningly.

"She put soda on the bite first, then mixed an egg, salt, and gunpowder into a salve to spread over the bite."

"All-all right." When it was done, she allowed him to take her into his arms, and she wet his shirt with a few relieved tears. They'd done what they could.

Nellie came again astride her large plow horse with a note from Miss Denton.

Jocelyn opened the note, a smile breaking over her face as she read. "This is such happy news." She gave Nellie, standing by her horse with reins in hand, a hug. "Thank you for bringing this to me and thank Miss Denton. Please tell her that I'll be there." *Herman Taggert had broken his silence: he wanted to come to school. He could read some, write a little; he wanted more. Monday he'd start school. Jocelyn was invited to be there.* Jocelyn danced a little quick step in the dust.

As happy as she was, she had to wonder what'd happened? Did Herman and his mother come to a peaceful agreement? Somehow, she doubted that. Did he have plans for sneaking off to school each day? That might work for a time, but then what? Had he called his mother's bluff and won? Whatever it was, she hoped it worked. She was proud that she'd reopened the old school, but this was the proudest moment yet. *Mrs. Gorham was going to love this.*

Driving her wagon and mule team, Jocelyn arrived at the school on a sunny Monday morning. Miss Denton stood just outside the door ringing a bell. Children, giggling and shoving until they found teacher's warning stare, filed past her into the schoolroom. At first, Jocelyn didn't see the tall young man, Herman Taggert, in the shadows cast by the porch roof.

She gave him a quiet smile at the same time her heart pumped excitedly. He stood, sweat-stained hat in hand, hair carefully combed, sweat running down the sides of his face. There was worry in his eyes; he looked ready to clap his hat back on and run.

"Good morning, Miss Denton." Jocelyn smiled at the teacher. "Good morning, Herman."

There was a moment of thick silence.

" 'Mornin', Missus Pladson." His voice was so soft and low it could barely be heard. He wiped his face with his sleeve, his Adam's apple bobbed, and he made an odd sound in his throat.

Jocelyn nearly tripped on the step, she was so glad to hear his greeting. "It's nice to see you here, Herman." She spoke cautiously. "You're going to like it. Miss Denton is a wonderful teacher." There was so much more she wanted to blurt out, hopeful words to encourage him, assure him he was in the right place. That she'd help him in every way possible, but she feared being too pushy would scare him away. "We're all of us glad you came."

Miss Denton had stilled her bell, the other children now all inside. She said to Jocelyn, "Herman was the first one here to school today, weren't you, son?"

"Yup," he said with the barest of a smile. "First."

"He cut and stacked wood for me," Miss Denton nodded proudly toward him. "I've already shown Herman around inside—the blackboard, the library books, the alphabet along the wall above. George Washington's and Abraham Lincoln's pictures. He knows his desk, his tablet and pencils, his reader, and his speller."

"Wonderful!" Jocelyn said, with a hand to her collarbone. "I can't stay"—she motioned toward her wagon—,"but I brought milk and ginger cookies for everyone, a little celebration. Herman, would you like to come take these for Miss Denton?"

He hesitated, frowning as though not sure what to do. His mouth opened but nothing came out. He tugged his ear. Finally, rubbing his hands on his pants leg, he came and took the jug of milk and cookies bundled in a dish towel. He took shuffling steps back from her and mumbled softly, "Thank you, Mrs. Pladson. For these. Thank you for the school. Ma hates your school. I like it." He turned and hurtled toward Miss Denton on the porch.

Jocelyn swallowed a lump in her throat. Such a sweet young man—and nobody knew! Why hadn't this happened long before now? She waved and watched Miss Denton and Herman disappear inside. Heaving a sigh of immeasurable satisfaction, she climbed into the wagon and took up the reins. "Hi-yup, Alice, Zenith, our day has only just started." The wash to do, bread to bake, garden to weed. But she felt such a sense of accomplishment, already.

Three days later, Jocelyn was out front of the house talking to

Mr. Raynor, the mailman, when a blur of a rider went by her lane in the direction of the schoolhouse. A woman, riding hard, skirts flopping, hat pinned back. Jocelyn stared, and her heart climbed into her throat. *Icel Taggert.*

"Beg your pardon, Mr. Raynor, but I have to be after that woman who just rode by. It's urgent; someone could be hurt." She clutched her skirts and turned toward the horse corral to saddle her mare or a mule. The mailman stopped her.

"Climb in here with me, Mrs. Pladson. I'm a'going that way."

"Fine, but we have to move fast." She shoved the letter he'd handed her into her apron pocket and clambered up into his buggy beside him. "Go! Please hurry."

It was only four miles, and the distance closed quickly. Jocelyn leaped from the buggy and raced for the schoolyard, where Icel was trying to get around Miss Denton, who blocked the door to the schoolroom. Mailman Raynor followed Jocelyn a few steps and halted.

"Hush, ma'am, please," Miss Denton pleaded with Mrs. Taggert, "you'll scare the children."

"Move out'a my way, or call my boy out here. He ain't got no business here, an' he's goin' home with me, now."

"If you have a good reason to interrupt his school day, of course I'll let him go."

"The reason is, I said so. An' he does what I say, or else."

"That's not a good enough reason, Mrs. Taggert." Jocelyn moved into the fray. "Herman loves school, he likes Miss Denton, and he wants to learn."

"I'll learn 'im, with a whip, when I get my hands on 'im. Now move, teacher, afore I snatch you baldheaded and throw you in yonder ditch."

"N-n-now j-just a minute," the mailman sputtered, a hand lifted to calm the fuss while his face turned ashen. He backed toward his buggy and took up the horse's reins in a white-knuckled grip.

Boiling with anger, her body fueled with indignation, Jocelyn had started toward Icel when the schoolhouse door was flung open and Herman stepped out. "Ma, what're you doin' here? Yellin' at teacher that'a way. You go on to home." Visibly shaking, he took a few steps toward his mother, and she tried to grab him. She failed when he jumped back. "I said go home, Ma, and leave me be. I want to go to school. I been tellin' you that for a long, long time, an' you won't listen. Now I'm big enough to do this, an' you ain't goin' to stop me. My bein' here ain't hurtin' nothin'. These ladies ain't hurtin' nothin', neither."

Icel lunged forward and grabbed both of his arms, attempting to drag him off the porch. He broke her hold and leaped away. "Go home peaceable, Ma. No more arguin' over this. Now go."

She gave him an icy look. "You'll be sorry, boy, you didn't heed my orders. You get on home before chore time, or I come for you with a gun. An' you might not be the only one feels a bullet's burn. You hear me?"

He swallowed. "I heard you. But I'll be doin' what I want from now on, not what you order me to do. Things I never wanted to do."

He looked stricken when he realized that he might have said too much.

Jocelyn looked on in shock, her heart hammering, wishing to know exactly what his expression meant, what it was he didn't want to do. *Rustling, maybe?*

CHAPTER TEN

Icel's lips were tight, alarm and hate for her own child in her eyes. She whirled and climbed back on her horse. "Get your horse, boy, and come with me right now, or else." She hard-eyed Jocelyn and Miss Denton not to mix in.

Herman started for the horse shed out back of the school, and both Jocelyn and Miss Denton grabbed at him. "You don't have to go, Herman," Jocelyn told him. "We'll look out for you, have the marshal talk to your mother about this, go to the county sheriff if we have to."

Herman hesitated and looked at them wistfully. "I have to go. Ma would hurt you if I don't. Teacher, could I take my reader with me?"

"Yes, you can take your reader, your tablet and pencils, too." She hurried inside for them.

"By fall, Herman," Jocelyn told him, "when school starts again, this matter will be taken care of, and you'll be able to come to school without all this fuss."

He nodded, took the book and supplies Miss Denton brought to him, and tucked them under his arm. "You been good friends. I won't forget. Never."

The two women watched him ride away. "Damn that woman!" Jocelyn said.

Miss Denton wiped her eyes with her handkerchief, straightened her shoulders, and turned to go inside to her other students. She said over her shoulder to Jocelyn, "Double damn her."

The mailman's hand shook as he took Jocelyn's elbow to escort her back to his buggy.

It had been a difficult day, after many of the same. At home again, the letter Jocelyn took from her apron pocket didn't serve her mood well. Muscles quivering with anger, she read the letter aloud:

"Mrs. Pladson, you stingy, greedy, liar you! Taking all our dear Aunt Letty's things for your ownself. All of it, no sharing at all. You'll pay for this, wait and see, you wicked of the wickedest. Burned in hell, that's what you got coming . . ." Sick with disappointment that anyone would think this of her, Jocelyn tore the letter to pieces and added it to her cook fire. All of it was untrue, so she needn't feel guilty, but still, it hurt. And she was tired. Weary of always trying to do right and having whatever it was fly in her face. She sat slumped in a chair until it came to mind what she needed: *A short visit with Francina in Topeka would be medicine to all this upheaval. I would come back restored, stronger than ever to face whatever was due next.* She heaved a deep sigh. *In the name of Hannah, I hope that to be true.*

Jocelyn had to stand on the crowded Topeka electric streetcar, but after the train ride from Skiddy, she welcomed the opportunity. Had gladly given her seat to an expectant mother who entered the streetcar after she did. Attempted to feel no ill will toward the portly gentleman across the aisle who filled a seat and a half, who pretended not to see the young mother-to-be, or Jocelyn. Lacking courtesy, he likely was also against women's right to vote. She turned away in disgust. A few minutes later, her spirits rose when she saw that they neared the corner where she'd leave the streetcar and walk the rest of the way to Francina and Olympia's cottage.

Olympia answered Jocelyn's knock, and with a warm smile, she drew her inside, then stepped back out to the porch to grab Jocelyn's satchel. Back inside, she called, "Francina, our Jocelyn is here."

Almost from the beginning of their meeting many months ago, the women considered Jocelyn the same as a daughter. She loved *them* and thought of the pair as Aunties, if not two mothers.

Mrs. Gorham fluttered in from the sitting room, where she'd been rearranging doilies. Her thin arms reached for Jocelyn, a smile on her upturned face, her pale-blue eyes filled with joyful tears. "My sweet Jocelyn, so glad to see you! From the moment we received your wire that you'd be coming, Olympia and I have been so excited. Wait until you hear our plans for your visit. For one thing, we're going to a performance at the Crawford Theatre." She released Jocelyn and motioned for her to follow, her small figure moving slowly ahead. "There's also the Kansas Equal Suffrage Association gathering we'll attend," she said over her shoulder.

Francina asked as they settled with tea and lemon cookies, "What's happening at Nickel Hill, Jocelyn? How is our young cowboy, Pete? Doing well with his cattle enterprise, I'm sure."

She briefly described ranch goings-on of the past few months that she thought would interest Francina, telling about their new calf crop, the spring grass poked up through the old grass and growing like magic. The young man, Herman—who she was sure would be in school next fall. Cleaning the henhouse and being bitten by a, fortunately, harmless snake. "I should've been paying better mind; snakes are common to Kansas farms and ranches after all. I was daydreaming about the supper fixings I had for Pete, new potatoes and peas, lettuce from my garden, and a young chicken to fry." She related the antics of her red mule colt, Shay, his curiosity about everything—bugs, turtles, and her sheets on the line! She explained about the last: "When he got through a corral gate accidently left open. It'll be a few years before he's the size to ride or to work. By then I'll have to teach him that everything's not a game."

The two older women chuckled. "We love your stories about Nickel Hill," Francina said, and Olympia agreed with a nod of satisfaction.

"Thank you, and I relish being here! I can hardly wait to go to the suffrage rally tomorrow." In the past she'd delivered literature and flyers about KESA, but this would be her first rally.

Francina and Olympia looked at one another, their expressions guarded. "Dear," Francina lowered her voice to a whisper, "we no longer refer to the gathering as a suffrage *rally.*"

"Oh, there's no rally?" She took a sip of her tea.

"Well, yes, there is, but we call it a *fair.* You see, there are many women, if you can believe it, who aren't interested in having the vote. They are indifferent; they feel that the vote, or working for the cause, would not be ladylike. Attendance at our meetings can sometimes be very small."

Olympia added, putting her cup down on the table by her chair, "Senator John J. Ingalls, who refused to commit himself on woman suffrage as a national issue in 1886, may have been a bit correct when he stated, 'In my judgment the principal obstacle to the cause which you represent will ultimately be found to exist in the indifference of women rather than in the hostility of men.' Unfortunately, lesser politicians leaped on his ideas hoping to defeat the cause. Kansas women who strongly believe in the freedom of suffrage will never give up until they prove Ingalls and the others wrong."

"There are ladies who believe suffrage is the right of women and want the vote, but they do next to nothing to help it happen." Francina stared at her palms as if there were an answer there. She looked up at Jocelyn, and her eyes widened. "I hate to say it, but there are ladies who believe that if we just wait long enough, men will recognize the need for suffrage and extend it of their own free will." She shook her head. "It's already taken far too long." Her cup rattled as she took it from the saucer. She sipped her tea. "We must educate and prepare for when we do have the vote, and we've taken on new methods to attract more women to hear us."

"How is that?" Jocelyn quirked an eyebrow and smiled.

"For starters we offer proof of our womanhood. We hold bazaars, sell fancy goods. We arrange our presence at fairs, picnics, all kinds of gatherings, with a booth for providing meals, for a price of course, which helps to earn funds for KESA. It's quite simple to carry on conversations and hand out literature about our group at these affairs."

Olympia took a long sip of tea and blotted her lips with a linen napkin. "Financing is too often a problem. Advertising the cause is not free; speakers must be paid, some suffrage columns in newspapers need to be paid for, and money is often needed to cover workers' expenses. It's difficult to keep interest in women's suffrage alive between campaigns, but we absolutely must continue . . . do all we can until we finally succeed." She took a bite from a small lemon cookie.

"Which brings us to our fair tomorrow." Francina's elfin face glowed. "Women will flock to the gathering for the show of women's handiwork. At noon, a speaker will give a suffrage talk." She giggled. "It works like magic."

Amazed at the enthusiasm, intelligence, and fortitude of these women she dearly loved, Jocelyn could only answer, "I can hardly wait!"

Magic was hardly enough to describe the fair next day, held in a downtown auditorium. Within minutes, Jocelyn was aware that she was viewing the finest, most beautiful women's handiwork that she'd ever hope to see. There were chattering women at aisle upon aisle of tables displaying embroidered samplers, filet lace tablecloths, paintings, tapestry pillows, and doilies galore. Paisley shawls, lace collars and capes, aprons, and bridal veils. An opera cape of gold silk brocade and lace, on a plaster mannequin, took her breath away. Of their own accord, her fingers had to pick up a baby's delicate, linen christening gown. Tears sprang into her eyes, and she bolted to the next table.

In every spot of the room, finely dressed city women were buying as fast as money could be removed from their handbags—needlework, jams and jellies, cakes, pies, bouquets of flowers—much of it the work of country women.

Jocelyn had to smile at pens of noisy baby chicks and ducks, playful kittens and puppies. The fair was truly a wonderland. She hesitated at a table of delicate handkerchiefs, of fine linen, with either crochet or tatting worked directly on the hem. The rosy-cheeked woman minding the table said, "The very small, square handkerchiefs have only recently come into vogue. A touch of finery every woman needs. And at the price of only a couple of coins."

She wanted the handkerchief badly, but she shouldn't spend money on frivolous things she didn't really need. Jocelyn chewed her lip in indecision. If she bought it, though, she would be helping the suffrage movement. And she'd still have the payment on the ranch to give Francina, although she still hadn't decided how to make her accept it. With a satisfied smile, she took twenty cents from her reticule and handed it to the woman. "I'd like this one with the pale-blue tatting, please."

In a room off the main area, Jocelyn, Francina, and Olympia sat at a table in a roomful of other women and were served a lunch of dainty sandwiches and strawberry punch against a background of soft female voices and tinkling china. On the stage at the front of the room, Mrs. Maude Laurence, a fine-featured Amazonian woman, smiled out at the audience, lifted a hand for quiet, and began:

"Dear friends, I thank you very much for your presence here today. As many of you know women's suffrage, our notable movement, began in Kansas in 1859. For forty-three years we have fought for women's rights, for equality. Beginning with that day Mrs. Nichols, Mother Armstrong, and Mary Tenney Grey sat in the Wyandotte convention, 'unelected and uninvited,' with their knitting in their hands, to hear the ruminations of that body. And try, if possible, to have the word 'male' left out of the franchise clause. They failed, that day, but from that time on, wise, determined women have directed their efforts to having it stricken out.

"We do not, will not, give up the fight for equal rights for women until we have them. Kansas Equal Suffrage Association was formed on June 25th, 1884. This year of 1902, our suffrage forces have come under the leadership of a young and most enthusiastic person, Helen Kimber.

"Helen is a hard worker, a woman of fine ideas, with plans we will join her in bearing fruition. We're sorry she could not be here with us today. Among the things she would tell you is that a woman should not support any political party with funds, with writings, anything—until she has the right to vote. Still, we must not forget that only men can grant us the right to vote. The way to gain suffrage is to treat our husbands with kindness and respect."

I already do that. Jocelyn sat easy and calm, thinking of him, *but it's because I love him dearly, not for gain. Regardless, Pete already believes women should have the vote and one time helped me to distribute KESA flyers.* She brought her mind back to the moment and to the speaker, Mrs. Laurence.

"Some suffragists have made the mistake of antagonizing

newspaper editors. In one instance a group of women ridiculed an editor, who was an opponent of the suffrage movement, by pointing out errors in his newspaper. One hundred-eight misspelled words, mistakes in grammatical construction, punctuation, and so on. They sent him a letter telling him they would provide him with a copy of an English spelling book, and English language lessons. Unfortunately, he was in place for the last word, and his diatribe published the next week did women's suffrage no good."

She went on to discuss matters Francina and Olympia had already talked about—financing, and advertising, and making suffrage events more than speeches.

"Today's fair is an overwhelming success," the speaker said, "and we owe a huge thanks to the workers and to the talented women who provided and sold their wares with great profit going to KESA. The rights of women in our state have been a long, long struggle, but we will win, ladies. With your continued help we will soon have our place at the polls alongside our mates, voicing *our* concerns, *our* wishes!" When the clapping settled, she said, "Good day. Please continue to enjoy the fair."

That night, Jocelyn was shown to the slim bed in the cottage's curtained screened porch where she'd slept before. Small tables—one holding a wash bowl and pitcher, the other a mirror and brush—and two chairs completed the porch furniture. The bed was almost hidden by a tall potted palm. The feather mattress was heavenly, but her heart, and her busy mind, were so full it was hard to sleep. To think, that one day she'd be voting alongside Pete. Their daughters would have the vote as well as their brothers without having to go through the struggles that women met now.

She missed Pete already, and she'd only been away a day and a half. She fell asleep thinking of him. And awoke surprised to see bright sunlight through the curtains. Humming to herself, she washed with a wonderfully perfumed soap, brushed her hair, and dressed.

Olympia had prepared a delicious breakfast of graham gems with raspberry jam, coddled eggs and ham, and a steaming pot of tea. Helping, Jocelyn organized the food on a large tray and carried it to a table in the cottage garden, where Francina insisted they have their meal in the spring sunshine. Later, a muffin in hand, Jocelyn studied the raspberry jam, remembered drinking raspberry-leaf tea, and caught Francina watching her, attentive, waiting. She took an extra spoonful.

"I remember the beautiful summer flowers in the gardens at Gorham House, where you lived before moving here," Jocelyn said, when they were finished eating and sitting leisurely with their tea. "But I miss seeing those gardens when spring comes. Were you able to bring some of the plantings or seeds with you?"

"We couldn't leave all of them there, though we left many," Francina said. "Olympia saved seed or bulbs from several, to replant here. The red and yellow tulips are all but finished blooming. The fragrant purple heliotrope, peonies, poppies, and four o'clocks have only just begun." She pointed them out. "And with summer the delphinium and hollyhocks will bloom by the picket fence."

"Yes," Olympia nodded, "and there is plenty of seed left over. Jocelyn, you must take some flower seeds and starts back with you."

"I'd love to make a flower bed or two at the ranch. I'm obliged to you both."

"It's our treat to give them to you." Francina sipped her tea and, with her faded eyes alight, changed the subject to their next outing. "You will enjoy the theatre this evening, Jocelyn. The Crawford Theatre engages renowned acts and actors from around the country. Would you know, the famous Polish actress, Helena Modjeska, performed one of her popular Shakespearean plays on the Crawford stage?"

Jocelyn in embarrassment admitted, "I've never been to anything like that, only to a circus or two with my father. And school recitations."

Francina caught her hand. "You will enjoy it more for that reason, dear. Olympia and I love the theatre and have taken in many notable plays, and even vaudeville. A few years ago, Thomas Keene performed as Macbeth but overdid everything in his ranting performance. Didn't he, Olympia? A review said that he 'tore every passion to tatters. His first performance, *Sight of Banquo's Ghost,* was an exception. There his action was high and noble, not merely noisy.' " She laughed.

"Walker Whiteside, among the foremost Shakespearean actors of the American stage, also performed at the Crawford theatre." Olympia fingered her long string of pearls and frowned. "Unfortunately, two years ago the poor fellow lost all his scenery, costumes, and effects in the burning of the Coates Opera House in Kansas City. According to news accounts," her face brightened, "he's received offers from many managers and gained contracts to appear in New York City. He's been sent out now in a series of strong romantic plays, but I'm sure a Shakespearean repertoire, too. Perhaps we'll see him again at the Crawford."

Jocelyn listened in wonder as the women prattled on. They might as well be speaking in Pawnee Indian language, however, for all she knew about *Shakespeare, Camille, The Merchant of Venice, hell-broth, repertoire* . . . For certain, tonight at the Crawford theatre would be a grand, new experience.

That afternoon, the older women napped while Jocelyn bathed, washed her hair, and pressed her very best dress, a simple dark blue with white lace collar and cuffs. Turning in front of the mirror, later, she decided she looked presentable enough. She smoothed her hair, pinched her cheeks, glad she'd been faithful using cow cream on her skin against the ravaging sun. Lastly, she put on her yellow flower- and ribbon-trimmed hat. She was as ready as she'd ever be.

Francina decided that, in their finery, it would be more suitable to hire a hack to drive them to the theatre than ride the trolley.

The theatre, on Kansas Avenue, was an imposing brick building on the outside and cool, cavernous elegance within. A patterned, sky-high ceiling, a huge stage with scenic curtain, six ornate balconies, three on each side, row upon row of seating—it was grand beyond Jocelyn's imagining.

They found their seats according to their tickets, smiled at one another, and sat back to read their programs. "Vaudeville, tonight," Olympia said.

"Which could be entertaining, though I'd hoped for Shakespeare," Francina replied. "My goodness," she added, "who is this featured performer, John L. Sullivan? The name sounds somewhat familiar."

Jocelyn had heard of him. Pete and Red talked about him. "John L. Sullivan," she told the other women in a soft, controlled tone, "is an Irish prize-fighter."

"A what?" Francina asked, whirling to stare at Jocelyn, and then her program.

CHAPTER ELEVEN

The two older women were aghast. Jocelyn was surprised as they were, but she was also finding it hard not to laugh. What had they gotten themselves into? Francina and Olympia were whispering over one another so fast—a pair of buzzing, confused queen bees—she could hardly understand a word.

"Should we leave?" Olympia asked Jocelyn, then turned to Francina, eyebrows raised.

"I certainly don't want to watch two men in their underwear jumping around pounding one another to bruises and blood," Francina said staunchly. "That's not performing. It's—it's, I don't know what to say about it. Vulgar silliness, I suppose."

"We can leave if you want," Jocelyn told them, sitting forward in her seat.

"Yes, leave!" a loud male voice said from the row behind them. "Wife and me are here to listen to the famous John L. tell his stories, not listen to the carrying-on of you blasted women."

"Stories?" Francina turned to ask in a small voice.

"Yes, this is his vaudeville act, not a prize fight. Now be quiet, will ya?"

The three of them looked at one another with eyes wide for a studied moment, then sat back, deciding to stay. Within a few minutes, a huge, silver-haired, well-dressed walrus of a man entered from the wings. He walked slowly to center stage and was introduced as the one and only, John L. Sullivan, prize-fighter, but tonight a monologist.

"He's in a nice suit, not underwear," Francina whispered and sat back satisfied.

For the next hour and beyond, the women were entranced by the great fighter's Irish stories and jokes and by his short speech about his career as a bare-knuckle boxer, and about people he'd met, including Theodore Roosevelt, who also loved to box; the Prince of Wales; and two well-known women—Nellie Bly, the investigative reporter, and Carrie Nation, crusader against liquor. Buffalo Bill had invited him to watch his Wild West Show with dignitaries such as William Tecumseh Sherman and ride in the famed Deadwood stagecoach through a fake battle.

The man's wonderful stories held his enthralled audience's attention every moment of the hour and a half, ending with an uproar of applause.

"Wasn't Mr. Sullivan wonderful?" Francina sat back in the hack on the way home, her hands clasped contentedly in her lap.

Jocelyn nodded. "Yes, he was."

Olympia agreed. "He certainly was, and who would have thought it? A prize-fighter so delightful with his stories. My heavens, yes!"

Later, Jocelyn lay quietly, her last thought before closing her eyes, *Pete will never believe all I've seen and done on this trip. And I will remember to tell it to my children, and my grandchildren, as one of the best times in my life.*

Next day, while the other women were otherwise occupied, Jocelyn slipped the payment due Francina under a bouquet of yellow tulips and ivy in the sitting room and packed her things for the trip home.

"I had such a wonderful time," she told Francina and Olympia a short while later. "Thank you both, so much." One at a time, she held their hands, kissed their cheeks.

"We loved having you with us, Jocelyn," Francina said, hugging her. "And you must come see us again, soon."

"Yes," Olympia echoed, "soon. You made your time here so pleasant for us."

"I'll be back, as often as I can." She waved and hurried down the street to catch the streetcar to the train station.

Three hours later she flew off the train at the Skiddy depot into Pete's arms. "Even for just two days, I missed you, Pete, so much."

"Me, too, honey."

They separated when a male voice said, "Howdy, Pete. Mrs. A mighty fine day, ain't it?"

Jocelyn turned to look. A bowlegged fellow standing in the open doorway of the small depot café lifted his hand in a wave. He ogled them with a wide, tobacco-stained smile and moved onto the sidewalk. He looked familiar, but she couldn't remember where she'd seen him. She returned his smile and nodded.

"Sure is," Pete answered. He tucked his arm around Jocelyn's waist.

"Do we know him?" she asked as they headed toward their wagon tied ahead. "He looks familiar."

"He works off and on at the stockyards as a helper; name's Barney Hauser. You saw him at the recent stock sale when he gave us a hand. I've heard he has a small place down toward White City but doesn't do much ranching. Mostly, he works for others."

"I remember him, now. He was a big help and, for such a rough cob, very courteous to me." She climbed into the wagon, details of her visit with Francina and Olympia taking over her mind. As they headed for home, she told Pete the highlights. "They are such dear women, and fun." She finished with a story about their evening at the theatre, and he laughed with her.

"Honey," he said, "I have something to tell you. The boy, Rommy Trayhern, is back."

For a moment she was silent, surprised at his words. "Back?" Her voice rose over their wagon's clatter and rattle. "With his father? Why? What happened? I thought they'd be all right at home in Nebraska."

"His father is not with him. He left the boy off at our place in the night. Red found Rommy asleep in our barn right after we left to take you to the train for Topeka. Alone. Just him." Pete took a deep breath. "He was so happy to be back and begged to go to school. There's more. The young'un seemed fine enough, but when I picked him up after school, he was feeling poorly. Miss Denton believes he might be suffering consumption."

"Consumption! That's a very serious lung disease. How is he? Pete, you should have brought him with you today, to see the doctor."

"I wanted to, but he disappeared. I needed to be here to pick you up from the train, and I couldn't find him. Red said he'd keep looking. The boy has to be around the ranch, somewhere." He thumbed his hat back. "Sometimes a body can be so excited to do a thing, like him wanting to go to school and see Miss Denton and the other kids, it makes them feel well, for a time. He seemed fine. I'm afraid that his teacher could be right, though, that he's really sick with tuberculosis, as they call consumption now."

"We have to find him right away and take him to the doctor."

"We will, honey, we will." He put his arm around her and pulled her close.

Red met them at the corral as Pete pulled their team to a stop. "I found him," he said, "at the school." He nodded toward the barn. "Now he's asleep in my bed in the tack room."

Jocelyn hurried into the barn for a peek at the pale, sleeping boy. He was thinner than when she'd seen him last, his clothes faded and tattered. For several minutes she stood there, tears welling in her eyes. She wiped them away on the back of her hand, walked quietly from the barn, and strode to where the men stood talking.

". . . looked everywhere on the ranch for him," Red was saying, "and was about to give up when I thought he might'a gone back to the school, though it's closed now, for the summer. That's where I found him, too sick to walk the four miles back here. He's a sad little feller, for sure. The button was fixin' to run away. He went to the school thinkin' to tell the teacher goodbye, but she was gone."

Pete nodded. "Miss Denton had mentioned that she might close the school early, so that the children exposed to Rommy, if he had consumption, could be doctored if needed."

"Poor Rommy," Jocelyn said, her heart in her throat. "We have to do everything possible for him."

"Turns out," Red said, "that his uncle showed the boy and his father the door. He didn't want his family to come down with the disease. They come here because Mr. Trayhern thought you two might be able to help his son get well."

"We will. We have to." Jocelyn swiped a tear from her cheek.

Pete said, "Once he was here, he was thinking to run away—from us? Why would he want to do that? Where to, for God's sake?"

The three of them moved out of the way as a whirlwind of dust twirled through the barnyard.

Red pounded his dust covered hat against his thigh. "He thought that if the teacher didn't want him near the other children, and his uncle had thrown them out because of his sickness, that you two wouldn't want him, either. Told me he'd find an empty shack somewhere and live by himself, not bother anybody."

"That ain't going to happen!" Pete growled. "Hell of a note. The sprout is only ten years old."

"Thank you, Pete." She gripped his arm. "No little boy should be so alone and sick. He's ours now; we're taking care of him."

As glad as Jocelyn was to see Rommy again, she was deeply worried about him. He was thin and weak. Stopping every few words to take a breath, he told them, "Here with you all is where . . . I most wanted to be. I wanted to go to school with my . . . friends hereabouts. Pa didn't know what else . . . to do when my uncle said we had to leave. My Pa is crippled from having his foot shot up . . . not much help in Uncle Dirk's cooper's shop makin' barrels, or on his farm, neither. Uncle Dirk said he couldn't . . . afford to feed us and his family . . . couldn't pay doctor's bills for me . . . an' I wasn't gettin' any better."

"If talking is too tiring for you, Rommy, we can talk more later," Jocelyn told him, frowning.

"Naw . . . I can talk. Pa wants me to be well . . . but there was just no way for him . . . to make that happen. He would have liked . . . to be here, too, but he . . . couldn't take the chance of being . . . being caught for a cattle thief . . . again, and this time hanged . . . for sure."

"Do you know where he planned to go, what he was going to do?"

Rommy shook his head. "All I know is . . . he promised to come . . . back for me one day when I'm better . . . and time enough . . . that Pa's stealin' the one steer . . . don't matter no more. He . . . brought me here because . . . you're such good folks . . . and you don't have no children . . . I'd make sick like

133

me. But you . . . don't have to keep me . . . if you don't want to, I can go."

"We're keeping you; that's final. And we're doing everything we can to make you well, starting tomorrow. You and I are going to Skiddy to see Doctor Ashwood."

Later, Jocelyn and Pete lay quietly in bed, Rommy tucked in, on a cot curtained off at the other end of the room, Red sleeping outside until his other bedding could be replaced. "After he sees Doctor Ashwood, the boy may have to go to one of those fancy health sanatoriums, somewhere warm like in Arizona," Pete said. "I'll sell half the herd to pay for it, if I have to, Jocey."

She smiled and kissed his chin. "I've heard they have these health spas in Colorado, too; that'd be closer. You may not have to do this, but bless you for wanting to, Pete. I love you so much." She snuggled closer, and he turned and pulled her into his arms.

"Likewise, darlin' girl."

Time ticked by much too slowly for Jocelyn, waiting in the front room of the doctor's office for his calculations. At last he came from the back room, alone, one hand in the pocket of his white coat, the other lifted toward Jocelyn. She charged from her chair, "What is it, Doctor? Will Rommy be all right?"

"It could be tuberculosis," he said gravely. "And until I know for sure, Jocelyn, you should not be anywhere near him. Tuberculosis is a contagious disease, deadly for some, and a long, nagging illness for others. I know how much you want a baby, and for that alone you have to take care of yourself."

She hid crossed fingers in her skirt and asked, "But couldn't there be other sicknesses that have signs like consumption—tuberculosis—but aren't as bad?" *And Rommy wouldn't die like so many other children had from the terrible disease.*

He leaned back on his heels; his eyes meeting hers expressed hope. "Yes, there are other infections of the lungs that resemble tuberculosis. An old tuberculosis infection that didn't 'take' but damaged the lungs. It could be bronchitis or pneumonia. Or some other infection caused by contaminated drinking water, or swimming in bacteria infested water. The boy could have any one of those, and not full-blown tuberculosis. That's why I want to keep him here for a few days until I have a better idea of the cause of his condition. You likely know that our hospital is at the end of the block, the small stone house with green shutters, nothing fancy. Rommy must be quarantined, and close by so I can continue seeing to him. We'll take care of him, Jocelyn, and you may go home."

"I can't see him at all?"

"No, I'm sorry, but you may not. There's nothing you can do for him, and you might as well be home."

"Maybe I can't be in the same room, but I want him to know that I am close. I'll take a room at the D. J. Shore Hotel. Will you tell him that for me, that I am close and talking with you often?"

"We can do that. Knowing how much you care," he mused "could aid in the boy's getting better. My nurse is with him now, preparing to move him to my hospital. Let's sit over here, Jocelyn," he motioned to chairs lining the wall. "I'd like to talk with you a bit. We know how serious a disease tuberculosis is. We used to call the malady 'consumption,' a wasting disease that 'consumes' the body."

Her heart quaked. "Surely that won't happen to Rommy?"

"We're finding some answers about the disease and pray that a curative will be next. About twenty years ago, a German microbiologist, Robert Koch, after many trials using a microscope was able to isolate the cause of consumption, a bacterium—a bacillus present in the victim's sputum. A single cough or sneeze containing hundreds of bacilli could spread the disease to others, which is why we separate the consumptive person from the healthy community nowadays."

Jocelyn nodded that she understood. But still . . .

"I intend to speak with a good friend, Doctor Crumbine, from Dodge City, and a member of the state board of health, about Rommy's case. Might be he'll have new suggestions for treatment. He fights hard to halt unnecessary disease in ways that were never thought of before. Years of horror surround the history of tuberculosis. People like Koch and Doctor Crumbine are about to change all that. My friend, Crumbine, wants people to kill flies, stop their spreading germs."

Jocelyn nodded, remembering the lecture Francina and Olympia had attended.

The doctor was saying, "He discourages folks, and children, from spitting on sidewalks. Three years past he led the nation in abolishing the drinking cup in public places, including railroad coolers. In one year, twenty-four states passed laws to forbid the common drinking cup, and our folded paper cups were invented. Doctor Crumbine in that regard has saved so many lives." He sat back, smiling. "I'm more honored than I can say to be acquainted with a man of Doctor Crumbine's accomplishments."

"I've heard of him," Jocelyn said quietly, "from an elderly friend in Topeka who went to hear him speak—about ways to better everyone's health. She was fascinated by his every word and deed. I understand Doctor Crumbine, among other things, is against the roller towel and invented the flyswatter?"

"Yes, an improvement on the 'flybat,' a screen attached to a yardstick, produced by Frank H. Rose." He chuckled. "A good man, Doctor Samuel J. Crumbine. A Pennsylvanian, with one year completed in medical school, he ran out of money and headed west to Dodge City. He told me that it appeared that he knew more about medicine than anyone else there, so he hung out his shingle and went to practicing medicine."

Jocelyn answered his smile, hoped to hear more.

The doctor stroked his jaw. "A few years later he returned to the Cincinnati College of Medicine to complete his medical training and become a real doctor. That done, he returned to doctoring again in Dodge City. In those years he made the acquaintance and formed friendships with well-known lawmen—Wyatt Earp, William 'Bat' Masterson, Luke Short, and Bill Tilghman. Pretty exciting time, he's said. Recently, he was called to become the secretary of the Kansas Board of Health in Topeka. No better man for the job. He'll be saving hundreds of thousands of lives by his simple, *miraculous* improvements regarding Kansans' and the nation's health. The whole country owes him thanks."

"We sure do."

Doctor Ashwood stood. "If it turns out that the boy has tuberculosis, the parents of the other school children must be told. They, and their teacher, must be examined by a doctor to check for signs they may be coming down with this"—he frowned—"this 'white plague,' as they call it in Europe. As should you, and Pete, and anyone else the youngster's been in contact with. Now then, I have other patients I must see." He held up his hands, the cleanest hands Jocelyn had ever seen. "Washed the dickens out of these paws before coming out to talk to you. That's one of the things we all need to do, often. Gloves, too."

As he turned to go, she reminded him, "Please let Rommy know that I'm right here in town."

He smiled. "I will. Now you take care of yourself, dear lady. Shoo." He waved toward the door.

She gave him a weak smile, left his office on watery knees, and drove her team and wagon to the livery, leaving it for the time she'd be in Skiddy. At the post office, she wrote a note to be delivered to Pete by the mailman, saying that Rommy would be in the hospital for treatment for a couple days and not to worry. *They would be fine and home soon.* She refused to believe anything else.

CHAPTER TWELVE

Jocelyn spent the next two days walking the streets of Skiddy. She visited with Mrs. Noack at the mercantile, where she discussed Rommy and other matters small and not so small. Brushed, fed, and watered her mules, Alice and Zenith, at the livery. Drank cup after cup of coffee in the hotel dining room. Nighttimes she tossed in the hotel bed, gripped with worry about Rommy. He might as well have been her own child. Finally, on her twelfth visit to his office, Doctor Ashwood shared his conclusions.

"I'm fairly sure, after thorough examination and asking young Rommy many questions, and discussing the matter with Doctor Crumbine, that he does not have tuberculosis."

"He doesn't?" Tears sprang to Jocelyn's eyes. "Thank heaven. Oh, my"—her hand went to her chest—"I've been so worried." She quickly wiped her tears on a handkerchief snatched from her jacket pocket. Her voice quivered. "I have to know: what is it then, that ails him?"

"I believe that it is a lung infection that started with a bad cold, which became weeks of severe bronchitis, and now worsening pneumonia . . . a very sick boy. I want to keep him here at the hospital for another week."

Listening, Jocelyn's heart raced from anxiety to gratitude and back again.

"If he responds well to treatment—complete bed rest, nutritious food, mustard plasters to the chest, and a serum to treat

139

infection—we'll know better that his problem is not tuberculosis. Someday there may be tests to tell a decided difference between tuberculosis and other ailments of the lungs, but so far there are none. Time and treatment, God willing, will prove me right in this."

"Thank you so much, doctor." She clasped his hand. "Thank you."

A week later, Pete and Jocelyn drove to Skiddy for Rommy. They sat on a lumpy sofa in the clean but sparsely furnished front room of the small hospital, both tense, holding hands. The room had a clean, liniment-like smell. Everything was so quiet, Jocelyn thought she could hear her heart beat. "Rommy!" she cried when he came through the door from the back room, the doctor with him, hand on the boy's shoulder. Rommy was still thin and white as milk, but his eyes were less feverish, his grin of gladness to see them, boundless.

"I'm lots better," he burst out. "Doctor Ashwood is the best doctor in the world." He looked up at him, then at Jocelyn and Pete. "But I can hardly wait to go home with you, if you're still thinkin' that way? How's my horse, Handsome? Bet he misses me. Your little mule, Shay, too."

"My goodness," Jocelyn declared, "you said all that without gasping for breath, once. You *are* much better!"

"I still cough some, but not as much." He looked at them with a twisted grin.

Doctor Ashwood cautioned them, "Rommy is better, but because his lungs are weakened, total recovery will take weeks, or months. For that he must have adequate rest at night, naps during the day. He should drink plenty of ginger tea as well as water." He handed Pete a brown bottle. "Give him a spoonful of this serum twice a day." He nodded at Jocelyn. "Mustard plasters to the chest if his congestion seems to return. Fresh air and sunshine will help, but no strenuous activity for the next five weeks."

"We will see to that," Jocelyn said, beaming.

Pete asked for the bill, paid it, and shook the doctor's hand. "Thank you, Doc. You've saved this boy's life."

"With your help, Pete, and yours, Jocelyn. Without you he wouldn't have had treatment in time."

Red's help, too, Jocelyn thought.

"We'd like to bring you some beef next time we're in town," Pete said.

The doctor smiled. "Take back this money, then."

"Nope." Pete shook his head and herded Jocelyn and Rommy from the hospital.

With Rommy tucked in bed, in his curtained-off end of the upstairs bedroom, Jocelyn and Pete went to their own bed. "I was so worried about the boy, afraid he would die, like so many others do, with tuberculosis," she told Pete, hugged to his side, arm across his chest. "I'm so comforted I could shout my relief to the moon."

He laughed softly. "Just like a mama would."

"I feel like I could be his mama, and he does need one. He will get well with us."

Pete kissed her brow. "Don't doubt it for a minute."

Rommy's progress to recovery was slow but steady. With the passing days his cough and fatigue lessened, and his color returned. From eating one bowl of milk-soupy oatmeal, he went to two thick bowls—brown sugar and raisins added—plus biscuits. He spent hours in the sunshine exercising his big, homely horse, Handsome, and petting and scratching Jocelyn's mule colt—getting acquainted. The latter was turning into a love match. Jocelyn noted that, like many mules, Shay showed affection leaning in and nuzzling the boy.

Neighbors came to visit, bringing fresh fruit from their orchard, cookies, or a pie. Rommy gloried in the attention, yet remained the good-natured, unspoiled youngster he was before the sickness. More so, Jocelyn decided, in peaceful pride.

By midsummer he was well enough to do small chores, feeding and watering his horse and the mules, gathering eggs and feeding chickens. The next visit to Skiddy, Doctor Ashwood proclaimed him healed, as healthy as any boy his age could be.

From then on, Rommy joined Jocelyn hoeing corn and toting water to the garden. Red taught him to rope, using an old rawhide riata that had been Pete's. Astride Handsome, he could build a loop and with a quick wrist-twist sail it to land over a calf's head. Or have it land in front of the critter's hind feet so that it stepped into it, and he speedily drew up the riata's slack, proudly grinning as he let the calf free. He practiced almost constantly, roping stumps, fence posts, Shay, and Jocelyn's chickens. He usually got a hug along with the scolding for the last.

Red proclaimed that he was becoming a "helluva cowboy" and his mount, Handsome, a "helluva cowhorse." Both would be useful at branding time.

They'd heard nothing from his father, and Jocelyn felt only slightly guilty for being glad. Not that she didn't wish Mr. Trayhern well . . . she did.

Rommy was out with Pete checking cattle, Red working on the bunkhouse, and Jocelyn outside beating dirt from rugs, grimy with dust, when she heard the rattle of a buggy coming up the road. She hesitated, broom in hand and shaded her eyes. *If this wasn't the worst time for somebody to come calling. Mrs. Goody and a smaller person beside her,* she saw in another few minutes.

Putting on a smile, Jocelyn brushed at her hair, shook dust from her apron, and went to meet Mrs. Goody and the young woman she didn't recognize. "Good afternoon, ladies," she said hesitantly, her eyes on the girl, who looked to be fifteen or sixteen. She was slight of figure, her corn-silk hair in a coronet of braids, wispy curls around her rather plain face. Her hazel eyes held an expression of uncertainty. She glanced from Jocelyn to Mrs. Goody and back, her lips parted in question.

"Brought you a surprise," Mrs. Goody chortled. "Found this young lady in Skiddy, sitting on the bench outside the drugstore, nobody to look after the poor little thing. Come all the way from Missoura to see you folks." Mabel Goody and her passenger climbed from the buggy.

"Oh?" Jocelyn went to the girl and offered her hand. "I'm Mrs. Pladson, Jocelyn Pladson." She licked her lips. "You came all this way, alone?" Who was she? She surely couldn't be Flaudie Malone. Who hadn't, now that Jocelyn remembered, written any more scolding letters. "What is your name, dear?"

"I'm Nila Malone." Her eyes blinked rapidly, her voice low and nervous as she continued, "I came on the train. Ma— Flaudie Malone—she wrote you some letters, said I could find my own way from the Skiddy station out to here, Nickel Hill Ranch." Her glance darted to Mrs. Goody. "Thank you for your kindness bringing me here." She couldn't seem to stop blinking. "Don't mean to be a bother, though."

She stood there, in shabby but clean and neatly mended clothes, holding her blue gingham bonnet and looking as though she'd like to turn and run.

Jocelyn's heart melted. "You're not a bother. Come inside, Nila," she motioned, "Mabel. I have some orange raisin cake and iced tea." She smiled, her eyes widening when the young woman struggled with a battered trunk and blanket roll in the back of the wagon. She went to help. This had the look of more than a short visit.

While they ate cake and drank tea, Nila explained, her expression tense, "I'm plumb sorry about this, but Ma made me come. She says her Aunt Letty raised you, and now it's your turn to do by me." She blinked several times, her face rosy. "I don't agree with her, seldom have, but she wouldn't hear of me staying to home, or going to the city for work, like I wanted."

Jocelyn felt a moment's amazement at the Malone woman's audacity, at the same time a weighted sympathy for Nila. "If you'd like to stay, I'm sure we can work it out." Her mind scrambled, thinking of her suddenly full table, hired hand Red, her and Pete, and Rommy. Now this young girl. She took a gulp of tea. "You can stay, Nila; everything will be fine."

The girl's face brightened like a morning sun. "I'm good at housework, tending garden, and barn chores, too." She held up her brown, chapped, and calloused hands as proof. "I'll earn my keep, Mrs. Pladson. I worried some that you might not want me here. I know Ma wasn't nice to you in her letters. That must have plagued you mighty."

Jocelyn cleared her throat. "A little." *A lot!* She stood up. "We have a spare cot on the screened porch. There are canvas curtains to make it private. We can make it your room, at least for the rest of summer." She wished Pete and Red would hurry with building the new bunkhouse—if her family was to grow any more.

Mrs. Goody followed to the screened porch, excitedly offering suggestions. "If it's cold this winter, heated bricks in your bed would keep it warm. A small keg painted and turned upside down makes a fine bedside table. Wood crates can be stacked and curtained for a dressing table, a looking glass hung above. If you need help, or an extra quilt, whatever 'tiz, you come ask me. I don't have children, and I like to share."

"Thanks, Mrs. Goody, we'll hold those suggestions in mind," Jocelyn said. "As you can see, here's a small table and two rockers on the porch already, though we may move them to the front porch. Look, Nila, you have a nice little view of the creek. It's cooler back here, too, because of the creek, or at least it feels that way to me."

Nila's slim shoulders drew up, her elbows tucked into her sides in guilt. "I'd be putting you off your own back porch, away from this pretty view. I don't want to do that. I'll make my bed in your barn." Her chin lifted. "Done it many a time when Ma run me out of the house in an argument."

Jocelyn swallowed and spoke in certainty. "Red, our hired man, already sleeps in the barn until we get a new bunkhouse built. Might'nt be proper, for a young girl to be there in the barn, too."

"I suppose not," Nila said regretfully, amber eyebrows in a deep frown.

"Oh, goodness, no!" Mrs. Goody's fingers pressed her lips. "The barn is no place for a young woman, nohow."

"We hardly have time to sit on the back porch enjoying the creek, these days," Jocelyn said ruefully. "You might as well make it your room, Nila." *Before we married, Pete had courted me on this porch, although he didn't realize right away that's what his visits were.* She smiled to herself.

After Mrs. Goody departed for home, intending on the way to check on a new mother whose baby she'd helped to deliver recently, Nila joined Jocelyn to finish cleaning the rugs and getting them back inside. Together they prepared supper. Nila husked sweet corn, sliced bread, and under directions fetched fresh butter from the bucket-cooler in the well. Jocelyn stirred baked beans and prepared carrot and cabbage slaw.

When the two men and Rommy shuffled into the kitchen to eat supper, after washing up at the wash basin next to the door, they startled at sight of Nila, flitting about placing plates, forks, and knives on the table.

Red threw his shoulders back, and his grin widened. "Lordamighty, where did this pretty little thing pop up from?"

"She didn't 'pop up.' " Jocelyn's hands smoothed her apron, and she grinned. "She came on the train from Missouri to see us, and Mrs. Goody brought her the rest of the way from Skiddy. Nila, this is my husband, Pete," she caught his arm, "our hired man, Red, over there by the door, and this is Rommy Trayhern." She ruffled his hair. "He lives with us."

Nila placed a pitcher of milk on the table and gave them a shy smile. "Nice to meet you all." Pete smiled at the girl. "Howdy, Nila." Red echoed him, as did Rommy. The three of them pulled out chairs and tackled the meal like they hadn't already had a substantial breakfast and noon dinner, stealing curious looks at the girl every half-dozen bites or so. Red continued to tease and turn on the charm, asking questions about Long Lane, Missouri, where she'd come from, stating that a pretty girl like her had to've left a "fella" there, who for certain was spilling broken-hearted tears.

Nila's face and slender neck flushed red at his teasing, but she answered in a low, shy voice about her hometown—that Long Lane was, as you'd expect, named for the long road leading to the original town founded about 1845. She described their farm, where they worked with mules, and grew corn, melons, and potatoes. They raised pigs, had a lot of chickens, two geese, and three dogs. Her father also did blacksmithing for neighbors. She skipped the "fella" question.

"D'ya want to come with us?" Rommy asked Nila, when the men finished the meal and headed out to do evening chores. "You can see my horse, Handsome—that's his name—and Mrs. Pladson's little mule, Shay. That little critter, Shay," he said with a shy grin, "can play 'kick the bucket' by his own-self if I forget and leave a bucket where he can get at it. I can show you the ranch?"

"Tomorrow, maybe." She smiled at him, much more at ease

with him than with the adults. "I want to help Mrs. Pladson red up the kitchen, and I need to put some things away in . . . my room." She hesitated. "I brought books, Rommy. I have lots of them in my trunk if you'd like to read them sometime."

He made a face and hurried outside.

Nila looked surprised but shrugged and smiled and accepted the dishtowel Jocelyn handed her. After a few minutes drying dishes and returning them to the cupboard, she said, "Mr. Miller—Red—is a real personable fella, isn't he? And good-looking. He's single?" Her expression was open but interested.

Jocelyn's tongue went to the inside of her cheek; her grip on a wet plate tightened. Surely the girl couldn't already be interested in Red? Jocelyn was horrified at the thought. *Rowdy and wild, footloose as a leaf in the wind, penniless most of the time from spending his money on drink, gambling, and women.* Too old for the girl. "He's single, no wife." She took a deep breath and asked, "Did you have a beau back home?"

Nila laughed as she caught on. "Mrs. Pladson, I'd never set my cap for a man the likes of Mr. Miller . . . Red, if that's what you're thinking. He might be nice enough, but—no, I was just asking." She turned from placing a bowl in the cupboard. "There's a farm boy back home, named Tim, I kind of liked. And also a man Ma wanted bad for me to marry." She made a face. "Near as old as Methuselah's nine hundred sixty-nine years. Not a bad person," she amended, "money coming out of his ears, and he bought me books as gifts. Wanted to marry me as much as Ma was pushing for it. I didn't feel the least affection for him and didn't want to be married yet, to anybody." She exuded calm, her gaze steady. "I put my foot down that it wasn't going to happen, ever, with him. That's one reason Ma sent me off here, glad to have me out of her sight. I was as glad as her to leave. But I don't have to stay, if you'd rather I don't."

Jocelyn smiled slowly. "You seem like a wise young woman,

Nila, not wanting to marry for money, or because your ma pushed you to. What is it you'd like to do, until you're ready to marry, or not marry at all, if you choose that?"

Nila shook the dish towel in her hands, took on a dreamy look, and said in a happy, flutelike voice, "Mrs. Pladson, you're the first person to ever ask me that. I want to make something of myself. The sort of life I've learned about in books." She neatly folded the towel. "I want to own a newspaper, be a traveling journalist or explorer—see the world that way."

"Sweet Hannah," Jocelyn exclaimed, wide eyed, a smile quirking at her mouth, "if those aren't the most exciting plans I ever heard a young woman to have. I hope every bit of it comes true for you. Well—some. Don't know how being here at Nickel Hill is a help, but you're more than welcome to stay as long as need be."

She stood back and waited as Nila took the dishpan of water from her to empty outside. She could come to love having Rommy and Nila around to enjoy. Maybe these youngsters were the children she might never have of her own? Part and parcel of the legacy she and Pete intended to build?

CHAPTER THIRTEEN

One hand on her cheek, Jocelyn reached cautiously with the other for the letters Hobb Raynor, the mail carrier, held down to her from his buggy. God willing, neither would be another blistering letter from Flaudie Malone, Nila's mother. She scanned the envelopes, breathed deep, and smiled heavenward. One letter was from Addie Denton. Probably Addie had questions or suggestions about the coming school year. The other letter, also postmarked Topeka, was from dear Francina.

"Good news?" Hobb asked, head back and eyebrows raised, likely expecting her to share whatever human pith the envelopes held.

"I surely hope so. Thank you, and good day, Mr. Raynor." She turned away, explaining over her shoulder, "I have dinner cooking on the stove; best I not let anything boil over." She preferred to read her letters alone. To her relief, the disappointment in his face didn't last.

"I understand, Mrs. Pladson." He beamed. "Have a lot of work ahead, myself." He tipped his hat to her, lifted the reins and spoke to his horse, turned the buggy, and went rattling back down the lane.

Seated at the kitchen table and reading Addie's letter first, Jocelyn's eyes widened with each line. *Accepted a proposal of marriage . . . The wedding not to take place for a year or two . . . After that you'll find it necessary to find another teacher for Gorham School . . .* Hearing the clump and chatter of Pete and the others cleaning up on the porch for their noon meal, she quickly scanned the rest of the letter and raced to put steaks, greens, and yeast rolls and butter on the table.

Over dinner, she said, "I received some interesting news today." The clatter of forks against plates stilled slightly. "First of all, Miss Denton writes that she misses her students and their families and looks forward to her return to teaching Gorham School in September. Unfortunately, she'll only be teaching our school for another year, maybe two. She's had a proposal of marriage; the wedding itself will take place when her fellow returns from Africa."

Pete barked a laugh and shook his head. "You're joking, Jocey? I understand the getting married part, but *Africa*? And isn't this kinda sudden?"

"*Africa?*" Nila moaned in envy.

Rommy wrinkled his nose. "Who'd want to go to Africa anyhow? They got dangerous animals there, lions and tigers. They attack folks and eat 'em up."

"Yes, Africa, and this isn't a joke, nor is it about what you're saying, Rommy," she reprimanded with a frown. "Addie explained in her letter that she, and a beau from her past, have met again and come to the notion, together, that they are still in love." *Almost a repeat of how it happened with us,* she thought. Pete's eyes crinkled as his met hers in a private smile. She continued, "Addie wants us to know ahead of time so that we can be prepared with another good teacher. I'm guessing that she expects to be traveling some with her new husband. And there is the regulation against married women teaching school."

"That young lady'd go with him," Pete questioned, eyebrows raised in doubt, "big game hunting in Africa?"

"Not hunting for game, a *food hunting* expedition. Addie's intended, John LeMay, will join another Kansan, a botanist named David Fairchild, who travels the world searching for useful plants to bring back to America, giving our farmers more food to grow. He's tried to introduce a smaller pineapple, no larger than a banana, that he found growing in southern Africa. Addie wrote that there's some argument about that. Pineapple growers in South America claim folks will always want pineapples the size they are now." She placed her knife and fork across her plate. "Two years ago, Mr. Fairchild brought better hops from Bavaria to America for making tastier beer."

Red nodded at that, loudly clearing his throat in agreement.

"The man, Fairchild, is referred to as a 'food explorer.' "

"It sounds so exciting to me," Nila said, "traveling the world to find different foods."

"Back to Miss Denton," Jocelyn said, "she writes that she's excited to teach students where our foods first came from— bananas from New Guinea; tomatoes, onions, and squashes from Italy; oranges and lemons from China. Her groom-to-be, she writes, insists that almost every food we eat is an immigrant."

"I bet if I had to go all around the world looking for something to eat, I'd starve. Or probably a lion would eat me for supper first." Rommy took a last bite of steak. He paled, thinking about it, and gulped his milk.

Nila dabbed her green onion in a bit of salt on her plate and took a bite. "I'm having a taste of Italy."

"Enough," Jocelyn said, laughing and scooting her chair back from the table and grabbing up empty plates. "Time for us all to get back to work 'til supper."

Pete grinned, rose, and kissed Jocelyn's cheek. "Yep, my American beeves are waiting for me." Moments later he led Rommy and Red back out to the barn and pastures.

Nila gave Jocelyn a quick hug. "Can't thank you enough, Mrs. Pladson, for sharing the teacher's letter. I feel like I almost know that 'food explorer.' " She stood back, looking thoughtful.

"If I was to marry anybody, I think I'd like to find me a botany fellow like Mr. Fairchild." She helped clear the table and then pulled her straw hat on to return outside and weed more of the garden—immigrant vegetables—under the hot sun.

"I'd appreciate it, Nila, if you'd dig a few new potatoes so I can cream them with green beans for supper. You might pull some carrots, too, if Rommy hasn't fed them all to Shay and the horses." She hesitated. "And you don't have to call me Mrs. Pladson; call me Jocelyn if you want to, or *cousin* Jocelyn, if you like."

"I can do that, Mrs.—Jocelyn." She grinned, shrugged, and hurried out.

As soon as the kitchen was clean again, Jocelyn opened Francina's letter. She was somewhat startled when a shower of train tickets fell from the envelope. *What, in the name of Hannah . . . ?*

Reading the letter, she began to shake her head. Having learned of Rommy and Nila, now living at Nickel Hill with Pete and Jocelyn, Francina and Olympia wanted to meet them. They *must* bring the children to Topeka for a picnic at the famous Gage Park. Jocelyn's cheeks puffed out at that. She had so much to do, garden sass to pick and can, the school had to be readied for opening, and with so many in her "family" now, dirty clothes were piling up to be washed. Never mind the daily cooking and cleaning.

Even so, in a dozen lifetimes, she and Pete could never repay Francina for all she'd done for them from the first moment of their marriage. Funny, sweet, honest, and forthright, Francina had always been delightful company. Special, very special.

By supper time, she could hardly wait to share the invitation with Pete and the children.

Rommy held the tickets with awe. "We'll ride in a train? I never rode anywhere 'cept on Handsome, or in a wagon."

Nila glowed. "I've never been to Topeka, or Kansas City, or St. Louis for that matter. Only small towns on back roads. Sometimes I've thought I'd never see a real city. Now, I will." She bit her lip, shook her head, a smile widening. "If Ma knew I was getting to do this, she'd be madder than a horned toad on a hot rock. I'll be thanking you folks for the rest of my life."

A few minutes later, the young ones, and Red, headed outside to evening chores. Alone, both recognizing a rare moment these days of privacy, Jocelyn went into Pete's outstretched arms. "You look tired, honey," he said against her hair. "Maybe you ought not to make this trip."

"I'm tired a bunch these days, probably because of the hot weather, along with the work. But I can rest on the train to Topeka." She leaned into him, her cheek against his chest. "Seeing Francina will be fun, and it is the right thing to do. I want to go." She nodded, mumbling mostly to herself, "Nila and I can take care of the rest when we get back. The world won't fall to pieces if a few things go undone."

He stroked her hair. "I'm going with you, then. Red will be here to take care of the animals and other chores. The buttons could be a handful, as excited as they are. I can help look after them. It's been too long since I've seen Mrs. Gorham, myself." His head tilted back to look at her. "Let's take the morning train, have our visit and the picnic, and come back on the evening train. Just one day off the ranch won't hurt nothing." He gave her a long kiss, which she returned in full measure.

She hoped to Hannah that she wasn't coming down with ague, Jocelyn thought, as she prepared for the day of fun in Topeka. Being this tired was a blamed nuisance, but she'd be blessed if she'd let it interfere with this rare holiday with her new family and friends.

Next morning, the side to side shaking of the train on the

tracks for the three-hour ride to Topeka upset her stomach. *Dyspepsia then?* She held her misery in sway, laughing and chatting with the young ones. As best she could she shared their excitement of the train ride, taking pleasure seeing their eager faces pressed to the windows.

They arrived in the Topeka train station none too soon, in Jocelyn's mind. She steadied herself and stepped off the train, slipped her arm through Pete's the minute her feet touched ground, and turned to make sure that Nila and Rommy followed. The two were right on their heels.

"There the ladies are," Pete said with a chuckle, nodding toward where Francina and Olympia waited, waving and calling "hello" and "over here" next to a hack and driver parked just off the station platform. Jocelyn's heart bloomed at sight of them. When they rushed to meet her, she moved from Pete to take each woman in her arms by turn. "We're obliged to the skies for your invitation, and the train tickets, Francina. So good to see you both. You know my husband, Pete. These wonderful young folks are Nila and Rommy." She gave each of the young people a little shove toward her friends, proud and satisfied when her charges smiled and said a polite hello to the women.

Francina and Olympia, faces filled with delight, led them in a triumphant march back to the hack. Once there, they mother-henned the girl and boy onto the seats with them and directed Jocelyn and Pete to the other. "The park is not far, only four miles outside the city." Francina gave each of the youngsters a pat. "We'll be there in the flash of a butterfly's eyelash."

Rommy opened his mouth, about to oppose the veracity of butterflies having lashes when Nila smiled at him with a brief shake of her head to never mind. "Do you children have any questions?" Olympia asked. Rommy was about to speak again when Nila gave him a second warning grin.

"Tell us about Gage Park," Nila said. "How long has it been here? Is it very big?"

"Are there animals in the park?" Rommy wanted to know, giving Nila a slight frown.

"Gage Park is rather new," Olympia explained. "In 1899 a family, name of Gage, gave eighty acres of their farm property to the city, to be a center of recreation. A horticulturist named Anton Reinisch moved into the park and in these few years has planted lawn, wonderful rose gardens, clusters of shade trees, and twisting roads and paths magically connecting it all."

At Rommy's look of disappointment at no mention of animals, she quickly added, "And, yes, there is a bear in the park. He has a name, Tom. A fellow, Mr. Snyder, bought the bear from a traveling circus. A wrestling bear, one of those bears a man could pay two dollars to wrestle? If he had the gumption? Mr. Snyder keeps the bear tied to a tree while he's building proper cages for Old Tom."

"Old Tom doesn't sound like a very mean bear," Rommy said. "I wonder if he tries to snatch people, tear them to pieces?" He wore an expression of delight at the thought of the gore.

Jocelyn frowned and kept a hand on her stomach.

"I'm sure not." Francina took up the conversation. "The story is that Old Tom does get loose now and then. Somebody in the neighborhood goes for Mr. Snyder to come get Tom and take him back to the park." She gave Rommy another pat. "There are going to be many animals at the park, in time. I've heard there is a plan afoot to have a 'Monkey Island."

"Monkey Island? Whatever would that be like?" Nila grinned, her eyes lit up.

"I'm guessing a large pen all their own, like an island in the park. They say there will be a castle for the monkeys. Each castle window will have a sign above it, like 'Mayor,' 'Police Chief,' 'Doctor,' 'Lawyer,' and so on, like it's city offices or something."

Pete burst into a chuckle. Rommy said, "I want to see that, Monkey Island."

"It may be a long time being built and made ready, and I might not be right about everything, but you'll be able to see it, eventually," Olympia assured him.

When they arrived at the park, Francina told Jocelyn, Pete, and the youngsters, "We have picnic baskets of fried chicken, buttered rolls, pickles, cherries, and cake." She warned them, her eyes sparkling, "Don't get too close to the bear, or our food will get snatched."

Having arrived at midday, it was decided they might as well have their picnic before seeing the rest, and in short order a dandy spot in the shade was located, and they settled themselves in the grass. Olympia spread a fine tablecloth in the middle of their circle, and the food, plates, and utensils came out of the baskets.

As usual, Rommy tied into his loaded plate of food as though he hadn't eaten in several days. Jocelyn cautioned, "Rommy, son, don't eat so fast, or you'll choke. The bear will be there," she said, "so take your time. You want to enjoy these delicious fixings Mrs. Gorham and Olympia—Mrs. Stewart—made up for us."

"It ain't just the bear," Rommy said, "I can hardly wait for the cake and cherries."

Everyone laughed and turned back to their food. They ate quietly, each set of eyes mostly taking in the people, the hustle and bustle of activity around them. Children rolling hoops, others playing tag, a few zipping around on roller skates along the sidewalks. Young men and women strolled along, holding hands, laughing and talking. Older folks sat on benches, some asleep, others chatting.

Jocelyn could have spent more time seated in the grass, or lying down even, but the food disappeared in a snap, it seemed to her. Plates, cups, utensils, and napkins were packed back into the baskets. Nila reached down to Jocelyn and caught her hand, "C'mon, Mrs. Pladson, walk with me."

With Rommy skipping along in the lead, they strolled the meandering paths for an hour or more. Now and then—too often for Rommy—they stopped as a group to admire the flowers, naming those that they recognized, like phlox, sweet verbena, many types of roses. At last they came to the bear—a shaggy, old, brown animal, dozing in the sun, oblivious to the chain that kept him fastened to the tree, the circle of people watching him, whispering to one another. Occasionally one mother or another would yank back a youngster bent on petting old Tom.

"He looks more tired than ferocious," Francina commented.

"Old more than fierce," Olympia agreed.

"I wonder if he's hungry," Rommy said. "I wish I'd saved my chicken bones for him. Bet he'd like cherries, too."

"I'm sure he would, but we'll leave it to old Tom's keeper to feed him," Jocelyn admonished.

Later in the day, on the northern edge of the park, they came to a large, cement rimmed pond where several children waded. Others were out in the far middle dog paddling or swimming belly down, arms flailing, their face in the water.

Both Nila and Rommy looked at Jocelyn questioningly. She shrugged and looked at Pete.

"Go ahead," Pete told them. "Take your shoes and stockings off, and you can wade for a while."

"It'll do them good to cool off," Francina told Jocelyn.

Jocelyn, Pete, Francina, and Olympia found benches in the shade where they could sit and watch. For quite a while the youngsters waded, splashing one another when they thought no one was looking. Jocelyn breathed deep and relaxed, finding the day pleasant and peaceful, a good day. She was glad they'd come.

"I so wish you could stay for the fireworks this evening," Francina said. "Would you change your mind, please, and stay?"

She had earlier pointed out the giant sundial towering above the trees, built by Mr. Reinisch, park planner and horticulturist, using rails from a failed train experiment. "We're sorry," Pete said, his eyes on the sundial, "but that clever gadget says it's close to time that we head back to the train and home."

"We have to go, I'm sorry," Jocelyn said, "but we've had a wonderful time. It's been good for the young'uns; they work so hard on the ranch . . . we all do. We'll surely come back any chance we have."

It had been a good day, but going home felt very good, too, Jocelyn thought as the train rumbled along toward Skiddy. After a while she stirred, sitting straighter in the seat. She must have fallen asleep near the entire way, she realized. Outside the train window the sun was a rosy coin in the west, sinking behind mounds of rolling prairie as they pulled into the Skiddy station.

Jocelyn was pleased how well she felt the next early dawn. So much to do, and, by Hannah, she was up to it. She dressed in the dim light, noticed that Pete was already up and out to feed and water the stock. As she took the stairs down to the kitchen, aromas of coffee, biscuits, and frying bacon floated up. Nila bustled about the kitchen, turning bacon, placing plates on the table.

"Morning, Nila. Thank you for cooking breakfast. I'm sorry for not stirring myself sooner. Don't know why I slept like that."

"You were tired from our trip to Topeka and not feeling well before that. I don't mind fixing breakfast. Sit down, now, Mrs. Pl—Jocelyn, and I'll bring you a cup of coffee."

'Thanks, Nila." Jocelyn gave her shoulder a pat. After a few minutes in the kitchen, the greasy smells of the bacon began to upset her stomach. *Again.* Fumes from her cup of coffee made her lightheaded. Clutching one hand to her mouth and the other to her stomach, taking an instant to fling the door open, she ran from the kitchen. Around the corner of the house, she emptied her stomach. After a moment, she wiped her mouth with her apron and went back to sit on the porch step, thoughts whirling. *What on earth? Could-could it be that I'm . . . ?*

CHAPTER FOURTEEN

"I set breakfast in the warming oven," Nila said, coming out to sit on the porch step beside Jocelyn. "I'm so sorry, Mrs. Pladson, that you're still ailing."

"Don't be sorry." She fanned her warm face while her heart pounded in happy expectancy. "If my upchucking and all is from what I'm thinking now, there's the grandest reason behind it that ever could be. And we can thank yams and raspberry-leaf tea."

Nila looked puzzled. "But that's not what we had to eat yesterday. It was fried chicken and lemonade."

"Yes, it was. About that part I was just funning. Nila," she turned to her with a wide smile, warmth radiating throughout her body, "I think I might be with child. I've been sitting here on the step, pondering, and I think I missed my monthly. Maybe more than one; I've been too busy to pay mind. After all this time, wanting to have a child so badly, I believe it's going to happen." Heartbeat racing, she swiped at happy tears flooding her eyes, a mountain of a lump in her throat.

"That's purely wonderful, Mrs. Pladson." Nila slipped her arm around Jocelyn's waist. "That you may be with child and not under the weather with some cruddy sickness. Why don't you go lie down for a little while, until the queasiness gives way? I can see that the men and Rommy get their breakfast, and I can take care of the chickens and other critters. You rest."

"I can't. I'm going to the barn right now to tell Pete." She

160

stood. "Then I'm fixing to drive to Skiddy for Doctor Ashwood's opinion. I want to be as sure about this as possible." Her heart was full and mind spinning. She turned back two steps later. "No, I don't want Pete to know until after I've talked to Doctor Ashwood first. Please don't tell him; don't mention this to anyone, yet. I'll tell him I'm going to Skiddy this afternoon to buy flour."

"Are you sure you feel well enough to drive there, alone? For flour?" Nila grinned.

"I'm perfectly fine." She rested her hand on her only slightly mounded midsection and stood up. "This is an upset stomach, or it is a baby. Either one is no reason I can't do this." Her smile was so big it nearly hurt her face as she hurried to get ready. *Please let this be a baby, please, please . . .* her mind pleaded.

Sitting on the examining table in Doctor Ashwood's office, clothing down to her chemise and pantaloons, Jocelyn forced calm answering his many questions as fully and carefully as possible. An eternity seemed to pass before he stood back with a smile and told her, "I'm pleased to say, Mrs. Pladson, that you have all the typical signs of a baby on the way."

Jocelyn closed her eyes, her hand on her chest in gratitude and joy, so happy that she scarcely heard the doctor continue with his findings. "Weight gain, cessation of the menses, swollen breasts, morning sickness. Let's have a listen to your heart and lungs while you're here." He held the cool stethoscope to her chest, and again to her back. "Very strong. You'll get through this just fine, little mother."

At her soft laugh, her tears, he held up his hand. "Now clear proof won't be for another two or three months, when the quickening will be felt. Even so, I'd bet my medical practice that you'll have a baby in your arms come March or early April." He took her arm and helped her from the examining table.

"Now then, now then, don't cry. This is good news."

"I know." She swallowed and wiped her eyes. "I'm so happy. Thank you, Doctor." She went to the hook on the wall where her dress hung, and quivering all over with the most happiness she'd ever felt, she pulled the dress over her head and fastened the tiny buttons up to her neck. She reached for her jacket on the back of a chair.

"We're not quite finished. Mrs. Pladson." He motioned for her to follow him back to his desk in a side room and held a chair for her. "I have a few more things you need to know." He picked up a pad of paper and continued, "Your tiredness may be attributed to the pregnancy itself, or work, or possibly a touch of anemia. I'd like you to try a new tonic, liquid iron, a blood builder." He scribbled a few words on a slip of paper. "Ralph Waterman over at the drugstore carries this. Take one tablespoon every morning."

Jocelyn paid him with a bag of vegetables from her garden, a small basket of fresh eggs, and two dollars. She would have readily paid him in gold if she had it.

Floating from the doctor's office, she stopped short when she spotted Icel Taggert leaving the drugstore down the street. Determined that the woman wouldn't dampen this rainbow day, she stepped back into the shadows of Doctor Ashwood's office and waited. Icel climbed into her wagon, unwrapped what looked like a bottle, and took a long drink, a second, and a third.

Jocelyn restlessly stood on one foot and then the other while Icel corked the bottle, uncorked it and took another long draught, hesitated, and then slowly wrapped it in a garment of some sort and put it at her feet. "Hup!" she hollered at her team. The crack of her whip sounded like a gunshot. She was off in a cloud of dust—suddenly wheeling the team about and bringing them ripping back in Jocelyn's direction. Jocelyn

squinched back against the building as Icel whipped by without
a glance her way.

Shaking her head, Jocelyn made her way along the boardwalk
to the drugstore.

The druggist muttered over his shoulder as he took a bottle
of tonic from a shelf, "I reckon coming here a few minutes ago,
you saw the Widow Taggert leave my store?" He rubbed at his
ear, frustration in his face when he turned and placed the dark-
blue bottle on the counter.

"I saw her, yes. But I wasn't close enough to say hello," she
said truthfully.

"Damn woman—excuse my language, Mrs. Pladson, I didn't
go to say that in front of a lady like yourself. But that Taggert
woman gets my goat." He wrapped the bottle carefully in paper,
tied it with string, and handed it to her. "I'm sorry for spouting
off." He sighed. "Please forget I said anything."

"What happened, Mr. Waterman?" Jocelyn asked sympatheti-
cally, struggling to keep her happy feelings about the baby
intact. The poor man was sweating, his brow creased deep with
worry. He needed to talk.

He looked relieved at her prompting, her willingness to keep
the conversation going. The lines of his deep frown eased. "Sorry
to bother you with this, but I'm blamed if I know what to do
about her. She's been coming in here this summer buying liniment for her boy, and more 'medicinal' whiskey than anybody'd
hardly need for use as *medicine*. I saw her, right there from my
window," he nodded in that direction, "guzzling the whiskey
she'd bought from me just now like she's dyin' in the desert.
Supposed to be medicine, and she hasn't any ailment I know
of. She could get me in trouble with the marshal, don't you
know? For breaking the prohibitory laws—I'd be charged fines I
can't afford or, worse, a sentence behind bars." He backed away
from the counter, shaking his head.

Jocelyn gave a deep sigh. There'd been strong efforts to "dry up Kansas" for many years. The constitutional amendment prohibiting *the manufacture and sale of intoxicating liquors,* passed in 1881, was largely ignored. Beer and whiskey were shipped from Kansas City, Missouri, that state not having prohibition. Open saloons boomed in nearly every Kansas town—Red Miller one of the many gents proving that. Saloon owners made deals, asking officials that they simply *arrest them once a month,* allow them to pay a fine, and let them get back to business. The ridiculousness of it all plagued Jocelyn, not least of which was Carrie Nation's determination to destroy all saloons in Kansas with rocks and her hatchet.

"I'm sorry, Mr. Waterman. I hope Mrs. Taggert won't bring trouble down on you and your drugstore. The whiskey wasn't for Herman's ailment, was it? Just the liniment?" Icel's threats against her son in the argument about his intention to go to school loomed large in her mind. She had to know. "Did she mention what his problem was that he needed liniment for, just sore muscles or something?" She searched her reticule for the proper change to pay him, hoping she looked innocent of actual prying. Finding the right coins, she looked up at Mr. Waterman with a half smile.

"Says that he took a spill with his horse. The horse fell on Herman, crippled him plenty bad for a while she's been saying. According to her she shot the horse; its legs were broke, too. Claims the medicinal whiskey is to ease the boy's pain he's been in all summer."

"*All* summer?" Hair on Jocelyn's arms was beginning to lift. She smoothed her arm with her hand. *Herman was ailing all summer?*

"Yep. I'd bet my last nickel he's not had a drop of the Old Grand-Dad Medicinal Whiskey, and that she drinks it up. I don't believe her story about the horse falling on the boy, either."

"Wh-what do you think happened?" Feeling Herman's pain to her very core, fearful of the answer, she began to tremble.

"I'll tell you," he said vehemently. "I think she beat that boy to within an inch of his life early last summer. I've told her over and over she had ought to take Herman to the doctor for the injuries she described to me—her reason to get the medicinal whiskey—but she wouldn't see the doc. Says she set his bones herself, believes liniment and a sip or two of whiskey time to time for pain will do the rest."

"*Set his bones?* Herman's been laid up that long? I hadn't heard a word." Jocelyn gripped her purchase in shock, a niggling of guilt beginning to climb in her mind.

"Yep, all summer, and Widow Taggert complains mightily about that—that she'll be going to the poorhouse if he doesn't get well pretty quick and back to running the ranch with her."

Jocelyn's fingernails bit into her palms, and heat flushed through her body. She shouldn't jump to conclusions, but the druggist, Mr. Waterman, wasn't the first to talk about Icel bullying her own son. *Had she beat Herman for wanting to go to school, that day months back? So badly that he'd been laid up since then? Am I partly to blame, wanting him to have his chance at schooling?*

Pain filled the back of her throat; it was hard to think, hard to talk. "Mr. Waterman, I know you don't want the marshal to learn that you've been selling a great deal of whiskey to Icel that she's using to drink and not as medicine. But you could turn the tables so she'd no longer press you to sell her whiskey. You could use the information, tell Marshal Hillis what you believe she's done to Herman. If you're right, she's guilty of horrible abuse to her own son. She could beat him to death, next, if not stopped. The law has to step in."

"She could be arrested, right?" The druggist closed his eyes for a moment and nodded. "Damned if I won't do that! She won't be coming in here anymore, putting my business at risk.

Thank you, Mrs. Pladson," he pumped her hand, "and begging your pardon again for my swearing. That woman has agitated me near to my grave, causing me to forget my manners. I'm very sorry."

"I have a husband and a hired man. I've also used the word *damn* a time or two myself. Never mind being sorry; the word was fitting to the circumstance."

Now I can go home and tell my husband not only the wonderful news about their coming child, but that she believed Clem may have been correct suspecting that Icel Taggert and Herman were behind the rustling of so many folks' cattle. The thievery had halted suddenly this summer. Was that because Herman had been gravely hurt at his mother's hands, was laid up, and couldn't fulfill her lawless orders? It seemed very probable.

Or was the slowdown of cattle theft and his being down with injuries simply a coincidence? Time would tell. Ralph Waterman's talk with the marshal could bring the answer soon.

She shook off her pondering about those worries and returned her thoughts to her condition. "With child"—were there ever more beautiful words? Not in her language, or Pete's. He was going to be so happy.

CHAPTER FIFTEEN

Jocelyn and Pete meant to keep news that she was in the "baby way" to themselves, especially until they were a hundred percent sure. Somehow their secret sprung a leak and spilled over the neighborhood in a flood. Maybe her growing body, or her soft "ow" whenever she bumped her painful bosom, had given her away, at least to women. Little more was needed for gossipy tongues and concrete opinions. She'd made a special trip to Topeka to share the news with Francina and Olympia. Francina became so excited there was brief concern for her heart. Like happy birds on the wing, letters about the joyful event to come were constant between Topeka and Nickel Hill.

Her friends Mabel Goody, Tarsy Webber—new baby daughter in her arms—Maggie Rowland, and Emma Hunter arrived one day together in the Webbers' buggy. They sat in a circle in her front room, furnished several months ago with second-hand chairs, tables, and a fat, new burgundy sofa. The old buggy seat that once served as a sofa was taken back to the barn.

From her corner of the sofa, Emma asked, "How is Pete taking the news that you two are having a little one?"

"And what about Nila and Rommy?" Mabel Goody asked. "I don't suppose you've told them yet?"

"Rommy and Nila know, and they can hardly wait," she answered Mabel first. "They're out haying with Pete and Red, baited by promise of a picnic and a swim in the pond. Nila would have liked to be here, but she caved in to Rommy's begging that she go with them. Too, it's her nature, seems like, to pitch in and help when work's to be done. As far as Pete is concerned about the baby," she said smiling, "he's tickled as I am, but a little scared, too. He claims he knows how to take care of other kinds of babies—a calf, a colt, a fox kit, or a tadpole even before it becomes a frog—but not a human baby." She laughed with the others. "I know he'll be fine; he's a loving man."

"What do you believe made it happen?" Maggie asked, brushing a flyaway tendril of her red hair behind her ear and leaning forward eagerly, "Dancing under a full moon, eating honey with cinnamon, sitting where a pregnant woman had sat, eating yams?"

"The raspberry-leaf tea? The you know . . . headboard? Which one?" Mabel Goody, local midwife, looked excited.

Jocelyn's face heated. "I don't know. I tried all of your suggestions except . . . that last one."

"No headboard needed." Mabel burst out laughing.

"I have coffee," Jocelyn said abruptly, swallowing her laughter. "Who would like some?"

"And I brought peach hand pies." Mabel Goody swung off the sofa to her feet.

They all stood and went in to the kitchen table. Tarsy, pretty, downy-haired baby Lucy held under one arm, set out plates and cups, Mabel brought her peach pies, Emma laid out forks, and Maggie poured coffee. Jocelyn brought a small pitcher of cream from her icebox and had already placed the sugar bowl in the table's center.

"Remember the time we were together like this to plan the opening of our school?" Maggie asked.

"It's gone very well, hasn't it, Jocelyn?" Tarsy turned with a smile, lifting her baby to her shoulder and patting the infant's back.

"I'm proud of Gorham School," Jocelyn answered. "Addie Denton has done a wonderful job for us, but she wrote to me recently to say that she plans to marry in a year or two and will be leaving us."

A couple of her guests murmured in surprise, and Mrs. Goody protested, "But we've only had her for a short time . . . Well," she continued, pressing plump fingers to her smiling lips, "it is natural for a young woman to want marriage. The young man is lucky. Miss Denton is a fine person."

"I'm glad she'll be teaching our school for a while yet. We can be thankful for that," Maggie added. "What do you know about the man she's marrying, Jocelyn? Anything?"

"A little, and it is fascinating." She sat forward and excitedly told her friends about Addie's prospective husband, John LeMay, assistant to a world traveling" 'food explorer." About their purpose to introduce new foods from foreign lands to America. "We'll miss Addie, and replacing her might not be easy. Luckily, we'll have plenty of time to think on it, keep our eyes open for the right person to teach Gorham School."

"You're right; we'll miss Addie," Emma said. "But what an exciting life she'll lead, seeing the world searching for different foods, with the man she loves."

When a few minutes of chatter about Addie's probable adventures ended, Jocelyn said, "I can't say our first school year was perfect. I wasn't happy with the two boys shooting at one another over us grownups' cattle rustling troubles. Broke my heart that Mrs. Taggert wouldn't allow Herman to attend school." She hesitated, drew a breath, and told them about her talk with the druggist, Ralph Waterman, how she'd advised him to turn Mrs. Taggert in to the marshal for misusing the ample supplies of whiskey she bought "for medicine." And to let the marshal know of Ralph's suspicion that the woman had seriously injured her son in a beating meant to bend him to her will.

"Mr. Waterman turned her in to Marshal Hillis, and Mrs. Taggert is in jail? She ought to be." Tarsy set her plate aside, only a few bites taken.

Jocelyn frowned, sipped at her coffee, hating to tell them. "He lost his nerve. From what I've heard our druggist friend was afraid of 'being jailed with the rock pile for entertainment.' He never went to the marshal with any of it." She nodded agreement to her friends murmurs of indignation, the rattle of forks to their plates. "Pete believes that Mr. Waterman could have other customers who buy whiskey not necessarily for medical use. Doesn't want to scare them off with an investigation, lose their business altogether."

"Widow Taggert got away with nearly killing her son, then?" Emma looked close to angry tears. "It can't be true. Do you know how Herman is—he's all right now?"

"Our hired man, Red Miller, saw Herman out riding the Taggert range the other day. When Herman saw Red watching him, he rode hard in the other direction. So, yes, Icel Taggert got away with her cruelty, and it appears that Herman is still under her thumb." She sat back in her chair. "I want so badly to go to the Taggert ranch again, talk long to Herman, tell him we're here to help. Bring him out of there."

Maggie said, lips tight, "I'd tell Mrs. Taggert exactly what I think of her and drag her to jail by her hair." She gave her own red hair a hard swipe back from her face.

"I wouldn't mind doing that myself. Pete forbids my doing anything about this, says the men will take care of the matter. He doesn't want harm to come to me, or our baby."

"I can understand that. A body can never tell when that crazy woman'll take up a gun and shoot to kill." Tarsy scowled and chewed her lip. She hugged her infant closer.

"Yes, Pete's right," Mabel said. "Keep your baby safe, and yourself, too." The other women murmured agreement. A few moments later, they plied Jocelyn with baby gifts they'd brought—tiny crocheted booties, caps, and bonnets, soft blankets, tiny, delicate garments.

As the gifts piled into her lap, Jocelyn felt a faint stirring in her belly, a poking movement she'd never felt before. Her eyes opened wide in surprise the second time the small bump happened. She pressed her lips to hide her smile and lifted a tiny bootie to her cheek.

"I'm ready to go," Jocelyn told Nila a few days later. She set a pot of beans at the back of the stove to soak, to be boiled later. "We can have that schoolhouse shining to a fare thee well for Addie and her students in no time." They hurried outside to the wagon and team Nila had readied. Behind the seat were their tools: rags, yellow soap, beeswax polish, two buckets, a broom, and a mop. Jocelyn climbed up and took the lines, enjoying as always driving her beloved mismatched mules, sorrel Alice and tall, grey Zenith.

At the newly white-washed schoolhouse, Jocelyn staked the team to graze while she and Nila would be busy inside. She cleaned the blackboard, globe, and charts, while Nila swept down cobwebs from ceiling corners. Nila continued with the broom, sweeping the floor, while Jocelyn followed with mop and bucket. Together they shined desks with cloths and beeswax polish, finding a love note in one desk to chuckle over. Scribbled by a boy named Abe to a girl named Lilly Ann. Abe wanted to know if Lilly Ann would like to share her lunch sandwich with him and be his girl. The answer was "nope" in very large letters. Books were dusted and tidied up on the shelves. Nila treated the volumes like they were gold, now and then flipping one open to read and smiling.

"It plagues the mind," Jocelyn said, "how people can be so different about books. Pete's father had no use for them, believed books ruined young'uns for work. On the other hand, my Papa was a school teacher who loved books, maybe too much—certainly more than he cared for farming."

"Back in Missouri," Nila began, "I helped at school. Taught the littlest ones to sound out words, to learn to read. Especially young'un's having the most trouble reading. Other times, while the teacher graded papers and the like, I read aloud to all the students—I love to read. I kind of acted out the words, making the story come alive, you know? The books in my trunk, they're all gifts from the old gent wanting me to marry him. The one good thing that come out of that kerfuddle, he saw that I loved books." She drew a breath and let it out. "Do you suppose Miss Denton would like me to partner with her at school, sometimes?"

"We'll ask, but I'm sure she'd welcome you. She has her hands plenty full, and we're expecting even more students this coming year."

"I loved school." Nila carefully placed a book on the shelf. "The teacher borrowed books from the Springfield City Library for me to read. She let me write a play for the school to perform for all the Long Lane folks. It had a lot of singing and not much acting. Waltz songs like *Sweet Violet* and *Only a Pansy Blossom.*" With hand to her breast and head thrown back, Nila began to sing *Golden Slippers,* with Jocelyn joining in full voice and equal drama.

Still laughing, Jocelyn sat down to rest for a few minutes, then grabbed the bucket of dirty water to empty outside. She had lifted the bucket to throw out the water, thinking what a beautiful day it was, when her gaze drifted toward home. She jerked. A flag of smoke lifted and bloomed from where the Nickel Hill barnyard would be. Fear and dread sent chills through her body. She dropped the bucket into the dirt and yelled, "Nila, come!"

She pointed as Nila sprinted out the door into the yard. "Fire!" she cried, her voice shaking. "Nobody's home; the men and Rommy are out working the cattle pastures. We have to hurry."

Nila gasped, picked up the fallen bucket, and threw it into the wagon. With flying fingers, the two of them hitched the team and climbed into the wagon. Jocelyn grabbed the reins and slapped them hard over her mules' backs.

"Hyup! Go Zenith, Alice!" They swung out onto the road, the wagon rocking as the team bolted along. Jocelyn's frantic thoughts traveled ahead. Pete had kept a fireguard plowed around the home place against prairie fires, but this fire was inside the plowed area. *Why? How?* The few miles sped under the mules' hooves, and yet they seemed to stand still.

Jocelyn pulled her team to a hard, dust-rising stop at the house. She climbed down and whipped the reins around a porch post to hold the team away from the fire. Over her shoulder, her strained gaze took in the blazing henhouse and her neighbors, Mabel and Lyman Goody, racing with sloshing buckets from the horse trough to dash water on the fire and back again to the trough. As her full heart thanked the two dear souls, she also saw sparks setting fire to the nearby grass. *Dear heaven, no. Everything could burn.* Her knees were clabber, her heart a jack hammer under her breast. How in the name of Hannah had the henhouse caught fire? With no one at home to cause it? She couldn't fret that now.

The hayfield, the house, everything could be next. Her fists tightened. Buckets of water wouldn't be enough; they had to do more.

"Nila, run to the barn and bring a horse blanket and grain sacks." She took long, deep breaths, forcing a feeling of calm against her fear. "We can wet them in the trough or at the creek. I'll bring a blanket from the house. We can *smother* the spreading grass fires that way." Jocelyn spun toward the house. Nila was already halfway to the barn.

CHAPTER SIXTEEN

Jocelyn dragged her wet blanket toward the crackling fire creeping into the grass beyond the burning henhouse. She winced from the eerie squeal and loud *crack* as a side of the henhouse collapsed in an explosion of flame and smoke. It became even harder to see, and to catch a breath, as smoke poured around her, but she continued to haul the heavy blanket along, pain threading through her shoulders and arms.

"Honey, you can't do this alone," Mabel shouted as she ran up and grabbed the other corner of Jocelyn's wet blanket. Mabel's face was deep red and shiny with sweat in the blistering heat. Together they chased a burning section of grass, dragging the wet blanket over it. Once, twice, again, they raced flames and smothered them out.

Smoke continued to swirl thick around them, flames licking up hither and yon. It was hot from the sun, hot from the fire. Jocelyn wiped her face with her apron, blinked her burning eyes, and returned to the creek to wet the blanket again.

Mr. Goody still stormed after the henhouse blaze with buckets of water. Nila helped with wet feed sacks smothering smaller flames as soon as they flared up.

Jocelyn was not aware that Pete had ridden in until he was beside her on Raven. He leaped from the saddle and grabbed the blanket from her.

"Jocey, you get to the house and stay there!" he shouted.

She started to argue, but having breathed so much smoke,

she choked and coughed and couldn't speak.

"Now!" he ordered. "Take care of yourself and our baby. We'll put this fire out." He motioned to where Red was alongside Mr. Goody throwing buckets of dirt on the henhouse fire. Pete shouted over his shoulder, "Rommy, tie the horses in the holding pasture on the far side of the barn, herd the mules over there, too, then help Nila."

"I could help," Jocelyn mumbled through heat-parched lips. She saw that Pete would carry her into the house if he had to, and it would be wrong to waste his time. She nodded, hesitating to look back as she stumbled to the house. She choked on a sob at the scene behind her. What was going to happen to Nickel Hill? This couldn't be the end.

From the kitchen window, after washing up, she watched neighbors drive their wagons fast into the yard. Men leaped out, grabbed buckets and shovels from the wagon beds, and ran to help. Women hurried into the house with baskets of bread, ham, jars of pickles, and pies previously intended for something else. Several brought jugs of lemonade or tea. They hurriedly made sure Jocelyn wasn't in early labor from the ordeal and went outside to help fight the fire.

It seemed only moments later that Jocelyn saw Nila coming to the house holding her hands in front of her. They looked blackened. She ran from the house to meet her. "You're hurt; what happened?" She put her arm around Nila's slim shoulders, her blood chilling at a closer look at the girl's burned hands.

"S-some bur-burning grass blew onto my hands. Stuck like— like glue. Red, Mr. Miller saw. He ran right over and shoved my hands into the water trough and held them there a few minutes. That got the burning grass off, cooled them some, but they— they hurt something fierce."

In the kitchen, Jocelyn hurried to the cupboards for tea leaves to make a poultice, milk to cool the pain, and vinegar to stop

176

the itch, her Gram's sure remedy for burns. If Gram didn't have those, she would have used camphor, and if no camphor, hog lard. "Red did the right thing; the cool water will help keep your hands from blistering. But we'll wash them carefully again, with a little soap." As gently as she could, she washed Nila's hands, then had her hold them in a large bowl of milk while the tea leaves soaked in water to make the poultice.

They both looked up as the door opened and Red came in. "How're you doin', little girl? Hurtin' like he—hazelbub, I betcha. Brought you this." He held up a half-full bottle of whiskey. "A little sip won't hurt you none, and it'll ease the pain." He looked at Jocelyn, suspecting an argument. She shrugged, not sure what to say. Nila, her young face crumpled with pain, took the bottle from Red and, with a shaking hand, milk dripping, took a swig, followed by a shudder and a clock-stopping grimace.

Jocelyn's lips pinched not to laugh but she said, "We're almost finished here, honey, then you best lay down for a spell." She patted her shoulder and said to Red, "Thank you. And thanks for all you're doing out there with the fire."

He nodded. "Hated to see the girl hurt like this. You done your part, too, Nila." He started for the door. "I better get back out there, but with so many fightin' the fire, we done got it all but out. Henhouse is just a smokin' dirt pile with only a few red coals here and there. The grass fires are dyin' down and mostly out."

In time, Jocelyn's kitchen was crowded as folks began to set aside their shovels and buckets and drift toward the house in twos and threes for a drink and a bite to eat, some going back out to make sure the fire was taken care of. Jocelyn and the other women had quickly made platters of ham sandwiches and now poured cup after cup of lemonade or tea.

Some friends sat at the table, some stood with plates and forks in hand, others took their food back outside.

"Seems awful odd to me, that a fire would start in the henhouse. Chickens couldn't have done it," Mable said, her eyebrows furrowed in her sweaty face. Her dress was dirty and water stained, and a tiny burned hole showed at the top of her right leg-o-mutton sleeve, another in the hem at her ankle.

Jocelyn agreed. "I've been thinking the same, that it shouldn't have happened, natural. There wasn't a storm, no lightning strike to cause it or hay put away wet that would combust and start a fire. I can't imagine how it happened; none of us were home. But we want to thank you all for your help."

"Yep," Pete said from the open door. He wiped a sleeve across his face, streaking dust and sweat. "We could've been burned out today, down to nothing but the land and that belonging to Mrs. Gorham."

"Which makes me wonder if somebody set the fire a'purpose," Lyman Goody spoke up, pushing his chair back from the table and rising. "I pondered that from the start. Now, I don't want to point fingers at nobody innocent, but not long before we saw the fire and hitched up to come here, we saw Herman Taggert ridin' right smart t'other way."

Silence followed, Jocelyn finally breaking it. "Herman might've just wanted to be left alone, not stop to talk; he's like that."

"He also has a mother who is meaner than an ol' bear with a sore ear, and who can make Herman do whatever ornery thing she wants," Jess Hunter said, using a whittled matchstick for a toothpick.

That's true, too, Jocelyn thought, thinking of Herman's want for schooling. Nobody mentioned that Herman was likely responsible for the fire, but Jocelyn was sure all of them were thinking it. She wondered, herself, at the same time she prayed that he had nothing to do with it.

Clem Kittridge made the comment that all of them pondered.

"If set, why the henhouse? A firebug got a pesterin' dislike a' chickens?" A few strained laughs responded.

"They were scattered, far from the henhouse and chicken yard, Clem," Jocelyn told him. "Pecking and scratching in the cornfield, and down by the creek scratching for bugs. Fortunately, Nila turned them out early this morning."

"Maybe the henhouse was set a'fire first because whoever done it reckoned it'd be the torch that'd spread and take everythin'?" Red offered. Rumbles of anger traveled around the room. He ate half a slice of apple pie in one bite and continued, "Or worryin' that they'd get caught and didn't finish what they was set to do?"

No one had an answer. With the fires down to smoky ashes, tired folks began to pack up their tools and empty food baskets and leave for home. When most had gone, Pete said, "Red, if you'll stay and watch that the fires don't spark up again, I'll ride to where we left those penned calves we intended to brand, finish up, and make sure they're fed and watered."

Mr. Goody spoke up. "Nah, Red, you go on with Pete; the two of you can take care of the brandin' quicker. I'll stay and watch that the fires stay out. Mabel can sit here with your wife and the girl and visit a piece."

Hours later Pete and Red still hadn't returned. Jocelyn could only wonder what happened to keep them as she made repeated trips to the kitchen window to look out into the dark. Nila and Rommy had gone to their beds. Mabel, worn out from fighting fire followed by hours of chatting, had fallen asleep splayed on the sofa.

Around midnight, under a full moon, Jocelyn, at the window, watched Pete and Red ride in. They stood talking to Lyman Goody several minutes before putting up their horses. Red stayed at the barn, while Mr. Goody and Pete came to the house.

It took only minutes for Lyman to say goodnight, brush off Pete's and Jocelyn's thanks, and herd his sleepy wife outside in the moonlight to their wagon.

"Jocey, you oughtta be in bed," Pete scolded, his face tired and dirty. "You go on now; this has been a tough day for you, for everybody." He motioned toward the stairs. "Go on, sweetheart. I'm sorry we took so long with the calves and you felt you had to stay up for us. I'm dirty as sin. I'll be to bed directly."

"Wash up. I'll wait. Then we're going to sit down, and you're going tell me what happened. *Why* it took so long to brand a few calves."

Fifteen or so minutes later they sat holding hands across the table while he explained. "We got up to where we'd left them seven calves in a pen, but they weren't there . . . pen was empty."

"They broke out? But you found them?"

"The critters didn't break out; they were stolen. And, yes, we found them, trailed them straight to the Taggert ranch. They were in a brush-filled gully in an old dugout you could hardly see, the door barred. If a calf hadn't bawled wanting its mother, a faint sound at that, we never would have found them."

"Did you go to Icel's house? What'd she say? What'd you do?" She squeezed his hand for answers.

"We went to the house, had to threaten that we'd break down the door and come in with guns if they didn't open so we all could talk. Herman let us in." He paused. "Shaky as all get out, but he admitted what they'd done. There'd been a fierce argument between him and his ma before we got there."

Jocelyn drew a sharp, surprised breath at that. *Herman fought back against his mother? He admitted to the fire, their rustling?*

Pete continued. "He'd been ordered to set fire to our house and barn, everything. She knew the fire would keep us and all our neighbors fighting it, while she stole our cattle, and maybe some others'."

"But he didn't set fire to everything."

"Nope. He didn't want to burn us out at all. He lied to his ma, told her that he'd accidently dropped all his matches in the henhouse blaze and didn't have any left to burn everything else with. She went crazy, claiming he could've found a torch of some kind and done as he was told. Which he could've but didn't want to do. She was so mad, she grabbed a loaded gun and was bent on shooting him, her own boy." He gritted his teeth, shook his head in sick disbelief. "Now, though, he's bigger, stronger, had had enough."

Finally!

"They tussled over that same long-barreled Buntline Colt Revolver she threatened you with. Herman says it was an accident that he pulled the trigger and she was hit. He was trying to yank the gun away, he said."

"She's dead?" Jocelyn was cold with shock, yet glad it wasn't Herman.

"Not when we saw her last. Red let the Nickel Hill calves out and hazed them toward home, then we took Icel and Herman to Skiddy and turned them over to the marshal and the doctor. She could be alive, or not; I don't know." He ran his hand through his hair. "Glad the fire didn't start up again. How are Nila's hands? Sure hated to see that happen to that sweet girl. She's done nothing but do her best to help us."

"I'm going to take her in to Skiddy in the morning, allow Doctor Ashwood a look, in case there's something else can be done to ease her pain, heal those sweet hands. You're right about her helping. Nila was a godsend today doing a large part of the schoolhouse cleanup, so it'll be ready. She was alongside the rest of us, fighting fire."

"Godamighty, what a day," Pete said tiredly. "You're sure you're all right, Jocey?"

She nodded. "While I'm at the doctor's with Nila, I'll have my second checkup for the baby." *And find out what's happening to Herman and if his mother, darn her soul, will survive.*

CHAPTER SEVENTEEN

Doctor Ashwood held Nila's palms resting on his while he scrutinized the red skin and tiny blisters. "First-degree burn, only to the first skin, and that is a good thing." He had listened carefully as Nila told him how it had happened, dry burning grass lifted by the wind and sticking to the top of her hands, and now he looked at Jocelyn. "What have we done for these pretty hands, so far?"

"I followed what I remember my Gram did for burns. She cared for neighbors who were burned by a spill of boiling water, or hot paraffin when sealing jars, or burned touching the stove somehow. For Nila, I made a poultice of wet tea leaves in a thin cloth to put on her hands to draw out the pain. To be sure we'd done everything we could, I also had her hold her hands in a bowl of milk for fifteen minutes, then vinegar to relieve the itch and help her hands heal."

"Excellent. Granny medicines are often the same as what I'd prescribe. Your quick treatment will likely help the burns heal faster. I could prescribe a calamine lotion, and I'll use it today on her hands, but cow's cream would do just as much good. Occasional applications of honey can keep the burns from being infected, and, later, oats softened in water will lessen the itch as the burns heal. Be careful not to break the skin—keep the hands covered with light bandage."

As he began to wrap fresh bandage on her hands, leaving her fingers free, Doctor Ashwood continued. "Doctors and scientists have recently discovered that protein in the diet is an aid to healing in the case of burns. Eat meat and eggs, and drink lots of milk, Miss Nila."

Both Jocelyn and Nila smiled. That was already happening.

Doctor Ashwood provided extra bandage, and Jocelyn put it in her reticule. At the same time, she removed her list of groceries. "Nila, while I have my examination, would you take my list to Noack's General Store and ask Mrs. Noack to gather what we need and have it ready? Please? I'll be along directly."

"Yes, I can do that." She nodded and took the list carefully in her fingers. "Thank you, Doctor Ashwood."

She held her other bandaged paw toward him, and he took it gently in his. "You're most welcome, young lady. I understand from Mrs. Pladson, here, that you have some fine plans for your future and in the meantime will assist the local teacher out your way. Very lucky youngsters, to have a bright, pretty helper like you, miss."

Doctor Ashwood let his stethoscope hang free and frowned as he helped Jocelyn from the examining table. "You're doing fine, Jocelyn. Your heartbeat and lungs are strong, as is the baby's. Everything seems in order and on time for baby's arrival come spring. But I have a feeling something is bothering you; let's hear what it is." He looked at her kindly, waiting.

She nodded and drew a deep breath. "I do have a question." She touched the light scar through her upper lip and a fraction of it on into her face. "Where we live now, nobody but Pete and I know that—that I was born with a cleft lip." Now that she'd voiced it, telling the rest was simpler. "I worry that my baby . . . might be born disfigured . . . like I was for a while, and I hope you can tell me what the chances are, that it could happen? Not that I wouldn't love the baby with my whole being," she said earnestly, "I just wouldn't want the child to be treated as an ugly freak, how I was before I had surgery that corrected the cleft when I was twelve." In her mind, she could still hear the crowd of neighborhood youngsters' taunting chant, almost every day at school, everywhere she went, *"Harelip, Ugly Crip, Hole in her lip."*

She'd always fought hard to not show how much the teasing crushed her inside. But there were scars there, not just on her face.

He smiled gently and smothered one of her hands in his. "My dear, how many times since you've been coming to me for examination have I asked you to please open your mouth wide and say, *'aaahhh'*?"

She clapped her other hand over her smiling mouth, realizing what he was about to say.

"I could guess fairly easily that you had a repaired cleft in your lip." He patted her hand. "I was just pleased to note that it didn't also involve the roof of your mouth, the palate, which happens during the embryo stage when the two sides fail to join. Clefts are not uncommon; they happen in every seven hundred births. From what I know, there is a fifty-fifty chance this baby could be born with a cleft."

She nodded hesitantly and smiled. "That leaves a fifty-fifty chance that my little one would *not* be disfigured like I was."

"Correct. But should a cleft occur," his eyes were reassuring, "it could be repaired when the babe reaches three months in age. We would see that you'd have the best surgeon in Topeka, or Kansas City, for your baby's care. There are many folks of renown that have been born with a cleft palate or lip or both, you know. Doc Holiday, the dentist turned gambler and town marshal of Dodge City, friend of Wyatt Earp, is one. His parents had his cleft repaired when he was very young. Unfortunately, about fifteen years ago, he died of tuberculosis, a disease you and I have already talked about. Tad Lincoln, the youngest son of Abraham Lincoln and Mary Todd Lincoln, is another born with a cleft. His cleft was also repaired in his infancy. He died at the age of eighteen, also of tuberculosis. I could name numerous others today, people who fortunately led happy, successful lives—like you, but"—he removed his stethoscope from around his neck—"I won't keep you. I'm sure you have errands."

"I do. Thank you, Doctor. You've made me feel so much better." She hesitated. "One more thing. Pete says that he and Red brought Icel Taggert in to you last night to be treated for a gunshot wound. I suppose she—that she'll be all right . . . she'll live?"

His lips tightened, and a slight frown creased his forehead. "She could, but it's doubtful. I'm doing the best for her that I can, but she bled profusely before she was brought in to me."

"I may drop into your hospital to see her, if that's all right?" She hesitated. "Do you think she'll be able to talk to me?"

"She's talked, however with some difficulty. She answered my questions about her condition. She spoke with the marshal regarding her rustling activities, arguing against the charge actually, and described the shooting that put her in the hospital, blaming her son. You can try talking with Mrs. Taggert with the marshal's permission. You'll find her under guard of sorts. The marshal's deputy—his wife, Cora—is with Mrs. Taggert making sure she doesn't attempt to leave. In my opinion she couldn't if she wanted to, but the law has to follow their rules."

Jocelyn thanked him again and hurried to Noack's store. She found Elsa Noack putting together the tag end of her list of goods—flour, rice, sugar, tea, and coffee—while Nila waited in the wagon, examining a book.

"Too bad about the fire out to your place, the girl's hands getting burned," Elsa said as she and Jocelyn carried groceries to the wagon.

"We were lucky so many came to help, and the fire was

stopped before it took everything, us with it."

"I heard that the Taggerts are to blame? That the boy is over to the jail and Icel under the doctor's care at his hospital and may not survive?"

Jocelyn sighed. "All true, I'm afraid. I just wish Icel hadn't been so hard on her own son. If she hadn't been, maybe none of this would've happened."

The two women said their goodbyes, and Mrs. Noack returned to the store. Jocelyn started around the wagon to climb in and hesitated. She looked up at Nila, who sat with her nose in the book. "Would you mind being here in town a trifle longer, Nila? I'd like to talk to the marshal for just a minute or two." She waited, knowing that Nila would guess her call at Marshal Hillis's office would have to do with the Taggerts.

A team clattered by on the street, the grinning driver giving a friendly nod and spitting brown tobacco juice over the side of his wagon. After he'd gone on, she realized that it was Barney Hauser, probably on the way to a job at the stockyards.

In the yard of a nearby house a dog barked at laughing children in a game of tag.

"Sure, Mrs. Pladson, you go ahead. I'll wait here at the wagon with our team. I'd like to read this book some." She held up the tan, cloth covered book with the title *Warren's New Physical Geography.* "It has color maps and so much information. Mrs. Noack ordered it for Gorham School and has been waiting to give it to us"—she smiled—"because you're such a good customer, she says."

"Oh, my goodness. Fine. I'll remember to thank her. I'll be back in a trifle." She started down the street, saying over her shoulder, "Miss Denton's students will surely treasure the book and be happy to share it with you."

"Mrs. Pladson, how are you?" Marshal Hillis greeted Jocelyn as she entered his office after a brief knock. "That was some durned bad luck you had out at your place, that fire, wasn't it? Sorry for your loss of the henhouse and the hayfield but glad it wasn't worse. Nobody got hurt, did they?"

"Burned hands, lungs filled with smoke, tired backs, but that's all. Marshal, I came to ask after the Taggerts. Doctor Ashwood told me some about Mrs. Taggert, that she may not live. I'd like to have a few words with her, if I may, and with Herman, too."

He motioned her to a chair and sat back, scratching his head. "Don't know that there'd be any harm in your talking to them, but why would you want to?" A deep frown creased his forehead. "Never met a woman with so much of the devil in her blood as Miz Taggert. Do you know that she controlled that boy by telling him she'd hang him from a cottonwood behind their barn, with a barbed-wire noose, if he didn't do what she ordered?"

The very thought of it made Jocelyn feel sick, and tears filled her eyes. *Poor Herman.* Surely, Icel couldn't mean it, but what a terrible threat to make. *Or do, if she truly meant what she said.* She blinked her tears away, swallowed, and motioned for the marshal to continue.

"Taking the gun and trying to kill her own son, now that's pure criminal. She's the one could be hung—if she lives to be tried in court over the rustling and attempted murder of him. You might say she'd be damn lucky to not survive the gunshot." He nodded agreement to his own remark, his expression grim.

"I understand from Doctor Ashwood that, seriously wounded though she is, she was able to talk, answer your questions?"

"Oh, yeah, I questioned her. She knows the boy told us the truth, admitted to the cattle rustling that's been carried on out your way this last year. That's made her real mad he told us, but there was no use to her arguing different, though she tried. She appeared proud, too, of what they done, how nobody caught her and her boy at thieving and have no way of proving it."

"That's what I can't understand. They were suspected almost from the first, but nobody could find proof that they were the cattle thieves."

"Well, they was slick, that ornery woman especially. We're sure they had an accomplice." He leaned back in his chair, his hands behind his head, his expression shrewd. "But she won't talk about that, none at all. We figure that she or the boy or both together would drive off some ranchers' beeves to a meeting place, where an accomplice or two took over and moved the herd fast out of these parts. Sometimes they'd butcher a beef, bury the hide, sell the beef to a butcher, again through their accomplice."

"Who do you think that might be, the one or more than one, that's helping them?"

"We don't know for sure yet, but it's under investigation by the county sheriff as well as me. I'm not allowed to name suspects at this point. Herman Taggert refuses to tell who it is, claims he and his mother would be killed if he told." He scoffed. "The old woman pretends to be dying and unable to say, when we ask her. I swear she can bring on bleeding by herself, to show how bad off she is with that chest wound."

"I doubt she can call up bleeding in herself, but I've never known a more hard-hearted person. Particularly a woman toward her own child."

"From the way Mrs. Taggert talked, she'd still like to tie into her son for ignoring her orders—the fire calamity—that ended with her getting shot. Herman told me that his orders were to burn down everything standing on your place, even the house with you and the girl in it—if you'd have been there. He couldn't do it because of how good you treated him, trying to help him every which way to get schooling. To get out of his fix, he made up the story about losing all the matches in the first building he set fire to." He laughed, although the expression in his eyes was serious.

"I'd like to talk to him, now. Thank him for that fib, what he did, that saved our ranch and us." She got to her feet.

"If it wasn't for his part in stealing cattle, and the fact that we need him to find the other thief or thieves involved, I think I'd let him go." He left his chair and came around his desk. "Main thing, it'd be the first freedom in his life he'd know."

Jocelyn nodded. "I have no doubt of that."

As he led the way back to the cells, the marshal said, "His ma claimed that foreclosure was breathing down her neck and that's what she stole the cattle to pay for. Herman told a different story, that the money they got from thefts mostly went first for his mother's rotgut whiskey, and legal whiskey she bought at the drugstore. An' groceries from time to time. Payment to the bank coming last." His keys rattled as they reached the cell where Herman sat on a narrow bed, elbows on his knees and his head in his hands. His eyes, when he looked up at them, were dimmed with sadness, dark circles below them.

Her breath caught when he stood and came to the bars, limping like a broken old man.

His own mother hurt him like that? Afraid she might be sick, Jocelyn turned away for a few seconds.

"Mrs. Pladson wants a word with you. I'm going to let you come out to the hall here"—the marshal pointed to a pair of chairs—"because the cell is no place for her."

Shoulders slumped, Herman took his hands from the bars, his eyes not meeting Jocelyn's.

She said softly, "Herman?" and he started to cry.

CHAPTER EIGHTEEN

"I didn't want to start the fire at your house, Mrs. Pladson," Herman said, as they sat side by side in the jail hallway. He wiped his sleeve across his eyes and looked down in shame. "I tried to tell Ma that I wouldn't, that I couldn't, but she didn't listen. She never listens, just says I got to do what she wants, or she'll—she'll . . ." He turned his face away, his Adam's apple bobbing in his throat.

Jocelyn shivered. *Hang you with a barbed wire noose.* "I know that you didn't favor all that your mother made you do, Herman." She touched his arm. "And that's why I'm here, to thank you for not setting fire to more than the henhouse. The whole matter would have been much worse, Nickel Hill Ranch destroyed and maybe lives lost, if you hadn't chosen how you did. I'll be everlastingly grateful."

"Did anybody get hurt bad?" he asked plaintively and rubbed his jaw. "I sure hope not. I'm sorry for the whole thing, real sorry."

"A friend's hands were burned some, but the doctor's seen to them, and she'll be all right. It was a lot of work for a lot of folks putting the fire out and keeping it from spreading."

"My ma, is she . . . did she die?" Herman asked, his fists clenched, worry in his eyes.

Jocelyn couldn't help wondering if the look indicated concern for his ma's welfare, or fear for himself at her hands if she recovered? *A mix of both, most likely.*

Jocelyn put her arm around his shoulders. "She's alive, at the doctor's hospital." Her heartbeat slowed, wanting him to know the truth. "Your mother's wound is serious, but Doctor Ashwood will take fine care of her. He'll do his best, but even then . . . she . . . might not survive." *And if she does heal and get better, she'll never have a chance to lay a hand on you again, because she'll be behind bars.*

"I didn't mean to shoot Ma," he said, his voice quivering. "I'd never do that. I fought her to make her stop. I was tryin' to take the gun away." His hands gripped his knees. "Then the gun went off as we was each tryin' to grab it." He rubbed his hands on his pants. His voice lifted. "I hope she don't die. She hates me, though." He nodded and said seriously, "I think her ma and pa was mean to her, awful like. An' she don't know no other way than be mean her ownself. Ma's got a terrible temper."

That she does, Jocelyn thought, clenching her jaw, *that she does.* She gave him a minute or two and then said, "I want to thank you, too, for not lying about the cattle thefts. It's such a relief to not wonder, anymore, who was stealing our stock—glad that it's over." *Almost over.* She took a deep breath and added, "Someone else helped you and your ma rustle others' stock, right?"

He froze, then turned away without answering.

"I don't mean to pester you, but it would help everything, you most of all, if that person is named. They must be stopped and made to pay for what they've done. But we need to know who this person is, or persons if it's more than one. Would you tell me who, please, Herman?" She waited, a fluttery feeling in her stomach.

Time ticked by, seeming to Jocelyn more like hours than seconds. She looked at him and asked, again, "Please, Herman?"

He'd turned white, his voice hollow. "I can't tell you, Mrs.

Pladson. I can't. If I did"—he was visibly shaking—"they'd come kill me fast as spit. Right here in this jail, locked up behind those bars yonder, Ma for one would find a way to kill me." He was quiet a long moment. Then reluctantly he repeated, "Ma tried before to kill me; she'd try again, believin' our bein' found out is all my fault."

Jocelyn's scalp prickled, and she touched his arm. It was hard to believe such a thing of a mother toward her child, but Icel had attempted to take his life. She said stoutly, "As long as you're under Marshal Hillis's and Deputy Cora's watch, you can't be harmed, by anyone. I intend to do what I can, too, to keep you safe." *I think you'd be surprised at the number of folks on your side, Herman Taggert. They, too, know your ma's bent toward cruelty.*

He looked at her, his expression imploring her to understand. "I can't tell you any more than I done already. Keep my mouth shut, that's what I've been ordered to do. And I got to do it . . . keep my mouth shut."

At the approach of the marshal and rattle of his keys, they both looked up. "Times up. Back to your cell, young fella', 'til we get all this figured out."

They stood. Herman looked away, then turned to Jocelyn, his voice at a nervous pitch. "Mrs. Pladson, would you visit my ma, too, at the doctor's hospital? T-tell her again that I'm s-sorry that I fought her so, and she got sh-shot? Tell her for me that I hope she gets better?"

Jocelyn touched his shoulder in wonder that he could still care about Icel, mean to him as she was. "I'll go visit her right now, Herman, if the marshal will let me. And I'll tell her what you said." *And a lot more!*

He tried to smile, but he was shaking and white faced with fear as he moved toward the cell.

Feeling a trifle nervous but determined on the walk to the

small, green-shuttered hospital, Jocelyn told the marshal, "I'd like to talk to Icel alone, please. More a woman to woman conversation—about . . . about a person's child and how we should love them, do what we can to protect them. Not treat them like . . ." She couldn't find a word to describe Icel's treatment of Herman. "Just talk."

"Reckon that'd be all right, but you'll be wasting your breath, I expect." When they arrived, he motioned Jocelyn to follow him to a small back bedroom, where Cora, his wife and deputy, sat on a chair by the door, knitting resting on the baby bulge of her stomach. A holstered revolver sagged off her hip. "Cora," he said, "if you'd go stay over to the office for me for just a little bit, I'd appreciate it." She nodded, gathered up her knitting bag, adjusted the holstered weapon, and returned his hug. She stared for a minute at Jocelyn, shrugged, and started for the front door. "I'll be there directly, Cora," he called after her, "a little business to take care of here, first." He took the chair his deputy-wife had been sitting in and motioned Jocelyn on into the room. Icel Taggert's still form in the bed looked a whole lot less ferocious than usual.

Even so, Jocelyn's palms turned sweaty, and her scalp prickled, remembering other times. She did her best to quell her nerves and moved a chair close to the bed and sat down. Icel Taggert's eyes were closed; she was smallish, wrinkled, a stone-white, very ill imitation of herself. The quilt covering her lifted with her ragged breathing. Jocelyn licked her lips and said quietly, "Mrs. Taggert, this is Jocelyn, Mrs. Pladson, I—" Before she finished, Icel's eyes slowly fluttered open.

Icel croaked faintly, "What're you doin' here?" Her eyes closed, then opened again, wider, staring at Jocelyn. Deep wrinkles of confusion creased her forehead.

"I came to see if there's anything I can do for you, Mrs. Taggert," Jocelyn said in a soft, pleasant tone hard to come by.

"That, and to tell you I've talked with your son." She waited for a reaction, but there was none. She continued, her throat dry, not liking what she had to say but keeping her promise. "Herman asked me to tell you again how sorry he is that the gun accident happened, and that he wants you to get well."

"He—he's in the jail, ain't he?" she asked in a slow, weak voice. Wrinkles around her eyes deepened, causing a brief accusing scowl. She muttered, "He wouldn't even try to get away, like he ought. About as much good sense as God give a turtle."

"Yes," Jocelyn's jaw clenched, "he's in jail; that's where I talked to him."

She had to lean in to hear, as Icel continued, "Ain't nothin' can be done for him now, got his ownself where he is. Against me, all the time. My idiot boy spilled his guts to the marshal. An' I'm dyin'." Tears of self pity shone in her eyes, anger in her countenance building.

Jocelyn started to reach into her reticule for her lace-edged handkerchief that she'd bought at the KESA show, to hand to the weeping woman. She shoved it back. Icel Taggert could flood the state of Kansas with her crocodile tears. Unless—she was willing to help her son. She had started to speak when Icel interrupted.

"Why're you in here? Ain't none of this your bizness no how." Icel huffed, glared, and with shaking hands used the front of her gown to swab her eyes.

Jocelyn decided to be honest and fair as possible. She spoke carefully, trying to keep bitter feelings reined. "Several reasons, I suppose. I feel bad for you and Herman. I wish life could've been different for the two of you. I'm sorry for whatever caused things to turn out so rotten like they have."

Icel panted, pain showing in her eyes, "Don't—don't waste no sympathy on me, 'cause I ain't sorry for nothin' I done."

"If that's how you feel, that's your right." Jocelyn shrugged and took a minute to form the words she really wanted to say. "I thought you might wish you could do something for Herman, your own flesh and blood, who cares about you."

"Don't know what you mean." Icel mumbled with a frown, her bloodshot, ferrety eyes on Jocelyn's face.

"Save him from spending years in jail, for one." She took a breath and added cautiously, "Do a good thing for him that he'll thank you for all the rest of his life."

Icel snarled in disgust, "Ain't nothin' I can do for him from this bed, dyin' little by little, 'cause of what he done." Her hand trembled to the thick bandages above her breast where it was said the bullet struck. "He ain't got no help comin' from me; he don't deserve it."

Jocelyn's throat dried, and she felt sick, but she persisted. "You might live, Icel. Be able, someday, to start over." The doctor had said that she'd bled a great deal, and the bullet had done its damage, going in and being taken out. "Doctor Ashwood feels you have a chance to pull through." *Small, but a chance is a chance.*

Hope flickered for a second in Icel's eyes, replaced by cold, flat recognition of her fate. She scowled, and her tone was acid filled. "My chances are littler than an ant's nose, you know it." She moaned. "Better to lay here—an' die"—eyes closed, her breathing shallow, silence ticked by for a minute or two—"than allow the law to put me behind bars. Th-that ain't livin'." She took several, quick, angry breaths, her eyes wide. "Let it be a curse on my boy for what he done to me. That's what." Her hands tore at her cover, and she sobbed in self pity.

"You threatened to hang him with a barbed-wire noose if he didn't fire our place."

She sneered, her face wet with tears. "Had to; he was bein' pure stubborn against me."

"That was terribly cruel, you know."

" 'Course I know." Her words came slow, with effort. "Scared me to my bone marrow when my ma claimed to do that to me. But when you don't do as you're told, you got such as that comin'."

"You've raised a good boy," Jocelyn argued. Tears threatened in her own eyes at the same time anger burned in her chest. "You could save his life, still, Icel. You still can. With just a little information, that's all."

"He done told everything." Her hand lifted, shaking. "Confessed what we done, brought this trouble down on both our heads—me, dyin', him behind bars and maybe gonna hang. Should'a listened to me."

"You must do this, Icel: you have to tell Marshal Hillis who your accomplice was. Things would go better for Herman." She scooted closer to the bed. "You could survive your wound and get well, you know. The law would go easier on you, too, if you give this information. Do the honorable thing, Icel, this one decent thing for yourself and your son. It's all up to you. It's not too late . . ." She waited, and waited, for Icel's reply while goosebumps crawled on her arms.

There was no movement, no sound from Icel. Her eyes remained closed, her skin pallid and her mouth slack. It startled Jocelyn when she finally spoke, her words faint. "Ain't goin' to jail. Leave me be. Go!"

Jocelyn waited several minutes. Then she stood and left the room. In the hall, she told the marshal, "I got no help from Mrs. Taggert, nothing. Not even to help her son. I'm afraid it's useless."

"I figured that's how it'd be. But I'm glad you tried, Mrs. Pladson."

She sighed. "I'm glad, too, I suppose. But in all my days I never met a more wrong-sided woman, and I hope I never meet another! Maybe she'll think about what I said to her and come

197

around, maybe not." Filled with disappointment and worry for Herman, she shrugged. "If she lives, I may talk to her again, but for now, I'm due home."

A longer time passed than she liked before Jocelyn was able to return to Skiddy and offer her hand against the dire situation there. The least she could do would be to visit Herman at the jail, do what she could to keep his spirits up. Give him hope *if there was any.*

Opening the door to the marshal's office, she was startled to see the newspaper editor, Stanley Murdock, leaning back in what was normally the marshal's chair, ankles crossed on the marshal's desk, pad and pencil held busy in his hands. The chair clunked into place as he quickly drew his feet to the floor. Color flooded his face. "Um, Mrs. Pladson. Good morning."

She took her tongue from inside her cheek and answered, "Good morning, Mr. Murdock. I don't see Marshal Hillis, or Deputy Cora. Are they around—maybe in the back?" She nodded toward the door leading to the back room's four cells and started that way.

"No, they aren't here, sorry." He stood and rubbed his hands together and smiled. "I'm minding the office momentarily. Cora left a few minutes ago to go to the mercantile for coffee beans." He nodded toward the coffeepot centering the round iron heating stove. "After that she's heading home for a few minutes to check on her children and the marshal's bandages . . ."

"The marshal's bandages? What's happened, is he all right?" Just a small accident, she hoped, with a hatchet, or lighting a fire—something like that. In her bones she knew better.

"He'll survive. We had us quite a frightening hullabaloo in our little town day before yesterday. Newsworthy, indeed. I'm writing it up for the *Reflex.* 'A SHOOT-OUT FOR THE ANNALS OF HISTORY.' "

Jocelyn's heartbeat nearly exploded, but before she could voice another word, Murdock's diatribe continued in high excitement, "I've already interviewed the marshal and his wife, but I came today to verify a few details with Cora. Also, to learn whatever she might add that will give more color to the written account."

"What *happened?*" Jocelyn's lips tightened, and her mind raged. *Tell me the facts before I grab you by the neck, Mr. Editor, and choke it out of you.* She leaned and planted both hands hard on the desk. "For the sake of Hannah, Mr. Murdock," her shoulders sagged, "tell me what happened?"

He took the chair again, scooted forward, anxious now to give details. "You don't know a thing about it, then? I would've thought you'd have heard." He licked his lips. "A couple days ago, Doc Asherwood gave the go ahead to move Mrs. Taggert from the hospital. If not totally healed yet, he believed she was well enough for jail, you see."

Jocelyn nodded. "Good." Her heartbeat headed toward normal.

"The marshal and his wife were walking Mrs. Taggert along carefully, one on either side, almost here to the jail when the prisoner suddenly moaned and started to fall. Deputy Cora leaned to see to her, and that blessed Mrs. Taggert snatched Cora's revolver from its holster, turned quick as lightning on the marshal—who was reaching for his gun to stop her—and shot him. Creased his scalp, made him dizzy, and blood pouring. Icel Taggert's next shot went wild when Deputy Cora struck the woman's arm."

"Good grief!" Jocelyn held her breath, and her skin tingled. She motioned for him to continue.

"Cora Willis is a fine deputy, no doubt about that! What a woman. She held Widow Taggert's wrist and wrestled the gun from her. Empty-handed, the Taggert woman then dove for the marshal's gun—he was trying to stand, couldn't focus his eyes, and there was all the blood, too. His gun aim wobbled, and naturally he didn't want to hit his wife by mistake."

"Wh-what happened th-then? How . . . ?"

"Cora held her gun on the Taggert woman and ordered her to stop right there: *Stop right there, don't move.* Mrs. Taggert screamed, 'My boy got me into this fix, and he's gettin' his after you'uns'! She ignored Cora's demand and scrambled for the marshal's gun, had it from his hand and aimed at Cora before the wounded marshal could move. Deputy Cora was quicker with her shot. Mrs. Taggert went down, her shot barely missing Cora."

Jocelyn found another chair and sat down, her insides all aquiver. It was a moment or two before she could speak. "Icel Taggert took the bullet? How . . . how is she?"

"Dead. The woman died before she could be moved off the street. Most likely died the instant the bullet struck her heart." He slapped the desk.

Jocelyn nodded slowly, her mind weighing how it would have been had the shooting gone differently, Cora the one killed. A good woman, fine at her job. If she'd died, she would have left a husband, three children, and likely her unborn would have died with her. Icel Taggert, no husband, one child that she'd treated horribly his whole life, whom she would have killed if she could've gotten to him at the jail with a gun. Justice had been duly served.

Moving to be more comfortable in her chair, Jocelyn's hand went instinctively to her tummy mound and the tiny elbow or foot poking at her from inside. She took several long breaths, needed to stay calm, not get so worked up, for her little one's sake. After a few moments, feeling better, she asked, "And Herman, how is he? Has he been told that his mother . . . is gone?"

Murdock was about to answer when the door opened, and

Deputy Cora came into the office, wearing a light-colored canvas coat over a man's shirt and pants and waddling tiredly. For a brief moment, Jocelyn cherished a sisterly feeling toward Cora Hillis that had nothing to do with the recent shooting, but rather their coming babies. She grew solemn. "Hello, Deputy, how are you? How is Leo? Editor Murdock tells me there was a serious shoot-out a couple days ago."

Murdock, surprisingly, jumped to, took the bag of ground coffee beans from Cora, and set about making a pot of coffee.

Cora Hillis struggled into a chair, barely fitting, her legs stretched before her. She sighed. "I'm fine enough, and so is Leo. Ready for him to take back this office—this job—while I allow number four into the world. Leo doesn't like being home today and insists a scalp wound isn't keeping him back, that he can take over the night shift in a few hours, and I'm about to let him. Thankfully, women neighbors are helping us at home." In the next few moments, she gave details of the shooting, her account matching Editor Murdock's—but with less drama.

"Did either of you talk to Herman about . . . what happened to his mother?"

"Both of us. I wanted to tell him myself that it was me that had to shoot his mother. How it happened. That there was nothing else I could do. Icel Taggert would have killed me, and probably this child I'm carrying, and Leo, too. I didn't tell Herman that his mother meant to shoot *him* in his cell."

Several moments of silence followed, each one in the room staring at the floor with their own thoughts. Jocelyn asked, "Have you since talked to him about who the accomplice might've been who aided him and his mother in the rustling?"

Deputy Cora nodded. "Herman seemed glad, relieved, really, to be able to tell the rest of what he knew. It seems that Icel Taggert met a man named Barney Hauser at a stock sale, both complaining that day how everybody but them was making

201

'real' money. They talked again a couple more times and cooked up a scheme for stealing stock. Icel and Herman would raid herds, take a few head, and herd them on quick to Barney at a meeting place. He'd take over from there."

"Just the three of them? Were they the only ones involved in the rustling do you think?"

"Far as we know, only the three. You never know about 'invisible' connections, though. That is being investigated."

"I know who Barney Hauser is, but only as a helper at the stockyards now and then, or seeing him around Skiddy. I wouldn't have guessed he'd be one of the rustlers, but maybe what he learned working at the stockyards, at Skiddy, gave him ideas for rustling stock, ways to get rid of them elsewhere."

"We think so. It appears the trio preferred calves that hadn't been branded yet. Hauser could then slap his brand on them, or skin the larger critters and sell them as beef to meat packing plants out of the area. When he was lucky, he could change a brand into his own with a running iron, then claim ownership when he went to sell. If he was dealing with shady buyers of live cattle or beef, we'll find them. The lot of them will be spending very long prison sentences. Had all this been a few years back, they'd hang."

"I worry about what will happen to Herman. I honestly believe he'd never have gotten into all this if his mother hadn't forced him with brutal threats of death."

"We'll see. He's a kid, but in the eyes of the law, regarding crime or marriage, at his age, he's considered an adult. My husband is frothing at the bit to do what he can to get Herman off."

"I can understand that. I learned a lot about the young man, and he's far more the victim than lawbreaker—and lucky to be alive."

"We'll see, when his case comes to trial."

"Yes," Jocelyn echoed softly, her heart in her throat. "We'll see."

CHAPTER NINETEEN

Jocelyn took a seat close to the open window of the old building that served as Skiddy's town hall. Herman's trial would begin any minute. Barney Hauser's trial had already been held, and he was looking at spending the rest of his life in prison. She was anxious for Herman's trial to be over with and prayed it would turn out how she hoped. With effort, she closed out the shuffling and chatter of others filing in around her, the racket of youngsters playing outside, and focused on Herman's court-appointed attorney, Grant Sanborn, a sincere, dark-haired young man seated beside Herman at a small table up front.

She liked Attorney Sanborn, but Herman's complicated case had her insides quivery with uncertainty. Would Sanborn be experienced enough? He'd assured her earlier that the circuit judge, coming from Council Grove to preside, was a fair man. When he named him, Circuit Judge Duane Rawlins, she'd felt a bit better, having met the judge in the past when he bought a mule team from her boss, Whit Hanley, while they were on the road.

Pete, having taken care of their team outside, slipped in to sit beside her. She whispered, "I thought Sam McCleary and Vern Rowland were going to be here for the prosecution? They were plenty riled when they found out who rustled their cattle. I haven't seen them."

"Backed out," he answered close to her ear. "They hated losing cattle to the scoundrels, but they don't like what's happening to Herman. Him, just a boy, in jail, his mother dead and buried, not here to say a word in his defense."

"It's likely she wouldn't have, in any event," Jocelyn whispered back. She felt certain of it, to be honest.

The bailiff, a man of middling size with thin, sandy hair, dressed in a rumpled, grey suit, looked out at the crowd and intoned, "All please rise for the judge."

Heart pounding, Jocelyn stood. She caught and squeezed Pete's hand, communicating her wish that all would go well.

Judge Rawlins entered through a door at the front of the room and took his place at a tall pine bench, placing a gavel in handy reach. Smiling, his plump hands motioned for everyone to sit down. Jocelyn sat back, letting relief sink in. From his shiny, bald head to his calm, wise, and friendly countenance, dressed not that differently from when she'd last seen him in a vested suit and black bowtie, the judge hadn't changed. Her heart settled with satisfaction.

With a nod from the judge, the bailiff chanted, "Court is in session." Bible in hand, eyes slumberous, he swore in Marshal Hillis. A streak of thinning hair and a healing scar along the side of the marshal's head was very obvious.

"Now, Marshal Hillis," Judge Rawlins said, "please tell us about the arrest, the why and wherefore of the charges against the defendant, this young man, Herman Taggert."

The marshal sighed, held his hat, and said, "I had to arrest Herman for setting fire to a ranch building that didn't belong to him. And"—he looked regretful to add—"for rustling cattle. Then there was this other thing, in which his mother was shot." He added quickly, "But that was pure self defense, and an accident."

There was a chorus of gasps around the room. Necks craned forward—so many, Jocelyn thought irritably, looking around, that if they'd been in a boat they'd all be dog paddling by now.

Everybody please spare judgment until you've heard everything, the true facts of it all. She faced forward chin up, and her hands clutched together.

The prosecuting attorney, a smartly dressed, heavy-jowled man with bristly hair, hauled immediately to his feet. He glared in the judge's direction. "Objection! The marshal's opinion is plain conjecture considering the shooting and shouldn't be allowed."

"Sustained." The judge said casually, "Marshal Hillis, we've only just started here, and it's up to this trial and me to determine the truth." He smiled quietly. "With the help of these two fine attorneys," he waved a hand and accounted, "the cooperating witnesses yet to be heard, and, finally, the jury, yonder." He then gave Grant Sanborn a nod to go ahead and question the marshal if he so chose.

"No questions," Sanborn declined. "I'd like to bring a witness for the defendant to the stand—but first I have a few words of my own in defense of the accused."

"So be it," the judge agreed.

"As Herman Taggert's attorney," Sanborn began, "I will prove that practically from the time young Taggert was born, his life was one of self defense. It's been hell, if you will. Self defense against threats, self defense against beatings and maiming at the hands of his own mother. I would like to call Miss Addie Denton to the witness stand."

Jocelyn had suggested Addie to Attorney Sanborn and was so glad to see the young woman had agreed to be there, guaranteeing on the Bible to tell the truth of what she knew.

"Now, Miss Denton—Addie—you are a school teacher, correct?" Sanborn asked.

"Yes, sir."

"And there was an occasion when young Taggert wanted to attend your school. He was prohibited to do so by his only parent, his mother. She strongly *disagreed* with his desire to go to school," he emphasized to the room, "*disagreed* with this young man's longing to learn!" He turned back to Addie. "Would you describe for us what happened, please?"

Addie looked at the crowd that had quieted to hear her and spoke in a clear, confident voice. "Although he was a teenager at the time he requested to attend Gorham School, Herman had had only a fourth-grade education. He wanted more. His mother was against it and came to school to force him back home."

"Force him, how, Miss Denton?"

Addie hesitated, moistened her lips, and took a deep breath. "She told him that if he didn't go with her, she'd go home and come back for him with a gun. That she'd shoot him, *her own child*, if he refused her again. She claimed, very convincingly I might add, that she'd shoot me and Mrs. Pladson"—she looked in Jocelyn's direction—"who was also there, should either of us try to prevent Herman leaving with her."

"Tell us how Herman reacted; did he go with her?" Sanborn asked.

"He was very frightened. He voiced his genuine concern for my welfare, and Mrs. Pladson's, regarding his mother's threats to return with a gun. He begged us not to intervene, and, yes, he left school to go with her."

The other attorney was on his feet, huffing and waving for the judge to let him speak.

"Go ahead with your rebuttal, prosecutor."

"This is nonsense, Your Honor. Pure hearsay," he scoffed, his high-pitched voice reminding Jocelyn of a honking goose. "A mother wouldn't make such a claim against her own son. Oh, she might use those words, joshing . . . a strong measure to make him mind her. The witness exaggerates."

"That woman never said nothin' she didn't mean, not ever,"

a voice shouted from the back of the room. Jocelyn clapped a hand over her mouth, not that she didn't agree. She looked and saw that it was Clem, who wasn't finished. "If she said she'd kill her son if he didn't do what she said, she sure as hell meant it." The judge tapped his gavel and motioned Clem to sit down.

Voiced agreement rumbled here and there around the room followed by a babble of shocked exclamations, one of them declaring loudly, "It ain't no crime, no how, to want schoolin'. The boy was within his rights, not doin' nothin' wrong."

Judge Rawlins's hands motioned a downward signal for silence from the crowd, followed by one loud rap of his gavel. He turned to the prosecuting attorney. "The floor is yours, sir, if you'd like to bring up witnesses for prosecution?"

"I had two or three who could prove this boy is a criminal, Your Honor."

"Well, then, where are they?" the judge asked, eyebrows raised.

"They didn't come today, I don't know what happened, but I—"

The judge waved him silent. "You had plenty of time to notify me of that before we got this far into the trial. We might have rescheduled. I believe we have their true opinion, by their absence. Attorney Sanborn, do you have other witnesses"—he sighed—"that might bring clarity one way or another to your claim of innocence on behalf of your client?"

The prosecuting attorney plopped into his chair and looked with desperation toward the door. When it continued to remain closed, squirming, he shook his head. His face bloated with anger.

"Yes, I do, Your Honor. I would like to call Mr. Lyman Goody to the stand as a character witness for the defendant."

Jocelyn warmed to every word of Lyman's defense of Herman. "Herman Taggert is a good, decent young feller, the hardest working of any human I've seen his age. He always done as asked because Mrs. Icel Taggert was, after all, his mother. The boss. But as he got old enough to know better, he knew that a lot of what his ma asked of him was wrong. Dead wrong. That's when he resisted, because he wanted to follow his own feelings of wanting to do right, not break the law. Mrs. Taggert's awful bullying and beating him got worse. Her threats went from saying she'd kill him with a gun, to her worst of all: that if he didn't steal cattle for her as she ordered, she'd hang him . . . hang him from a tree with a barbed-wire noose."

Three women began to cry, handkerchiefs to their mouths; others gaped in shock. Men's stormy faces showed their disgust, their outrage.

Attorney Sanborn held his hand toward the crowd and then the jury. "Now what would any of you folks do, in a situation like that?" The room grew so quiet one could hear flies buzzing and bumping against the windows. Sanborn repeated the words in a hollow voice, "She would use barbed wire; she would hang her own child. Think about it, please. What would you do?" He sat down.

The prosecuting attorney, taking the floor, chuckled and shook his head, jowls quivering, his hand nervously playing with his moustache. He repeated, "Those were just words Icel Taggert didn't mean, empty words given in an overwrought moment. Nothing more." Continuing, his voice dripped with sadness, his eyes appealed to the jury and audience to understand Icel's plight. "The poor woman was inhumanely overburdened and overworked running a large ranch with just the inadequate help of the boy, who was known to rebel, to not heed her wishes." With an expression meant to shame Sanborn and flicking a hand toward him, he claimed, "Defense's case is nothing but over-blown hearsay, all of which must be ignored by those of us blessed with common sense and wanting justice. Herman

Taggert must pay for his crimes." He sat down and, shoulders back, looked at Sanborn with an expression radiating stubborn superiority.

Grant Sanborn got to his feet, gave a half smile, and shrugged at the opposing attorney as though dismissing a small insect as he strode to the center of the courtroom, his eyes more interested in movement at the back of the room. "Judge, it was my intention to bring Mrs. Pladson to the witness stand next. But if I may, I'd like for the jury to hear from Doctor Fraser Ashwood for now."

Jocelyn turned in surprise. Doctor Ashwood must have come late, as she hadn't seen him there earlier. She noted Sanborn's relieved grin, the relaxed set of his shoulders, as the doctor was sworn in and settled in the witness chair.

"Doctor Ashwood," Sanborn began, "I only have a couple of questions—we don't like to keep a busy man like you from caring for his patients. All right?"

The doctor sat forward, rested his arms on the arms of the chair, and nodded. "Fine with me."

"I believe you treated the defendant's mother for the gunshot wound that took place in the struggle for a weapon between her and her son, Herman. Did she tell you anything about that struggle?"

He nodded. "Yes, she did. She said that she might have 'gone a little crazy,' which she saw as all Herman's fault. She admitted she had every intent to shoot him, to kill him, and not be 'bothered with him and his ornery standing against her another time.' "

"Thank you, Doctor," Sanborn said. "I had asked if you'd try to visit Herman at the jail. Were you able to do that and examine him physically for proof of his own mother's ill treatment?"

"I was able to, yes, a few days before his mother passed."

The prosecuting attorney was on his feet huffing and honking frantic protest, his arms waving like he was flagging down a runaway team of mules. The judge motioned him silent with a sharp order to sit down.

"Would you tell us what you found, Doctor?" Sanborn continued.

"In a private room at the jail I was able to examine Herman Taggert. I found new and old scars from beatings. Broken bones—his ribs and his left leg, his other ankle—that due to lack of proper treatment healed improperly. I admit that I had a problem, myself, to believe that a mother would do that to her child. On my last visit to check on Mrs. Taggert at my hospital, I asked her about it. She said yes, that she was responsible—that the boy's, Herman's, refusal to carry out her demands brought on her 'temper fits.' "

He hesitated, waiting for that to sink in around the room. "She agreed that what she wanted of him, such as rustling others' cattle—never mind her abuse of him—was against the law but to her mind had to be done to keep her ranch. If this had gone on much longer, I'm afraid she would've killed the boy."

A long, serious silence filled the room, broken by a muffled sob here and there and ragged sounds of stifled anger.

The prosecuting attorney sat stiff in his chair and signaled with frustration that he had no questions for the doctor.

Called next, as another character witness, Jocelyn was sworn in. Moving with certainty, she settled in the witness chair, hands clasped in her lap. She doubted that her testimony was needed after the doctor's and hoped that what she had to say would not be thrown out as hearsay. With a nod from Sanborn, and the judge's smile of recognition, she told how, under threat, Herman chose to set fire to only their henhouse, contrary to his mother's orders for him to burn the house, barn, the pastures—everything at Nickel Hill. Icel, Herman, and another cohort would steal cattle while all the neighbors would be at Nickel

Hill trying to fight the huge fire. Because he'd not done her evil bidding as ordered, Icel took a loaded gun intending to kill her own son. Herman had tried to take the gun away, and, in the tussle, the gun had gone off, wounding his mother.

"Your Honor, may I say somethin'?" a voice very familiar to Jocelyn asked. She turned in surprise to see Red Miller on his feet at the back of the room. Judge Murdock nodded and motioned him to go ahead.

"This boy ain't the one should be on trial here; it oughtta be his ma, but she's dead, taken down by the law on her way to kill her son. If the jury's decision is that Herman Taggert goes free, I want them, and you, Your Honor, to know that almost anybody here in this room, anybody like Mrs. Pladson, would give him a home, a job . . . a good life."

There was rousing agreement around the room. Jocelyn was standing and trying to say above the noise that she would take Herman in.

"I'd learn him the ropes of being a cowhand," Red was shouting, "like me and Pete Pladson used to be over in Chase County on the 7Cs ranch for Daniel Curran and his wife, Adella. For God's sake, don't put this young fella' in prison. That'd be a helluva lot more wrong than what he's already had served to him."

Half the room was on their feet with offers to give a job, a place to stay, to Herman. Judge Rawlins, a smile quirking at his mouth, furiously banged his gavel for order. Finally, folks began to quiet down and slowly take their seats.

Marshal Hillis, still standing, was getting a last word in. "I recommend that Herman Taggert at the least be given probation but stay under my watch. Pay for his part in the rustling—even though that was against his will—by taking small jobs for folks here in Skiddy."

The sound of agreement filled the room.

Jocelyn blinked away tears.

Among those settling into their seats, she noticed the handsome, weathered, middle-aged couple, Daniel and Adella Curran, owners of the 7Cs, beside Red Miller. Had they, too, been bargaining to take in Herman? They were good, honest, successful folks like she and Pete intended to be. She gave them a tiny wave, remembering that she'd been invited to supper at the 7Cs when she and Pete were courting.

Judge Rawlins rapped with his gavel again to end the rabble. Giving in to a wide grin, he turned to the jury. "Do you all have to retire to another room to make your decision, or can you give a sensible verdict to us here, pretty quick?"

With heads together, soft murmurs traveled back and forth among the jury members for five minutes. The jury foreman then stood. "We have reached our decision, Your Honor. Because Herman Taggert's actions were in self defense for his very life, we've decided that to place Herman Taggert behind bars would be a miscarriage of justice in itself. However, he did take part in the crime of rustling—albeit under the cruel hand of his mother. The jury recommends that he be sentenced to a period of two years' probation under the eye and guidance of Marshal Hillis, wherein he'll surely learn to stand up for himself, as well as obey the laws of the county, and the state of Kansas, eventually to seek lawful and gainful employment."

Every person in the room seemed to hold their breath, waiting, eyes on the judge.

"So be it! Recommendation accepted in the sentencing of Herman Taggert." Judge brought his gavel down with a bang.

Jocelyn gasped in delight and hugged Pete, tears filling her eyes. She got to her feet and sped back to where Red stood, his hand being shaken by this one and that. Taking her turn, she threw her arms around him, "God bless you, Red Miller."

She shook hands with the Curran couple next. "Thank you

so much." She found Addie, and Lyman, and the marshal, and thanked them all.

Finally, she was able to hug Herman. Neither could speak by then, but thanks were mutual.

School started on time, with the students' beloved teacher, Miss Denton, taking over once again with calm joy and firm instruction. Two weeks after that, Nila—her hands practically healed—became Miss Denton's assistant. After a month of school, minus a few rough moments, students showed equal regard for both their teacher and the teacher's assistant. They repaid the two young women with attention to their studies, and fulfilling small chores to win their favor—Rommy one of that group. Nila loved her students and delighted in the few hours she spent each week helping them with their studies. In the distant future she might fulfill her dream to travel the world; for the present she enjoyed her time at Gorham School.

How Nila's mother could rid herself of her daughter, Jocelyn couldn't fathom. Nila, in every way, was a young woman anybody should be proud of and dearly want in her life.

One snowy day, a letter came for Rommy from his father. Jocelyn went to the back porch and called him from where he played games with Shay. Rommy lost his hat running after the reddish, long-eared mule colt circling inside the corral at a gallop. It was clear both were enjoying the contest, each determined to win. Shay stopped, planted his hooves, and brayed, "E-e-e-e-onk! E-e-e-e-onk, onk, onk!" Rommy laughed, turned, and shouted, "Can't catch me, fool mule!" Shay galloped after him, took Rommy's coattail in his teeth, and dragged him to the ground.

Jocelyn stomped her foot and called the second time, "Rommy, you have a letter from your father! And shake loose from that blessed mule before he ruins any more of your clothes!"

He hugged Shay's neck, and the colt nuzzled him back. He came, cheeks and nose red, eyes shining from boisterous play, and took the letter from her. He met her eyes with a grin and panted, "Sorry, ma'm." He opened the letter and read, eyes following the few lines, and gave it back to her. "You can read it, but I hope my pa never comes for me. I like it here at Nickel Hill."

She started to tell him that he couldn't mean that about his father, but he raced off to the corrals faster than she could blink. She scanned the letter, and, as it sank in, she thought she might understand Rommy's feelings.

His father was in Montana, according to his letter, working as cook on a ranch owned by a woman who he thought might agree to marry him. When that happened, if it did, he'd come for Rommy if *she* didn't mind. He couldn't come now. He hoped Rommy was okay and that the Pladsons were fine with his staying on. *If the prospective wife didn't mind?!*

It was all Jocelyn could do not to scream or stomp her disbelief into the porch planks. How could people treat their youngsters this way? It made no sense. Herman, Nila, Rommy, were precious young human beings. *She* loved them like they were her own. Maybe they were better off without their true parents, but it was still hard to understand. She rested her hands on her rounded body. *You'll know my love and caring every day to my last breath, I promise.*

CHAPTER TWENTY

"My goodness, Mrs. Pladson, you're up and about early." Nila nodded toward dark shadows outside the kitchen window. She took an apron from a peg by the cupboard and tied it on.

Jocelyn had already been at the bread dough for quite a while. "I figured to start the bread early, since I was having trouble sleeping." At the table, elbows out, she continued to knead the mound of dough, her fingers pulling the smooth, yeast-fragrant pile forward, the heels of her hands shoving it away, over and over. Satisfied, she spanked the dough into shape and put it into a large bowl to rise, washed her hands, and rubbed at the mild ache in her back.

"Mrs. Pladson, you just made a face, like you're in uncommon pain. Is it—maybe your time, and you should be resting?" Nila checked the fire in the stove and took down a skillet from a hanger. "It is March, you know." She turned to face Jocelyn, her eyes full of question.

"Posh, I'm only a little achy. Otherwise, I never felt better. As soon as breakfast is over, let's air our mattresses, all right? We can start with mine and Pete's, then yours, and Rommy's. Wash the bedding, too. Scrub floors—the rugs can wait until later." Nila, her eyes on Jocelyn's mammoth stomach, was starting to look nervous. Jocelyn chuckled and reassured, "I'm not worried. Doctor Ashwood said, 'Most first babies take a long time to come, and keeping occupied eases the early discomfort.' "

"I hope you're both right," Nila mumbled under her breath,

eyebrow cocked, and went back to fixing breakfast.

The men hadn't come in yet from morning chores when the first platters of bacon and eggs were cooked, so Jocelyn and Nila each fixed a plate, quickly buttered biscuits, poured coffee, and had their own breakfast first.

After the men and Rommy had eaten and were no more than out the door, the cleaning marathon began. One on each end, Jocelyn and Nila toted feather mattresses out back of the house to air in the grass by the creek. Quilts were shaken out and hung on the clothesline to air while sheets were washed. They emptied cupboards, wiped them out, and replaced the dishes, spices, and other foodstuffs. Jocelyn polished furniture with her beeswax concoction, straightening and taking a deep breath to ride through a twinge of pain. Since the spasms didn't amount to much, she chose to pay them little heed.

At noon, Nila made sandwiches and a pot of coffee, preparing to take them to the men repairing fence in a west corner of the ranch. Jocelyn stopped her at the door. "Don't tell them that I'm likely in labor. Pete would be bedeviled with worry, and the birthing is apt to be hours and hours away." *Sometimes labor lasted a couple days,* Doctor Ashwood had said, but they hoped that not to be the case.

After their own noon meal, the cleaning continued. Floors were swept and mopped. Mid-afternoon the mattresses were brought back to the beds. Warm winds had dried the sheets, and the beds were made. They were washing the windows outside when a pain struck Jocelyn so hard she cried out and dropped to the ground, sitting spread legged. She took dozens of deep breaths.

"It's time, isn't it?" Nila threw aside her soapy rag. "We need to take you inside."

Jocelyn picked up her cloth and climbed clumsily to her feet. "Not yet; that was just the first honest pain. There'll be more before this baby comes. Let's finish the windows."

Fifteen minutes later another pain struck. "All right," Jocelyn panted, "maybe I should go in the house." She hesitated, allowing the pain to fade away. "I still think it's very early, but maybe it's time you rode to the Goodys and told Mabel better be ready to come and assist. If the men see you riding off to the Goodys they'll likely figure for themselves what's going on. If they stop you, tell them the baby won't be here until probably supper time, or later." She considered, "And that the women can handle this better if they keep on fixing fence or whatever they've got to do."

In the hour and more that it took Nila to ride to the Goody farm and return—Mabel following fast in her buggy—Jocelyn's pains subsided enough that she was able to put a stew on the stove for supper, lay out the baby's things, take a bath, and dress in a fresh nightgown and wrapper. She was waddling back and forth in the front room, the pains returned fulsome, when Mabel burst through the front door. "How are you feeling, Jocelyn, honey? How are the pains? I'm glad we're here in time."

Seized and hobbled by a strong pain, Jocelyn halted and waited for it to pass. She took a steadying breath. "I'm glad you're here, too, Mabel. I feel fine, between these twitchy pains." She panted. "They are coming closer together." *And fiercer.*

Nila closed the door and stood watching Jocelyn. "I can see that you're hurting, Mrs. Pladson. Don't you think it's time we help you to bed?"

"Yep, it's time you're off to bed, and resting," Mabel said matter of factly, "where you'll need to be. You don't have to stay in bed if you want to walk now and then."

Jocelyn agreed with a shaky smile, clutched at her skirts, and slowly made her way partially up the stairs. Halfway, another spasm struck. She cried out and doubled over, holding her midsection. Biting her lip, feeling the pain recede in what seemed like forever, she climbed on, Mabel and Nila close behind.

In bed, and despite her pain, Jocelyn laughed. She panted, "Mabel, y-you're n-not really d-doing th-that, p-putting a knife under my b-bed?"

Still on her knees by the bed, Mabel answered, looking at Jocelyn, "Yes, indeedy, I put a knife under your bed to cut the pain." She wobbled to her feet, wearing a half-guilty frown, hands in the air. "I know, I know, some are starting to believe it's a granny tale that don't work. You never know but what it might, and it doesn't harm a thing." Jocelyn tightened her lips against a pain and rolled her head on the pillow in response. Mabel continued, hands confidently on her hips, "Nila has water boiling on the stove. I put birthing cloths, thread to tie off the navel, and scissors to cut the cord, into the heated oven to sterilize them."

Nila came to take a chair by her bed and held her hand, now and then wiping her forehead with a damp cloth. "Thank you both," Jocelyn said on a quick breath. She attempted a smile—a long eerie cry, *eeeoowwwoh*, left her mouth instead. "S-sorry."

Nila shook her head, tears shining in her eyes as she looked down on Jocelyn. "Don't you be sorry; you're doing fine bringing us a baby. I just wish that it didn't hurt so."

In the next hour, contractions came hard and fast, one on top of the next, with no time in between to rest, the pains such that Jocelyn fought hard not to faint. At some point, she believed she'd been told that Pete was back at the house, pacing the porch as he waited for word he could come be with her.

For the umpteenth time, Mabel peeked under the blanket that covered her knees. "Going to be any time now, sweetheart, you just hang on." She spoke loudly, to penetrate through Jocelyn's cloud of pain, her near unconscious state. Jocelyn nodded and gave a quivery moan she couldn't hold back. "I-I know, c-can't hardly w-wait. B-but that knife isn't w-working, Mabel."

"Almost ready . . . you forget that knife business. I want you to push when I say push," Mabel ordered, "and when I say push hard, you do that. D'ya understand?"

Jocelyn opened her eyes. "Y-yes."

Mabel pushed her nightgown up around Jocelyn's waist and slipped a birthing cloth under her to absorb the blood. She put a piece of leather in Jocelyn's shaking hand. "Bite down on that, honey; bite it in two if you have to."

Jocelyn took the leather in her teeth and bit down in a grimace. A deep groan tore from her throat.

"Now!" Mabel said in a few minutes from her position beyond Jocelyn's covered knees. "Push, honey." Jocelyn set her teeth and pushed until Mabel said, "That's enough. Rest now. Right, you take those deep breaths. *Long, deep breaths.*" Mabel disappeared again, looking under the blanket. "Push again, push! Lay back now, breathe, relax much as you can. There now." Mabel raised up and gave Jocelyn's leg a pat. "You're doin' us proud, girl. Real proud. Only going to be another few minutes."

A "few minutes" was a century.

Jocelyn felt like a mass of pain, and weary to the bone, feeling the baby would never arrive, when Mabel bobbed up from the blanket with a wide smile. "I can see a little head, lotsa hair. Push, Jocelyn, honey, push!"

She half raised and pushed so hard it felt her body would split in two. She threw back her head and wailed, took a deep breath, and pushed again, puffed and pushed, puffed and pushed.

"Oh, my goodness! My goodness," Nila said, leaning over Mabel's shoulder.

"Got us a child, a boy," Mabel shouted. "There, baby boy,

there now." She held the morsel up and swatted its tiny pink bottom. A quivering, sweet cry filled the room.

Jocelyn lay back, half laughing, half crying, sucking air into her lungs, her wadded nightgown soaked with perspiration. "M-my baby. Y-you, you said a boy?"

"A handsome baby boy, yes." Mabel turned to Nila. "Hand me the thread and scissors. I have to tie off the cord and cut it away."

In another few minutes, the crying baby, swaddled soft and tight, was placed under Jocelyn's arm. She raised up to look at him, touching his wet, silky-fine hair, her finger tracing his velvety face. Joy threaded through her tired body. His mouth was as perfect as a mouth could ever be. He was beautiful. She burst into happy tears, flooded with love for this little being that was hers and Pete's. She whispered, "Hello, my sweet little Andy." They'd already decided that if he was a boy, he'd be named Andrew Royal—Andrew Royal Pladson.

"Pete, where's Pete? I want him to see his son."

Seconds later, she heard Pete's boots on the stairs. He came into the room, eyes lit with excitement, brows furrowed in concern. "Jocey, are you okay?" He brought a chair close, leaned to kiss her temple. His eyes widened in surprise as he took a good look at baby Andrew. "He's so little, no bigger than a minute."

"Now he is, but babies grow fast. Would you like to hold him?"

"Are you sure? He's so—little." He reached hesitant as she passed their baby into Pete's hands. He held him close, his lips brushing the baby's head. "His name will be Andrew, right? And Royal for your last name before you married me, and Pladson?"

"Andrew Royal Pladson, yes, like we planned." She smiled up at them. It surprised her a trifle, how natural Pete looked holding his son. "You noticed his mouth, didn't you?"

"Why, what's wrong with it?" He shrugged. "Looks perfect to me."

"That's what I'm trying to tell you, that his mouth is fine, not like mine that I grew up with. You know how ugly my cleft mouth was. His is—all right." She wiped her wet cheek, smiling.

"Hardly noticed yours when we were kids," he said softly, his eyes meeting hers with teasing affection. "And this little button would have meant as much to me, either way."

"He would've to me, too. Francina will want to see him, the minute she knows that he's here. I want to take little Andy to Topeka, show him off to her and Olympia."

Pete laughed. "Don't be in such a hurry, honey; this young'un of ours isn't even an hour old." He relented, a grin still on his face, "Sure, sweetheart, when you're able, that'll be fine." He held the baby up close to his shoulder, his work-hardened hand behind the tiny head. "In the meantime, this little family needs to get acquainted."

The MKT, or "Katy," railroad train slowly chuffed its way into the Topeka station and squealed to a long stop. Jocelyn looked down at six-week-old baby Andy, asleep in her arms, and lightly fingered his wisps of silken, blond hair. Her throat grew thick with love for him, *such a good baby, he'd slept most of the three-hour trip to Topeka, waking and nursing under a discreet shawl twice.* She wrapped his blanket tighter about him, held him up close, and gathered her satchel. It made sense, she decided, to wait for the rush of debarking passengers to thin before making her own way from the train.

Outside in warm spring sunshine, Jocelyn blessed her good luck to catch a streetcar ready to depart, and she quickly found an available seat. Baby Andy stirred, his blue eyes settled on her face, his lips curling into an infant grin. Probably from gas, but a grin was a grin. She brought him up in her arms and kissed his face, which he took as an invitation to nurse and snuggled into her. She placated him for the time being with her knuckle in his small, pink mouth—he sucked it contentedly, eyes on her face.

The streetcar ride from the train station to where she needed to get off passed quickly. Excited for the women to meet her tiny offspring, she hurried the short distance from the stop to Francina and Olympia's cottage by the park.

With the handle of her satchel hooked over the crook of her arm and the baby high on her shoulder, she rang their doorbell and heard it tinkling inside. Olympia came to the door, opened it wider still when she saw who it was, the weary, worried expression on her face quickly changing to a smile.

"Come in, dear, oh, the sweet baby." She reached for him the moment Jocelyn was inside, smiling down at him in her arms. "Francina has been so wanting to see you, little fellow." She looked at Jocelyn. "We're glad you've come." She hesitated as though to say more but shook her head and led the way to the small parlor, where sunshine flooded through windows opened toward the park. A warm spring breeze lightly tossed the yellow lace curtains.

"Francina . . . ?" Jocelyn questioned, noting her absence to welcome her—which was not like her good friend. She took a place on the settee, across from Olympia, who'd taken a chair and was cuddling baby Andy.

"She's resting now," Olympia answered with a worried expression, "which gives me a few minutes to tell you—Francina has given us a scare, a bad scare, but—she—she is doing better."

Jocelyn waited and her heart climbed to her throat. "What is it? What happened? She's here at home, isn't she, and all right?"

Olympia nodded and sighed. "A few nights ago, Francina

had a fainting spell, at the Crawford Theatre. We had to bring her home in an ambulance. The doctor determined that she'd had a heart attack and felt that the end was near, that she'd not last until morning."

"Oh, my goodness, no." Jocelyn bit her lip, caught her two hands in her lap, and leaned forward to hear more. "She . . . she's . . . ?"

"Fortunately, Francina has rallied and, though weak, is somewhat back to her old self. She's quite a fighter, you know."

Jocelyn sighed and, nodding, managed a smile. "Yes. I can believe that." She had moved to the edge of the settee, anxious to see Francina for herself. *A heart attack.* "She is going to be all right, then?"

"As well as possible under the circumstances. We shouldn't have gone to the theatre that night at all; Francina hadn't been feeling well to begin with. She was adamant, though, in her wish not to miss the new musical performance by Mr. Theron C. Bennett, the young composer of ragtime music. Have you heard of him, Jocelyn? His kind of music is quite new."

She shook her head and tried to show interest in the conversation but was unable to shake her worry about her good friend and only half heard as Olympia continued, "He's just wonderful on the piano playing his tunes like *Picanniny Capers,* a very joyful piece." She fussed abstractedly with the baby's blanket and smiled down at him, murmuring baby talk.

"Ragtime . . . ?" Jocelyn stroked her forehead, puzzled. What did ragtime music have to do with Francina being ill?

"Yes, ragtime. I could hardly blame her for wanting to go. Theron Bennett is growing in popularity everywhere. His song *St. Louis Tickle* is all the rage right now, and there promises to be more songs as popular in the many he's composed, such as *Sweet Pickles,* a two-step. A Missourian, he's quite the ambitious young man, wanting to continue writing music, eventually to be a publisher of sheet music, we're told."

"Then, it's music to dance to? This ragtime?" Jocelyn settled back—might as well hear the whole story while Francina got her rest, strange though this was starting out.

"For the most part, yes. Listening to ragtime is exhilarating, too. Some folks were dancing that night—it was near impossible not to—and that's what happened to Francina."

"How do you mean?" Jocelyn's heart thumped. *What in the name of Hannah took place?* She itched for Olympia to get on with it, before she keeled to the floor with unmet curiosity.

"Francina loved the music," Olympia explained, "and she began a conversation with a young gentleman about the composer, Theron Bennett, who'd been an acquaintance of Bennett's at a university in New Mexico. First thing I knew, the young man had asked Francina if she'd care to dance. You know Francina—I tried to talk sense to her, but she would have none of that. I have to say the young man was very kindly, careful with her, and that dance was a dream come true for Francina."

"What happened? The heart attack?"

Olympia frowned and shook her head, tears sparkling in her eyes. "Francina was considering a *second* dance despite my warnings. She reluctantly gave in to my argument and sat out the rest of the evening unhappy with me." For a moment, Olympia's hand nervously smoothed the baby's blanket and cupped his head, and she kissed him lightly. She took a deep breath and explained. "Stepping from Crawford Theatre to our waiting hack, Francina simply passed out, faded down to the sidewalk like a broken doll. At first, I thought she'd died right there. She was still breathing, although her heartbeat was next to nothing. An ambulance and doctor were immediately on the scene, caring for her. She was brought home; she's very much against hospitals, you know."

Jocelyn hadn't known but remembered that Francina had

cared for her husband, Frye, at home, to his last moment. "But she'll recover? Be able to enjoy life, do things she likes?" *Francina had always seemed fragile, but in her own way full of life and good humor.* A drastic change in her friend, never mind losing her, would be near unbearable.

"With Francina, I'd say there is a good chance that she will be with us for some time yet. Of course, you never know. The doctor feels that the attack last week is a warning; another more severe attack will likely end her life, but she pooh-poohs that. He has insisted on complete bed rest for the time being, which she's fighting. She loves warm baths, which he has recommended, but dislikes the doses of calomel and bicarbonate of potassium she must take three or four times a day. As dear to me as she is, Francina is not an easy patient."

"Will I be able to see her?"

"Oh, yes. She wants so much to see you, and the baby." Tiny Andy had begun to *mew* and wiggle in his blankets. Olympia returned him to Jocelyn's arms. "I'll see if Francina's awake and be right back."

While she waited, Jocelyn measured what she'd just heard. Dancing to ragtime—at Francina's age? She smiled to herself at the same time her own heart thumped with worry. A person had to admire the dear soul. Not much that Francina did was a surprise, anyhow.

Olympia was at the door, motioning for her to follow.

She nodded, kissed Andy's sweet face, and followed.

CHAPTER TWENTY-ONE

Francina, in a white, ruffled bed jacket, was sitting up in bed, her lap covered with a pink, floral coverlet with fat, rose-colored pillows at her back. Despite being pale, with a bluish tinge to her lips and under her eyes, Francina's expression glowed. "Come, dear Jocelyn, and show me what you have in that tiny bundle." She chuckled softly, and her thin arms lifted to hug Jocelyn, struggling a bit with her stiff arm, and then she took the baby, drawing him a bit shakily to her shoulder. "Come to Grandma, my sweet babe." She patted his back, before cradling him down in her arms. "What a beautiful child you are, little Andrew." She cooed at him when he blinked his blue eyes at her, his mouth turned up in a sideways grin.

"Oh, I love him so much." She looked up at Jocelyn. "When I received your letter telling me your plan if the babe was a boy, I told myself, 'a cardinal name, Andrew Royal Pladson.' He is my honored grandson, right?" Warm excitement filled her voice.

Jocelyn's throat filled. "Today and always, your grandson, Francina."

For the next several minutes, Francina's rapt attention was on Andy. She cooed, squeezed him in her thin shaking arms, arranged and rearranged his blanket about him, only to remove the blanket and stroke his chubby, pink legs and arms and his cheeks. She looked at Jocelyn, who was smiling from where she sat by the bed. "Thanks for this, Jocelyn, dear. I can't begin to tell you how much it means to me, having this child in my arms. My, just the feel of him."

"It is my pleasure, Francina, and my baby's."

Francina sat very still, a half smile on her face, seeing in her mind's eye something she found most appealing. "I had such plans for this child and me, together." She shook her head and looked at Jocelyn, her mood changing to a look of disgust. "You've likely heard that the doctor believes I'm crowding death's door? Pure nonsense. I'm not ready to go, and I won't be rushed." Her gaze flicked upward, her hand in the air and her tone sarcastic as she finished, "I had a little spell at the theatre a few nights ago, and, suddenly, I'm supposed to have seen my last days."

"How do you feel, Francina? You look beautiful."

"I feel a little tired, weak, but that, my dear, is because they're making me stay in bed and take foul medicines. In another day, or two, I'll be up and around and doing fine. Did you hear that I danced to ragtime, Jocelyn?"

Jocelyn sucked in her cheeks, feeling slightly giddy at what she was about to hear, and cautioning herself to be careful what she said. "Yes, I heard," she said lightly. "You enjoyed the music, I understand?"

"Oh, so much so!" Francina smiled at the baby in her arms and traced his tiny cheek with a delicate, trembling finger. "They're trying to tell me that one dance with the handsome young fellow brought on my spell. *Pshaw.* I'm sure it was the codfish supper I had that made me a little ill, and I fainted. I tell you, dear, I loved that one dance to that happy ragtime song; the name of it is *Satisfied.* I was ready for a second dance to a jiggy tune called *She Was from Missouri,* but I was argued to stay put in my chair. Mercy sakes, where would I ever again have such an opportunity?" She frowned in Olympia's direction.

A roll of Olympia's eyes and her expression declared, hopefully, *none.*

Jocelyn tried not to laugh and made no protest either way. Each of the two women had a right to her own feelings and opinions. The rest of the afternoon was spent chatting and playing with baby Andy, with Francina taking time out for a nap while Jocelyn changed and nursed her child. She stayed to the last minute before she had to catch the late-day train back to Skiddy.

"You'll come again, soon?" Francina asked as they were saying goodbye. She held Jocelyn's hands in hers, looking tired but hopeful.

"Yes, I promise. I will come to see you as often as I can, and you do your best to get better."

The day had left her believing that Francina would improve and be fine for a few more years at least. With the baby asleep in her arms, and herself comfortably drowsy as the train rocked toward home, Jocelyn reflected that any day she'd ever spent with Francina—Mrs. Gorham—was surely among the best days of her life.

Jocelyn kept her promise, taking the baby and visiting with Francina and Olympia every few weeks for months in a row. It was obvious that Francina was growing weaker as time passed but was still fighting her illness, coming alive when they arrived at the cottage to see her, happy to cuddle Jocelyn's little one, and to have tea and cookies like old times.

One day a wire came as Jocelyn prepared for another trip to Topeka and a visit.

Francina had quietly passed away in her sleep. A funeral was to be held on the coming Sunday. Jocelyn found comfort, crying in Pete's arms. "I know that it was expected, had to happen sometime," she told him, choking back tears, "but it's so hard to believe. She's been one of my best friends, Pete. I loved her as much as I did my own Grandma Letty. Now, they're both gone."

Pete's eyes were shiny in union with hers. "How old was Mrs. Gorham?" he asked, swallowing, "eighty-five, or so?"

"I'm not sure, late seventies or maybe eighty. But she was never an 'old woman,' Pete. In spirit she was young to her last breath."

At the funeral, Pete held little Andy on his lap, his arm looped close around the young one's small body. Young Rommy sat to Pete's left, and Jocelyn sat beside Pete, her fingers woven in his free hand, soaking his strength into her own. Nila sat to her right. The young folks had good memories of their time with Mrs. Gorham at Gage Park and other occasions when in Topeka and had asked to be at her funeral.

Throughout the service—the organ music, the minister's welcome and preaching, his beautiful praise of Francina Gorham and the amazing, inspiring life she'd led, the prayers, and singing of old songs like *Abide with Me*—Jocelyn felt a deep, painful sadness, and yet a growing peace. When they sang *All Things Bright and Beautiful,* such a joyful, hopeful song, Olympia leaned over the back of her pew and whispered to Jocelyn, "That last song was particularly requested by Francina."

Of course it was. Jocelyn gave a little nod and smiled. The next thing she knew the minister was inviting one and all to the basement for punch and cake. While there, Francina's attorney drew Pete aside and reminded him and Jocelyn that there was to be a reading of Francina's will at the cottage, following a brief graveside service.

Only a few were in attendance, besides Jocelyn and Pete with their youngsters, when they arrived at the cottage. Olympia was there, with her daughter, who'd come to take her home to Indiana. Present was a representative of the Kansas Equal Suffrage Association. Appearing at the last minute was the director of a children's orphanage called The Children's House, and a fellow representing the park across the street. The attorney had them gather in the parlor and made short work of reading Francina's will.

The cottage was awarded to the park, with Francina's wish that it be turned into a small theatre, a close-by addition for park goers. Francina's jewelry and other valuables went to Olympia to share with her daughters. Nickel Hill Ranch now belonged to Jocelyn and Pete, free and clear, with monies to refresh their cattle herd, although Francina was hopeful that some of the latter would go to Jocelyn should she wish to return to the mule trade. The remainder of the estate, in monies, went partially to KESA—making the woman representative of the Kansas Equal Suffrage Association very happy—while the final, generous amount went to the very grateful director of The Children's House orphanage.

It was a beautiful September day, as beautiful as such a day could be. Jocelyn and Pete, and six-month-old Andy, lazed on a blanket in the shade of young cottonwood trees growing next to a Nickel Hill pond. Rommy and Nila splashed about in the pond, their ringing laughter making Jocelyn smile in contentment. They'd all enjoyed a picnic of fried chicken, corn salad, yeast buns and jam, and iced tea. Andy, sitting next to Jocelyn's knee, practiced his four new teeth on a chicken leg, but his eyelids were drooping sleepily. A short way off near the wagon, Alice and Zenith grazed.

"I never would've wanted to own a ranch in the way Nickel Hill came to us," Pete was saying, "if I was choosing. But I'll be grateful to your friend Francina Gorham the rest of my life. And I intend to make a success of this place in her honor, not let her memory down by failing a trifle."

"I know, Pete, I feel the same. Without Whit, her son, hiring me that time to cook on the mule drive, I never would have heard of Nickel Hill. And if not for Francina, the ranch wouldn't be ours now." She reflected, "We can be glad that we made her happy by taking on Nickel Hill when she didn't care a fig about it—and being her friend, filling an empty space in her life after she lost Whitman. Olympia told me that the times Francina spent with little Andy, her 'chosen' grandson, and leaving us the ranch gave her more pleasure than anything else could."

Pete, seeing tears in her eyes, caught Jocelyn's hand. "Everything's going to be okay, sweetheart. We're going to be fine."

"I know," she choked out, "but I'm going to miss her so much." She wiped her eyes on the back of her hand and changed the subject. Looking at Rommy and Nila splashing each other in the pond, she said, "It's so hard to judge folks. Who would have thought a woman could be so cruel as Icel was to her son, Herman? Rommy's father disappointed me, Pete. I thought he was a better father than he turned out to be."

"And Red Miller, what do you think of him?" Pete teased.

"Red Miller is a saint." She smiled sheepishly. Herman, as Red predicted, was doing fine. He appreciated his freedom, was a hard-working young man about Skiddy, a happy favorite of town folk.

Pete laughed, then sobered. "Speaking of Chester Trayhern, a man tries, you know, and I think he did what he could for a time. Sometimes a fella doesn't have what it takes to be a father, and his young'un is as well off without him, like Rommy, here at Nickel Hill with us. After the last letter, his pa writes to tell him that the woman who he thought would marry him picked otherwise. Ain't that bull—dung. Said he'd moved on, said Rommy was better off here; he wasn't sure *he'd* be coming back to Kansas." He moved his hat out of the way in the grass and lay back on his elbows. "I've come to think a lot of the young sprout"—he looked out at Rommy, now out of the pond and being chased by Nila—"and I don't believe I could ever find a better cowhand to help me run the place. Except you, son." He gave Andy's fat little leg a pat. Andy gurgled a sloppy grin at him.

"I hope Rommy stays with us 'til he's a full-grown man and after that, too, if it pleases him," Jocelyn agreed. "He already behaves as if he's Andy's brother. And Nila is moon eyes over our baby. We're lucky, Pete, to have Rommy and Nila with us."

They were silent a while, both pondering and coming up with the same idea, the same moment. "We could make it legal, adopt them, make them our children," Jocelyn said, "a part of our legacy we're always planning."

Pete's eyes gleamed. "And when it's our time to go to the heavenly corral up yonder"—he looked and thumbed toward the wide blue sky—"we can leave Nickel Hill to them, our kids. Born kids and adopted kids, equal."

"Do you agree with that, Andy?" Jocelyn said. He grinned, crawled into her lap, and burbled a sound that could be most any word. Jocelyn laughed and looked at Pete. "Did you hear that Pete? Our son just said yes."

Pete leaned to kiss Jocelyn's cheek. He looked down and chuckled. "Sounded like 'damn right' to me."

ABOUT THE AUTHOR

Irene Bennett Brown is an award-winning author who enjoys using Kansas, where she was born, as background for her historical novels. Previous to her nine novels for adults, Brown authored nine young adult novels. They include *Before the Lark,* winner of the Western Writers of America Spur Award, nomination for the Mark Twain Award, and other honors. *Miss Royal's Mules* and *Tangled Times,* Books One and Two in the Nickel Hill Series, are adult sequels to *Before the Lark.*

She lives with her husband, Bob, a retired research chemist, on two fruitful acres along the Santiam River in Oregon. Visit her website at http://www.irenebennettbrown.net.

The employees of Five Star Publishing hope you have enjoyed this book.

Our Five Star novels explore little-known chapters from America's history, stories told from unique perspectives that will entertain a broad range of readers.

Other Five Star books are available at your local library, bookstore, all major book distributors, and directly from Five Star/Gale.

Connect with Five Star Publishing

Visit us on Facebook:
  https://www.facebook.com/FiveStarCengage

Email:
  FiveStar@cengage.com

For information about titles and placing orders:
  (800) 223-1244
  gale.orders@cengage.com

To share your comments, write to us:
  Five Star Publishing
  Attn: Publisher
  10 Water St., Suite 310
  Waterville, ME 04901